On The Record

The Backlot Series - Book 3

Kimberly Page

On The Record

Published by: PageMedia, LLC

Cover Design by: Quirky Bird

This is a work of fiction. Names, characters, places, and incidents either are the product of the author's imagination or are used fictitiously and not to be construed as real. Any resemblance to actual persons, living or dead, events, or locales is entirely coincidental.

All brand names and product names used in this book are trademarks, registered trademarks, or trade names of their respective holders. The publisher and author are not associated with any real likeness, product, or vendor mentioned in this book. Any likeness referenced within the book has not endorsed the book.

ISBN: 979-8-9918472-5-4

Editing: Emerald Edits and First Editing

author's note

Dear Reader,

Welcome to my third Hollywood romance! While Lucas and Jess's wild ride from enemies to lovers is fictional, their story explores themes that feel especially relevant right now —the tensions between truth and spin, the challenge of maintaining integrity in your career while protecting the people you love, and how sometimes the most unexpected relationships teach us the most about ourselves.

Like my previous books, this one doesn't shy away from difficult topics. The story addresses workplace misogyny and sexual harassment, and there are discussions about losing a parent, even though that loss happened before our story begins. I've tried to handle these subjects with the care they deserve while still delivering the romance, banter, and steam you've come to expect from this series.

What I love about Lucas and Jess's story was how perfectly they represent that clash between public perception and private truth. As a journalist and a PR executive, they're professionally trained to either expose or protect secrets—but what happens when the biggest secret is their own growing feelings for each other? Their journey reminded me that sometimes the stories we tell ourselves about what we want are the ones that need the most editing.

I loved writing about two people who are genuinely good at their jobs, respect each other's skills (even when it's inconvenient), and have to figure out how to be partners in both professional and personal spaces. Plus, there's something deliciously meta about writing a romance where the characters' fake relationship is being documented in a real documentary —reality within fiction within reality!

I hope you enjoy watching these two stubborn professionals discover that sometimes the best stories are the ones you never planned to write.

Fair warning: This book would definitely earn an NC-17 rating for strong language, alcohol consumption, and open-door bedroom scenes. Lucas and Jess certainly have some scenes that are NSFW! 😇

Happy Reading!

The Night We Met - Lord Huron
I Forgot That You Existed - Taylor Swift
Maneater - Nelly Furtado
Love In An Elevator - Aerosmith
Wild Ones (feat. Sia) - Flo Rida, Sia
Can't Help Falling in Love - Elvis Presley
Teeth - 5 Seconds of Summer
Black - Pearl Jam
Sweater Weather - The Neighbourhood
Little Miss Can't Be Wrong - Spin Doctors
Gives You Hell - The All-American Rejects
That Don't Impress Me Much - Shania Twain
Love On The Brain - Rihanna
Shameless - Camila Cabello
Shut Up Kiss Me - Angel Olsen
Sweetest Thing - U2
Today - The Smashing Pumpkins
fOoL fOr YoU - ZAYN
I Can See You (Taylor's Version) - Taylor Swift
Don't Blame Me - Taylor Swift
All For You - Sister Hazel

Free Fallin' - Tom Petty
Heart Attack - Demi Lovato
Fine Line - Harry Styles
Good In Bed - Dua Lipa
One More Night - Maroon 5
Centerfield - John Fogerty
Magic In The Hamptons (feat. Lil Yachty) -
Social House, Lil Yachty
Ruin My Life - Zara Larsson
Drink You Away - Justin Timberlake
I Love You, I'm Sorry - Gracie Abrams
Fuck it I love you - Lana Del Rey
Kiss Me - Ed Sheeran
Real Love Baby - Father John Misty

prologue

. . .

THE LOCKER ROOM door explodes outward under my palm, a satisfying outlet for the frustration burning through my veins. My father's voice still echoes in my head—*Enjoy one of your last games before joining my campaign team*—like my future is already set in stone.

"Jesus, fuck!"

A blur of golden hair and tanned skin darts back from the swinging door. I freeze, my jersey hanging open, forgotten.

She's a vision in cutoff denim shorts showcasing legs that seem to stretch for miles. Her faded band T-shirt is cropped just enough to reveal a slice of toned stomach, and the way her cross-body bag cuts across her chest accentuates curves that instantly send my blood south. At least a hundred thin bracelets jingle at her wrists as she steadies herself against the wall. Her blonde hair escapes a messy ponytail, framing a face that belongs on magazine covers.

When I finally reach her eyes, a piercing blue that

reminds me of the California coast, they're locked on my exposed chest. Her lips part slightly, and whatever she is about to say evaporates as her gaze travels over my abs. The hunger in her eyes is unmistakable, igniting something primal in me.

I can't help myself. I flex subtly, and a jolt of satisfaction rushes through me when her cheeks flush pink.

"Hey, sorry about that," I say, my voice rougher than intended. My heart hammers against my ribs, and it has nothing to do with being late for the game.

I should be sprinting to the dugout, but I'm rooted in place, caught in her gravitational pull.

It's no hardship keeping my gaze trained on her beautiful face, but damn if I don't want to take my time looking slowly at the rest of her. The quick glimpse I allowed myself is stamped permanently on my brain. She looks like pure sin and sunshine poured into blue denim, with long legs, ample curves, and a barely there grin, but it's the hint of mischief in her eyes that has me imagining things that would make us both sweat more than nine innings under the sun.

"Can I help you with something?" I ask, reluctantly buttoning my jersey. Each fastened button feels like a crime, hiding what she clearly appreciates. As I walk backward toward the field, the roar of the crowd is a distant reminder of responsibilities I'd gladly abandon for five more minutes with this stranger.

"Dugout," she says, pointing down the tunnel. Her voice matches her appearance—a little husky, confident. It would sound incredible whispering in my ear at night.

"You're headed to the dugout?" I blink, thrown. That's not exactly an open-access area. "Coach Byrum signed off?"

She nods like it's no big deal.

I should probably wonder who she is—or what kind of strings she pulled—but the thought of her sitting in our sanctuary during the game sends a thrill through me. Nine innings with this view would be worth getting in trouble.

I wave for her to follow, stealing glances over my shoulder as we walk toward the field. The sway of her hips is hypnotic, and twice, I nearly trip over my own cleats. My focus is shattered, my mind already spinning fantasies of getting her number, taking her out after the game, and discovering if she tastes as incredible as she looks.

We emerge into the sunlight, and I spot my teammate Austin charging toward us, grinning like a lottery winner. He barrels past me and wraps his arms around the blonde goddess. Lifting her, he spins her with unbridled joy.

I blink. Wait—do they know each other? Are they together?

A flicker of something unsettled twists in my chest. Not quite jealousy, maybe something more like disappointment? Which is insane. I don't even know her name. But the way she looked at me, like she saw something worth noticing, I'd be lying if I said it didn't spark something.

Of course someone like her would already be taken. No way a woman like that walks around unattached. She's the kind of woman you just *know* doesn't stay single for long. And I missed my shot.

Austin approaches me, his hand clasped with hers, and my heart sinks.

"Hey, Lucas. Meet my big sister, Jess."

Sister. The word hits me like a fastball to the chest, but instead of pain, it's pure elation. I've never been so grateful in my life. Austin's big sister. My joy dissipates only slightly when I realize she's my teammate's sister—off-limits, according to the code—but I'm graduating, and some rules might need revisiting.

"We've met," she says, tilting her head with a smile that steals my breath. There's mischief in those blue eyes, a challenge I desperately want to accept.

"Oh, yeah? Where?" Austin asks, looking between us with growing suspicion.

I take too long to answer, lost in fantasies of how her lips would feel against mine.

Austin nudges me. "You ok?"

"Oh, yeah. We didn't technically meet, just ran into each other in the tunnel outside the locker room." I extend my hand, anticipating electricity with our touch. "Nice to meet you, Jess."

Her hand slides into mine, small but strong, and the contact sends a current racing up my arm. She holds my gaze with such unwavering confidence that I have to remind myself we're standing in public, surrounded by teammates and thousands of fans.

"Did you see all the press, man?" Austin asks, breaking our connection. He knows all about my father's political agenda hitting the news this week and his expectations suffocating my dreams.

"Yeah, I'm just keeping my head down. They are nothing but vultures." The words leave my mouth before I realize what I'm saying. "The worst of the bunch are the ones from the local entertainment trades."

Austin winces, and when I look back at Jess, the warmth has vanished from her face. Her eyes, molten with attraction moments ago, have cooled to ice.

"So, what brings you into the dugout for our annual USC alumni game?" I say in an attempt to recover, desperate to see that smile again.

"I'm an entertainment reporter from one of the local trades," she says, her words precise and sharp. Each syllable drives the stake deeper into whatever was building between us. Her eyes, which had undressed me minutes ago, now look at me like I'm something stuck to the bottom of her shoe.

Fuck me.

"Right. Um…"

"Don't worry, this vulture isn't here for you anyway." Her voice drips venom as she brushes past me. "I'm covering Sal Ruzzi, the alumni actor pitching against you today."

The contact of her shoulder against mine should feel like a victory after the electricity between us moments ago, but instead, it feels like goodbye.

Sorry, man. I didn't know, I mouth to Austin.

Austin watches her stomp over to the bench before turning back to me. "It's fine. She'll get over it."

He redirects my attention, and we line up to watch our first baseman approach the plate. I grab a bat and go through the motions of warming up, but my focus keeps drifting back to Jess. God, even angry, she's stunning, maybe the most beautiful woman I've ever seen.

I watch as Austin introduces her to the team, pointing out

players, and then I hear her ask about the unusual number of reporters present. My stomach tightens, knowing they're here for me—or rather, for my father.

"No idea," Austin tells her. "I didn't think alumni games pulled any press, but maybe Sal is more of a draw than I realized. I mean, that got you here."

"Well, I'm a baby reporter sent to cover the shit stories, so I doubt that's why any of those folks are here." She gestures across the field. "I mean, fucking Michelle Shocklam is here. She's one of the top political journalists out there. I asked my editor if she knew."

"Well, maybe she's got a crush on Sal. Or me. You never know."

Austin's joke falls flat as Jess becomes absorbed in her phone. Her expression transforms from concentration to shock, and her hand flies to her mouth. I look away, my stomach sinking, knowing that she's discovered the reason for the heightened media presence.

"Holy fucking shit."

"What?" Austin asks.

"Logan Carmichael is supposed to be at this game. That is why the reporters are here. That's what Michelle is doing here." Her voice rises with indignation. "I can't believe that piece of shit is coming to this game."

Austin catches my eye. I offer a shrug in return. I mean, she's not wrong, but I still flinch internally from the harshness of her tone. He might be a piece of shit, but unfortunately, he's still my father.

"He's not coming," I say, the words heavy in my mouth.

Jess's head snaps up, and her eyebrows knit together. "How do you know?"

"He's my father."

And just like that, whatever spark that ignited between us in that tunnel is extinguished completely. The first strikeout of the game—and it's not even happening on the field.

one

. . .

Jess

"OF COURSE I've got the exclusive! It's like you don't even know me!" I flash my most charming smile as I begin walking backward, away from the semicircle of industry men in expensive suits. They're nodding appreciatively at what I just said about journalistic integrity, but I catch the way Marcus Delgado's eyes track up and down my body before returning to my face with unmistakable interest. His wink is so obvious it might as well have come with sound effects.

That's my cue to spin on my heel and escape. Five hours in Vegas, and the National Association of Broadcasters Show is already chaos. I tuck a strand of my blonde hair behind my ear and fire off a quick email approving the podcast episode with Sophia Ford and Edie Lang. Their action film *Survivor* is releasing over Memorial Day weekend, and the buzz is already deafening. I snagged an exclusive with both of them that will kick off their media blitz and serve as a major win for my podcast, *On The Red Carpet*.

I love those women and can't wait to see them dominate a

traditionally male-skewed holiday weekend. The trades are already predicting record numbers, and my interview dropping first means serious traffic for my platform.

I glance up to get my bearings in the sprawling convention center, and I spot Lucas Carmichael lounging outside the room I'm headed for. I stop short before he notices me, my thumb frozen mid-swipe on my phone.

What the hell is he doing here?

There isn't a person on the planet who gets under my skin quite like Lucas Carmichael. I quickly flip to my conference app to make sure he's not moderating my panel session. I should know this already, but the past week has been a blur of prep calls and research.

The text notification interrupts my scrolling:

MARCUS

Where'd you run off to? I was hoping we could get drinks later and maybe watch some clips in my room?

Marcus Delgado, the bane of my existence. One martini-fueled moment of weakness a few months ago led to a regrettable kiss in the backseat of his car, but not because I was too drunk. I was just bored and maybe a little curious, or maybe trying to prove something to myself, like that I'm not destined to die alone. After mistaking a polite smile for an invitation and a vague raincheck for a binding agreement, he's been relentlessly trying to charm me ever since. He's not dangerous, not exactly, but he's definitely entitled, the type of man who assumes that the world is lucky to orbit him, and that includes me.

I wish I could blow him off completely, but Marcus has serious pull in this town. As head of TV production at Wonderland Studios, he's known for holding grudges and making careers—or quietly breaking them. He's never crossed a line with me, but I've heard enough from other women to know that he likes to test the edge. Nothing you can prove. Nothing that sticks. Not yet, anyway. And if the day ever comes when his name hits my inbox attached to a story? I'll be ready.

Until then, I craft a carefully worded response:

JESS

> I'd love to see you! Can you grab a quick drink at the Adobe mixer? Already booked tonight with interviews.

You don't have to be rude to people you don't like. You don't have to be rude to people you don't like, I silently repeat with my eyes closed, my personal mantra, centering myself before heading into the South Hall.

"Don't tell me the interview queen is nervous."

Just my luck. I suck in a deep breath through my nose, hold for a count of four, and turn to face the smug voice that's become my professional nemesis.

"What do you want, Lucas?" I ask, keeping my tone carefully neutral despite the immediate surge of irritation. Then I repeat internally once again: *You don't have to be rude to people you don't like.*

Lucas Carmichael, head of PR and comms at Wonderland Studios, is leaning against the wall, looking irritatingly put together in dark jeans, a crisp white button down under a navy blazer, and spotless sneakers. He's just the right mix of effortless and intentional. His dark hair is perfectly styled, and his smile is calculated to disarm.

His job is literally to make messy stories disappear, while mine is to drag them into the spotlight and force the industry to deal with them. We've been circling each other for years, me digging for truth, him layering on spin. Somehow, we always end up in the same places—red carpets, studio junkets, high-profile press disasters—me with a mic, him with a smug smile and a hand on the eject button.

I've never liked him—not since our run-in when he was still in college and dismissed entertainment reporters like me as "vultures," and certainly not since he started turning every professional encounter into an opportunity to needle me. He's too smooth, too confident, too infuriatingly good-looking for a man with that much power and that little shame.

And yet, when I need access to talent, he's often the gatekeeper. When he needs a story to break just the right way, he comes to me. Our whole working relationship is built on begrudging respect, mutual annoyance, and the unspoken agreement that neither of us will blink first.

"I've never seen you nervous before. What's that like?" he asks, pushing off the wall to stand at his full height, which, annoyingly, means I have to tilt my head up slightly to maintain eye contact.

"It feels like the rejection you experience every time you try to pitch a fluff piece to a reporter: normal and expected." I offer him my sweetest smile.

"You're hilarious," he deadpans, but I catch the slight twitch at the corner of his mouth.

"Great catching up. I gotta run. See ya never, I hope." I turn and stride through the double doors into the grand exhibition hall, searching for my fellow panelists.

"Hey, wait up," Lucas calls, quickening his pace to catch me.

"Isn't there some corporate award form you should be filling out right now? Or maybe reminding your executives that it's time to submit their Emmy nominations?" I don't slow down.

"You're on a roll today, but hang on." He reaches for me and gently touches my elbow to stop my forward momentum. I hate that it works, but I appreciate that he didn't just grab me like most men would—like most men do—when they want my attention.

I turn around with an exaggerated sigh. "You've got two minutes."

"That's all I need." He holds up his hands in mock surrender.

"That's what she said," I mutter.

"What?"

"Nothing. What do you want, Lucas? I'm on stage in ten minutes, and I'd like to meet my fellow panelists."

His expression shifts to something more professional. "Just a heads up. *Survivor* is releasing the same weekend as *Terminal Velocity*, and we've decided to collaborate on marketing. I was hoping you could tease it when you're doing promo for Sophia and Edie's podcast."

I consider this for a moment. It's actually not an unreasonable request, and cross-promotion could benefit everyone involved. "Fine. Send me the info. Is that all?"

"That is all." His face relaxes into something genuine. "Thank you."

"No problem, Senator." I can't help the dig, knowing how much he hates being associated with his father's political ambitions.

His smile vanishes. "Not funny."

I break out my best shit-eating grin, enjoying the way his jaw tightens. He's such an easy target. "Stick around for the session. Maybe you'll learn something about communications." I back away and head toward my cohorts.

I make a point of warmly introducing myself to each of them. I spent all last week learning about each panelist, their strengths, backgrounds, and even their weaknesses. Not that I'll use the latter here, but it's always good to know who you're dealing with. Our panel topic is "The State of the Creator Economy," essentially discussing how the information age is changing. Anyone can share news now; a degree in broadcast journalism is no longer required, though I'd like to think my Boston University education is part of why I've done so well.

I'm paired with Courtney Cooler, a YouTuber with 2.5 million subscribers who has a weekly show reporting on pop culture. The others are Jackson (that's it, no last name), a TikTok self-help guru with over ten million followers; Tyler the Comedian, a stand-up comic turned podcaster; and me, the entertainment journalist giving the trades a run for their money. We're the setup act for all the other sessions, showcasing what's working, while the later panels will discuss what could work.

"Jess Lexington! I'm so honored to meet you in real life!"

Courtney squeals as she wraps her arms around me in an enthusiastic hug. She's all oversized sunglasses, glossy brown curls, and contagious energy. She's the kind of person who could go viral for just existing at a farmer's market. I dare anyone not to fall in love with this woman. She's been one of my favorite content creators for years.

"Same, Courtney. I'm totally starstruck. I'm a huge fan!" I return her embrace, genuinely pleased to meet her.

"Oh, stop it. Tell me more," she says with a laugh. That breaks the ice with the rest of the group, and we take the few minutes before our session to get acquainted.

Our casual bonding proves valuable when Courtney smoothly references my first big break when I broke the story on several producers who were deeply involved on the wrong side of the #MeToo movement. It's something I'm incredibly proud of and work I know my mother would have championed had cancer not taken her too soon.

Before that exposé, I was covering D-list celebrities at charity events and alumni baseball games. After taking down an entire production company, I quickly rose to entertainment reporter at *Variety*. Since then, I've bounced between entertainment pubs before going independent almost three years ago.

I wanted to tell more immediate stories, to speculate and share opinions. I wanted the freedom to be biased, even if it's a journalist's cardinal sin, according to everything I learned at BU. My podcast gave me that freedom, and now I'm thriving.

Midway through the panel, as I'm scanning the audience, I spot my best friend, Blair, in the crowd. I can't suppress the smile that automatically appears. She's my ride or die, the one who was in law school when the #MeToo revelations broke, helping me navigate what I could legally report. When she shifts in her seat, I notice Lucas sitting behind her, rolling his eyes at something I just said.

God, he's insufferable. Why is he even here?

"Reach out to Courtney and Jackson for a possible episode on how mental health and pop culture are dominating conversations right now. Period," I dictate into my phone's voice notes immediately after the session. "Maybe ask Jackson how he feels about offering advice on a platform he's telling people to limit their time on. Period. Does he ever feel like a hypocrite? Question mark."

I'm standing just outside the conference room, tucked into a quiet corner of the hallway. Most of the attendees have filtered into other sessions by now, leaving the corridor oddly still. The carpeted floors muffle any foot traffic, and the only sounds are the distant hum of slot machines bleeding in from the far side of the casino and the soft, echoey clink of silverware from a nearby banquet setup. For the first time in hours, it's just me and my thoughts, and I'm trying to get them down before the next conversation pulls me away.

I finish just as Blair reaches me, her arms wide for a hug.

"That was fire, babe!" She embraces me tightly, and her familiar, citrus-vanilla flavored shampoo momentarily grounds me in the chaos of the convention.

"Thanks. I saw Lucas sitting behind you. Almost ruined

the whole session." I adjust the strap of my messenger bag across my body.

"I hardly believe you'd let him ruin anything. Seems like you'd crush him before he could ever bother you." Blair's perfectly arched eyebrow rises in challenge.

"Yeah, yeah." I wave dismissively. "How long are you here? Can you come with me for a drink? I have to meet up with Marcus for a few minutes."

"I thought you didn't like him?"

"I don't, but I need him to still like me until he doesn't like me anymore." I tuck my phone away.

"Sorry, babe, but I'm headed to the airport," Blair says, with her oversized tote slung over one shoulder and a giant iced coffee in hand. "I was only here to see you, and now I've gotta get back to LA. Promised Wyatt I'd be home in time for dinner."

A familiar rush of gratitude floods my chest. Of course she flew in just for this. Of course she rearranged her whole weekend to hear me speak for forty-five minutes and then immediately turn around and fly home. That's Blair.

She never makes a big deal out of these things, but they always land like love notes anyway. The fact that she came just to support me, no agenda, no networking, just...me? That means everything.

"Ugh. You're so in love. Disgusting," I tease, but there's no malice in it. I actually adore Wyatt and Blair together. They're the epitome of "meant to be." After crushing on each other and hooking up in high school, a miscommunication tore them apart before they left for college. That's when I met Blair and encouraged her to get over him by getting under someone else (solid advice, right?).

When she heard that Sophia Ford was looking for new representation, she realized that Sophia Ford was actually Sophia Bradford, Wyatt's younger sister. Paths crossed, old feelings rekindled, and now they're the most beautifully in-love couple I know. I couldn't be happier for my best friend, even if their perfect relationship makes me slightly nauseated.

"Safe travels and lunch next week, ok?" I give her one more quick hug.

"Definitely. Love you. Be safe!" She squeezes my hand before heading toward the exit.

As I navigate through the growing crowd, I spot Lucas again, surrounded by a pack of executives with slick hair and shark smiles. He's in full PR mode, nodding along like he's listening, with one hand in his pocket and the other gesturing just enough for him to seem thoughtful without committing to an opinion.

Our eyes meet briefly across the room. A zing of awareness shoots through me, annoyingly precise, like my body clocked him before my brain could remind it that *we do not like this man*. It's not attraction, obviously. It's just hyper-vigilance, like spotting a fire hazard—or a red flag with a nice jawline.

I look away first, but not because I'm flustered. I'm just smart enough to keep walking.

two

. . .

Lucas

SHE HAS to be the most infuriating woman I've ever met.

I watch as Jess crosses the casino floor, the long waves of her hair catching the light like she's in some damn shampoo commercial. But she's not the girl in cutoff shorts anymore. Now she's all sharp angles and sleek confidence in tailored black pants that hug her in all the right places, a sculpted black crop top under a structured blazer, and stilettos that make her legs look even longer than I remember. She moves with the kind of purpose that turns heads, every step a reminder that she knows exactly who she is and that she isn't afraid to make sure the room knows it, too. That cool little smirk of hers? Still infuriating. Still captivating.

When she notices me watching, I hold her gaze deliberately, refusing to look away first. It's a bad habit I've never bothered to break. It's addicting, making sure she knows I see her.

Mission accomplished. She rolls those ocean-blue eyes

and continues toward the bar. I smirk to myself before refocusing on the conversation beside me.

"I'm excited about the sports summit panel tomorrow. Rights for athletes are insane these days. Can you imagine being in college now and pulling in millions from sponsorship deals?" Dave Michaels, a mid-level exec from a rival studio, leans in with the excitement of someone who's never actually played a sport.

"Lucas, you played college ball, right?" asks Trent Alvarez, some tech guy who's been hovering around our conversation circle for the past twenty minutes.

"Yeah, baseball at USC." I take a sip of my whiskey.

"What do you think about all this? Feel cheated?" Trent persists, clearly hoping for some juicy sound bite he can repeat later.

"I come from a time where you played for the love of the game," I say, rubbing my thumb absently along the scar on my knuckle from a sliding catch gone wrong sophomore year. "But I understand the frustration of watching everyone but you profit from your likeness."

"Hello, gentlemen. Mind if I steal Lucas for a minute?" Grant's voice comes from behind me. When I turn, he nods toward the far side of the room, indicating that I should follow.

Grant Hall, my boss for the last five years and the closest thing this town has to a box office oracle. As the head of Wonderland Studios, he's built a reputation on picking winners, dodging flops, and staying five steps ahead of every media storm, which is where I come in. He produces the magic. I keep the mess out of the headlines.

I trust Grant more than anyone in this business. He's sharp and unshakable, and he plays the long game better than anyone I've ever seen. If he's pulling me aside mid-mixer, something's up.

I excuse myself and fall into step beside him. "What's up?"

"Our lead actor in *Pink Slip* just crashed his car into a tree."

My stomach drops. "Is he ok?"

"He's fine, but our legal team, his agent, and his publicist are currently making a deal with the LAPD so they won't arrest him for driving under the influence."

"Fuck." I run a hand through my hair, already mentally drafting press statements.

"I need you to get ahead of this. They should be calling you shortly, but I'm sure it's just a matter of minutes before the press catches a whiff."

"I'm on it." My mind races through potential angles. Levi Peterson is our biggest star right now, and *Pink Slip* just wrapped shooting its third season. We can't afford this kind of scandal right before the premiere.

Grant and I catch up on a few other things as we walk to the elevators. He's heading back to his hotel, where Sophia has joined him for the weekend. They're using this quick trip as an engagement celebration. I still can't believe that he actually got down on one knee on the Oscars red carpet to propose to her just last month. After all the drama they went through in getting together last year, I'm happy it all worked out for them.

"Where you headed?" The voice behind me is like nails

on a chalkboard. While familiar, it's incredibly irritating and impossible to ignore.

I turn to find Jess following me, her expression a mix of curiosity and determination. It's annoying how good she always looks. Only she could pull off a bare stomach under a blazer and still look professional.

"Why are you so interested in where I'm going, Jess? Are you stalking me?" I raise an eyebrow.

"You wish." She matches my expression perfectly.

A low chuckle escapes, but not because I think she's funny. I know she smells blood in the water. This woman knows everything about everyone in town. It's a sickness. As annoying as it is, it's also pretty damn impressive.

"I don't have any information to share with you yet. I haven't even heard the story myself."

"Great. I'll join you for the call." She steps closer to the elevator, making it clear she's not going anywhere.

I turn toward her and slide my hands in my pockets, sizing her up. "If you want to come up to my room, you just have to ask, Jessica."

"Jess," she corrects, her eyes narrowing. "And puh-lease. If I wanted a disappointing two minutes of bouncing up and down, followed by nausea and regret, I'd ride the Screaming Eagle at Six Flags, Luke."

"Lucas," I counter automatically, my lips twitching. "And that's...oddly specific."

The elevator dings.

I want to be surprised when she follows me in, but of course I'm not. She's relentless. She has been since the day we met at USC eight years ago. Back then, she had a notebook and a mission. Now she has an audience and a platform, but the effect is the same. She's always chasing the story. And somehow, it's usually mine.

I step in first and pull out my phone, already scrolling through the email from legal, trying to figure out what kind of storm I'm about to walk into.

Jess steps in right behind me, moving uncomfortably close—like, on-purpose close. I catch her leaning just slightly, trying to peek at my screen like she's trying to sneak a look at the answers during a final.

"Seriously?" I say, tilting my phone toward my chest. "Ever heard of boundaries?"

She shrugs, unbothered. "Ever heard of transparency?"

I slide my phone back into my pocket and glance down at her. She's grinning and completely unrepentant, looking way too pleased with herself.

The elevator doors close, sealing us into a mirrored box of tension and too little air. Her scent trails behind her: a hint of honeysuckle with a touch of ocean. Floral and sun. She's standing so close that I can feel the heat radiating off her skin, the brush of her arm every time the elevator shifts. I'm one second away from leaning toward her, just to confirm if it's her perfume or her hair that smells so good.

Then I catch our reflection in the elevator's chrome interior and see her with that smug little smirk, while I look like I'm five seconds away from doing something stupid. I take a tiny step to the right, just enough to clear my head.

She watches the movement with a glint in her eye, like she knows exactly what I'm doing. And maybe she does. That's the thing about Jess Lexington: she's always two steps ahead, which is exactly what makes her so damn dangerous.

And so hard to ignore.

"So, what happened? It was Levi's car that crashed, right?" she asks as the elevator begins its ascent.

"I'm not sure." I keep my voice neutral and stare straight ahead at the mirrored doors.

"Was he hurt? Or was he driving? Was anyone with him?"

"I'm not sure."

"Do you know anything?" Impatience creeps into her voice.

"I know that there's nothing to share with you right now."

She rolls her eyes and slumps against the wall, her thumbs flying across her phone like she's trying to summon national security secrets from thin air. I'm pretty sure she's already texting three sources, digging for details I haven't even confirmed yet.

The elevator dings again.

I step forward just as the doors slide open, and suddenly, there's a thud and a muffled *oof* behind me.

Jess barrels straight into my back, her face smacking between my shoulder blades as one hand grabs a fistful of my jacket to keep from falling.

We freeze like that for a second—me mid-step and her plastered to my back like the world's most annoyed backpack.

"Jesus, warn a guy," I say, turning just enough to glance over my shoulder.

She's still clinging to me like she might fall through the floor. "You stopped short."

"I walked. You crashed. There's a difference."

She pushes off me like I'm contagious, brushing nonexistent wrinkles from her blazer and avoiding eye contact. "Your back is annoyingly solid."

"My personal trainer will be thrilled to hear that."

She glares. "Don't flatter yourself."

"Oh, I don't have to," I say with a smirk as I step out of the elevator. "You literally threw yourself at me."

"Keep dreaming, Carmichael."

"Already am, Lexington."

Her huff is audible behind me, but her footsteps follow mine all the same.

"Thanks for walking me to my door. I'll see you later at the mixer." I swipe the key card across the lock, and it chimes the all-clear to enter. Just as I step forward, my phone chirps, and Jess practically crashes into me again, peeking over my shoulder before I can angle the screen away.

"Is it an update?" Her breath is warm against my neck.

We both go still when the text pops up.

MADELINE

Hi Lucas! Looking forward to our date tonight. Maybe we can pick up where we left off last time? I've missed your… company. See you soon! xoxo – Madeline

"Oh, hot date tonight?" Jess purrs, her voice thick with fake sympathy. "Setting someone else up for disappointment? Should I text her and warn her now or later?"

I grit my teeth as fury bubbles up from somewhere deeper than I want to admit. When my father called earlier to suggest I meet up with Madeline Bishop, his favorite donor's daughter, I gave him a non-committal "yeah, maybe." Apparently, he heard that as a green light, and now I get to look like an asshole backing out of a date I never agreed to in the first place.

Usually, I'd volley back something cutting. But right now, my blood is already boiling. Not at Jess. At him.

At all of it.

My father will explode, of course. Once again, I can play my usual role as the family's lead disappointment. My brother and sister might have fallen in line with the Carmichael political dynasty, but I had the audacity to choose my own path.

"I'll catch up with you later, Jess." I step into my room and close the door, not waiting for her response.

At least watching the door slam in her face brings me a little satisfaction and joy.

I toss my phone onto the bed and walk to the window, where I take in the Vegas skyline. My room offers a perfect view of the Strip, all glittering lights and illusions, kind of like how my job is all about making things look better than they are.

I've got fifteen minutes before the conference call about Levi. That's just enough time to come up with a strategy and tell Madeline the "date" isn't happening. I take off my jacket and grab my laptop, already drafting potential statements in my head.

Levi Peterson, star of Wonderland's upcoming Pink Slip, *was involved in a minor traffic incident last night...*

No. That's too vague. Everyone will assume the worst.

I take a deep breath and pick up my phone again. I need

to deal with Madeline before tackling Levi's mess. As I type out a polite but firm rejection, my mind wanders back to Jess. She's probably already working her sources, trying to beat me to the story.

The thought makes me smile despite myself. If nothing else, she keeps me on my toes.

My phone rings—it's Levi's agent. Time to get to work.

By the time I hang up, twenty minutes later, I have a plan. Levi wasn't drunk—he swerved to avoid hitting a cat that darted into the road. He's shaken but fine, and his "previously scheduled" trip to Scotland for his sister's wedding will give him time to recover. And possibly dry out at a discreet rehab facility that none of us will ever mention.

I'm just finishing up my press statement when my phone buzzes with a text:

JESS

Any update on Levi? Sources saying he was spotted at Cedars. Call me.

I set my phone face down on the desk without responding. Let her stew a little. By the time I'm ready to release a statement, it'll be on my terms, not hers.

three

. . .

Jess

I TWIST on the bar stool, scanning the crowded hotel bar for Lucas so that I can murder him when he arrives. The champagne in my hand is nearly empty, matching my patience level after waiting forty minutes for a response that never came.

Instead of a call or text, he'd sent me the same cookie-cutter press release that every other entertainment reporter received. Me, the one who's known him since college. He's friends with my brother! The dismissal stings more than it should.

"He swerved to avoid hitting a cat? Seriously?" I mutter, taking another sip of bubbly.

The press release landed in my inbox an hour ago, and it's the most transparent PR spin I've ever seen. Levi Peterson, the Hollywood golden boy and star of *Pink Slip*, risking his life for a stray kitten is exactly the kind of saccharine story that makes the public swoon and reporters like me roll their eyes.

I spot Marcus Delgado entering the bar, his expensive suit and slicked-back hair making him stand out even in a sea of polished egos. The second our eyes meet, he flashes that signature smile that is too confident, too practiced.

My stomach flips, and not in a good way.

"Shit," I mutter, sliding off the barstool and ducking down the hallway toward the bathrooms.

It's not that I'm afraid of him. Marcus hasn't done anything wrong, not exactly. He hasn't crossed a line, but he's been dancing on the edge of it for months. And I've let him, smiling when I didn't want to, dodging when I should have said no. I told him to meet me here. Technically, I invited this, and now I feel trapped in a dance I never agreed to choreograph.

You'd think, after everything I've written, after helping expose some of the worst predators in this business, I'd know exactly how to handle a man like Marcus.

But I don't. Because it's different when you're the one in it.

With those women, I was a champion. An advocate. I had perspective, power, and the distance to do something. But with Marcus? I'm too close. Too visible. Too aware of what one wrong word or accusation could cost me.

He's not dangerous, but he is powerful. And in this town, sometimes, that's just as terrifying.

I lean against the cool hallway wall and close my eyes, forcing myself to breathe. In. Out. In again.

I hate that I'm hiding. I hate that I'm playing the game, but I also know what happens to women who don't. I've reported on them, too.

"Please tell me you aren't trying to follow me into the bathrooms now."

My eyes fly open to find Lucas leaning against the opposite wall with his arms crossed over his infuriatingly broad chest, looking entirely too calm for someone who's been ducking me the past hour. His navy blazer is still perfectly tailored, and his hair is infuriatingly intact. Of course he looks good. He probably doesn't even sweat.

I roll my eyes, ready with a comeback, but then he tilts his head and really looks at me.

"You ok?" His tone shifts lower, less sarcastic. The question lands heavier than it should.

I blink, caught off guard. He's studying me, like he can see straight through the sarcasm I usually weaponize.

"I'm fine."

"You don't look fine." His brow furrows, and it's not that smooth PR concern, either; it's real. "Did something happen? Did someone upset you?"

Just for a second, I hesitate. My gaze flicks down the hallway, toward the bar where Marcus is probably already holding court with someone else, flashing that same smarmy grin.

For a beat, I think about telling Lucas the truth.

But that would be giving him something, and I'm not in the mood to give him anything.

Taking the opening, I step forward and jab a finger at his chest. "A press release, Lucas? Really? And you want me to believe he wrecked his car trying to avoid hitting a cat?"

He glances down at my finger, still pressed against him, but instead of backing away, he lifts his hand and gently curls his fingers around mine, just enough to stop the jab, not enough to hurt, but just enough for me to notice how warm his skin is. Just enough for me to forget how to breathe for half a second.

"He's a sucker for kittens," he says, his voice maddeningly calm.

We both look down at the same time at his fingers still wrapped around mine.

Then, as if realizing the moment has lasted a beat too long, he drops my hand like it burned him.

I take a quick step back, my jaw tight. He's still watching me, but his expression is unreadable.

"Enjoy your night, Senator," I bite out, retreating before the flutter in my stomach can make its case.

He turns on his heel and heads toward the bar, his back stiffening at the nickname. I can't help the twitch of glee on my lips from knowing it torments him.

When I found out Lucas was a Carmichael, I thought he would be to be a carbon copy of his father, a senator with presidential aspirations who's built his career on "family values" while quietly steamrolling anyone who threatens his image. As a journalism major, I'd heard how Senator Carmichael systematically buried exposés about shady campaign financing, blackballed reporters, and used power as a shield. He's the kind of man who makes you question why you ever thought the system could be fixed from the inside.

And yeah, I guess, lately, I've been feeling that way about a lot of men in power.

Lucas's mother, on the other hand, is accomplished and elegant, running education charities with genuine heart. Still,

I've never understood how she's stayed married to that man. Then again, political wives learn how to look the other way. It's practically a job requirement.

Lucas? He doesn't seem to think his father is corrupt, which is probably why we got off on the wrong foot eight years ago and never recovered.

"Have a good night, Jess," he calls over his shoulder, not even turning around.

I sigh and straighten my shoulders, forcing my game face back on. Time to fulfill my own dumb decision and meet Marcus for that drink.

As I make my way to the other side of the bar, I pass Lucas, who's now leaning casually against a corner wall with one hand in his pocket and the other wrapped around a glass of something amber. His navy blazer is draped over a nearby chair, and his shirt sleeves are rolled up just enough to show the kind of forearms that should be illegal on a Saturday night.

I studiously ignore him, but I feel his eyes on me. Watching. Tracking.

My practiced smile slides into place as I reach Marcus, who's holding court with a half-circle of ad execs and low-level producers. The moment he spots me, his face lights up like he's just won a prize.

"Jess! Come meet my people!"

He's already reaching for me before I can brace myself. I shift just enough that his hand lands on the side of my hip instead of wrapping around my waist, masking the dodge with a breezy laugh.

My jaw aches from smiling, and my fingers curl around the strap of my bag like it's a grounding stone.

I shake hands and make polite small talk, all while subtly dodging Marcus's orbit. Every time I step back, he steps forward. By the end of the introductions, the two of us have somehow migrated to the far side of the group, away from witnesses.

"You trying to avoid me?" he whispers, his breath too close to my ear.

I grin like we're sharing a secret. "Don't be ridiculous."

Inside, I'm vibrating. Every inch of me is tense. My shoulders are drawn, my back is tight, and my thighs burn from the constant repositioning. It's a dance I know well, one most women in this business do without thinking. Don't offend. Don't make waves. Don't let them think you're rude. Don't let them think you're available.

Marcus leans in again, and his arm brushes mine.

I pretend to spot someone across the room. I pivot to speak to someone else. I inch backward again. Then it happens. His hand lands on my ass. Not a graze. Not a misstep. A full-on palm disguised as an accidental touch.

I barely have time to react before another arm wraps around my waist and pulls me back, out of Marcus's reach.

"There you are," Lucas says, his voice low and calm. Too calm. "I've been looking everywhere for you."

His arm wraps lightly around my back, anchoring me to his side. One hand rests just above my hip, and his thumb absently strokes my waistline, right over my bare stomach. His body is close—too close—and I can feel his heat all around me. I can smell his cologne, something clean and warm, with a trace of cedar and leather.

It's disorienting how fast my body forgets how much I claim to dislike him.

I pretend not to notice how his forearms flex with every movement. His fingers are splayed, firm but gentle. When I glance up, he's looking right at me. Thankfully, his expression is not smug, and he's not smirking. Just checking, concerned. His eyes ask the question he doesn't speak.

Is this ok?

I give the smallest nod.

Lucas exhales softly. That's how I know he was holding his breath.

Marcus's expression shutters. "I didn't know you two were together?"

"It's new," Lucas says, his gaze still locked on mine.

"We've been keeping it quiet," I add smoothly, turning slightly into Lucas's body and resting a casual hand on his chest, right over where I can feel his heart beating a little too fast. "You know how complicated things can get when work and personal lines blur."

I tear my eyes away from Lucas.

"But Marcus," I say, bright and breezy, "you were telling me about that yoga instructor? Her pitch sounded amazing."

To his credit, Marcus blinks, adjusts, and slides right back into the story. Narcissists never stay bruised for long.

Lucas stays close the entire time. His arm doesn't budge, but his thumb makes lazy, rhythmic strokes against my side. It's more than a fake boyfriend move. It's more than a performance. And it's working.

But when Marcus leans in to kiss my cheek goodbye, Lucas's hand tightens so fast it borders on possessive. His fingers dig in just enough to make me feel the moment. And my traitorous body? It hums.

Once Marcus wanders off, Lucas guides me out of the bar, his hand still warm at the base of my spine.

"You didn't have to do that," I murmur.

"I know."

"You were watching me."

"I was."

The honesty makes my stomach flip.

"It's frightening how good your acting is," Lucas says as we step out of the crowd and into one of the quieter hotel corridors.

"Thank you," I reply, coolly professional again. "Now, what's the latest on Levi?"

"No change."

"Then why are we leaving?"

"I need a favor. Hoping I can cash in since I just saved your ass."

I stop so abruptly that he nearly collides with me, his hand still resting on my lower back.

I turn slowly. "Excuse me?" My voice is sharp enough to cut glass.

He holds up a hand in mock surrender. "Relax. I'm not saying you couldn't handle it. But I could see you fidgeting from across the room, Jess. I gave you an out."

"I don't need an out."

"Maybe not." His tone softens. "But Marcus was crossing

a line. You shouldn't have to pretend to be fine just to keep your career intact."

That lands harder than I expect.

The casino noise buzzes behind us, but I barely hear it over the blood rushing in my ears. He's not wrong. And the fact that he noticed? That he cared enough to step in without making a scene? It messes with my balance more than Marcus ever could.

Still, I can't give Lucas the win.

"What do you need from me?" I ask, crossing my arms.

"I need you to be my fake girlfriend for the next fifteen minutes."

I laugh. "Absolutely not."

"Jess—"

"Lucas—"

His eyes suddenly dart past my shoulder, and something flickers there. Panic? Anticipation?

"She's coming this way," he says, his voice pitched low. "I need an answer. Now."

I arch a brow. "So, let me get this straight. You want me to break some poor woman's heart just because you're too much of a coward to tell her you're not interested?"

Lucas doesn't flinch, doesn't blink. His poker face is infuriating. But then he leans in slightly, and his gaze locks onto mine with something real behind it. Something I didn't expect.

"Please," he says. Just that one word. Quiet. Honest. Vulnerable.

And just like that, I'm toast.

"Fine." I sigh dramatically, rolling my eyes for effect. "Tell me what my role is."

His eyes reflect relief, but before I can press for details, he's already moving.

As his hand slips behind my neck and his fingers thread through my hair in a firm but gentle grip, his other arm curls around my waist, pulling me against his solid chest, toned stomach, and broad shoulders. Every point of contact is heat, tension, and danger.

And then he kisses me.

Not a soft, chaste brush. Not a staged peck.

No, Lucas Carmichael *devours* me.

His mouth is hot, demanding, insistent. His lips part mine like he's been waiting to do it for years, and to my utter dismay, my body doesn't hesitate. I kiss him back like he's oxygen. My hands fly to his shoulders, gripping him like I might float away.

It's not what I imagined. It's better. More precise. More chaotic.

And for one breathless moment, I forget this is pretend. I forget about Marcus. I forget about the girl he's trying to avoid by kissing me. I forget about the casino, the story, and the bitterness I've carried since that day at USC.

All I know is the press of his mouth and body, and the maddening realization that I don't want him to stop.

four

. . .

Lucas

HER LIPS ARE SO SOFT. I knew they would be. She tastes like champagne and toothpaste, with a hint of cherry lip balm. Her tongue finds mine like she's actually into this, not just playing a part.

The casino noise fades into white noise. As I move to pull her closer, my hand finds the small of her back, and that's when she breaks the kiss.

The look of genuine shock on her face is priceless. I would laugh, but then I spot Madeline approaching, and I need Jess to pull it together. She can't look like this is the first time she's ever kissed me. Her hand flies to her lips, and I grab it, lacing my fingers through hers. I lean in, and my lips graze her ear.

"Get it together, Scoop. Now's not the time to start falling for me." The nickname slips out before I can stop it. It's what I used to call her when she'd show up at practices and games to watch her brother.

That does it. She snaps out of whatever daze the kiss put

her in and squeezes my fingers so hard that I think she might break them.

"Hey, Lucas," Madeline says, lifting her hand in a small wave, approaching with the practiced hesitation of someone who's been taught to appear demure. I watch as her gaze flits between Jess and me. She's probably hoping this blonde isn't actually "the girlfriend" I mentioned when responding to her texts earlier.

"Hey, Madeline. So good to see you again." I slip into PR mode automatically, my voice taking on that polished edge I use at press conferences. "I'm glad we were able to grab a drink. Let me introduce you to my girlfriend, Jess."

Jess steps forward and right on my foot. Hard. I just got these Common Projects sneakers last week for this event. Four hundred bucks, crushed under her heel.

"Madeline, so great to meet you!" Jess chirps in her "on camera" voice. "I've heard such lovely things about you. Lucas is a fan!"

Madeline's cheeks flush as she looks my way, and I imagine pushing Jess into the hotel's famous fountain. She has no idea the drama she's just ignited.

"Oh, wow," she says. "Well, Lucas and I do go way back. Our families have been friends for as long as I can remember."

I internally roll my eyes. If, by "friends," she means "political allies," then sure.

"Jess and I go way back, too," I counter, sliding my arm around her waist. "We met at one of my college baseball games. She couldn't take her eyes off me." I give Jess a wink and shift her weight off my abused shoe. "Limited-edition sneakers. Keep your monster feet off them," I whisper, catching the floral scent in her hair.

"I was there to see my brother play," Jess clarifies. "But I do remember Lucas tripping over his ego and faceplanting into a Gatorade cooler."

"I don't remember that at all, dear," I say with a smile plastered on my face.

"Oh, Lukey-bear, are you taking all your vitamins?" Jess pats my cheek condescendingly. "I don't want you to forget about our first real conversation, when you told me PR was 'just journalism with better paychecks and lower ethical standards.'"

I blink. God, she's sharp with an insult.

"Should we get a drink?" Madeline suggests.

I guide both women to a curved booth at the hotel bar. Jess maneuvers so that I'm squished in the middle, with her on my left, sitting as far away as possible without looking suspicious; Madeline is on my right, sitting inappropriately close.

"Lucas, tell me how work has been." Madeline leans in, her perfume is overwhelming and makes me miss Jess's fresh scent. "Daddy said your studio is making all the best movies right now."

"It has been a good year for us," I say, sipping my Macallan 18. I shift casually, trying to get Jess's attention. She's on her phone, and I need her to act like she's into me.

Madeline turns to face me more directly. Bringing one of her legs up onto the seat, she places her hand on my shoulder before starting into some political drivel about polling numbers and constituent outreach that I stopped caring about the day I chose USC over Stanford and baseball over becoming the third generation of Carmichael men in politics.

I kick Jess under the table. She kicks me back harder, still focused on her phone.

"Jess! You're not following me, are you?" Marcus's voice slurs after what appears to be one too many cocktails. He slides into the booth, pushing Jess closer to me. Well, that's one way to get her attention.

"Oh, Marcus, you are too funny!" Jess's voice drips with synthetic sweetness. "Looks like you're having loads of fun!"

Jess nuzzles into my side, placing her hand on my thigh. My skin prickles with unexpected heat, and then she's grabbing my leg so hard she'll leave a bruise. I take that as a cue to place my arm around her and pull her closer.

I admit that Jess is attractive, with her sun-kissed skin and effortless beauty, but her personality should make it impossible for me to notice.

"I thought you and Lucas were together?" Marcus stage-whispers. "Who's the hot babe with him?"

He's not exactly whispering, and we can all hear him. His voice carries across the bar, and a few heads turn our way.

I see red, but I smile anyway. The PR version of me might be polished, but the man part of me? That one's about two seconds from dragging him across the bar.

"Marcus," I say evenly, "Madeline is a longtime family friend. She's also terrifying in a courtroom, so I'd suggest not calling her a 'babe' unless you'd like to get acquainted with the concept of a cease and desist."

He laughs like I've told a joke, too drunk to catch the edge in my tone.

Marcus reaches across the table to shake Madeline's hand, and when she extends hers, he instead brings her fingers to his lips. Gross. But I look over at her, and she's blushing all different shades of red.

"Oh, how cute!" Jess lunges at the opportunity to get away from Marcus. "Madeline, let's trade places so you can get to know Marcus!"

Before I can process what's happening, she's sliding across my lap. Her ass scrapes across my crotch, and the pressure awakens parts of me that have no business responding to Jess Lexington. I realize that she's moving deliberately, slowly.

I use the opportunity to wrap my arms around her waist and hold her in place. My lips grazing her ear as I whisper, "If you want my dick, you just have to ask, Scoop."

That gets her moving, but not before I catch the slight hitch in her breath.

"We should get a bottle of Dom to celebrate old friends and new! Lucas's treat!" Jess announces, signaling a server. Alright, she wants to play?

"Honey, don't be shy," I counter, my hand finding the small of her back. "You can tell them we're celebrating our six-month anniversary and you confessing your love to me."

I smirk as I take a measured sip of my whiskey, watching her eyes narrow dangerously.

Confusion creases Marcus's forehead. "You've been together six months—"

"You love him?" Madeline asks simultaneously as the blood drains from her face.

Jess grinds her heel into my toe box, and I know that's going to leave a mark on both my shoe and possibly my foot.

"I felt bad that you had said it so many times," Jess says sweetly, "so I figured it was time to say it back."

I twist my fingers through her silky hair. "Well, I know you want more. I see the searches for wedding rings on the laptop when you 'accidentally' leave the web browser open." I tug her hair gently, feeling a hint of satisfaction when her pupils dilate slightly.

"Well, you did say you wanted to get married before you turn thirty," she counters. "I know it's coming up. I don't know if we'll make it, but at least you can say you're in love with someone."

The champagne arrives, and Jess tops off her glass. I'm not sure how many she's had, but she's getting braver and more handsy the longer this charade carries on. And this game of cat and mouse is unexpectedly entertaining. People nearby are starting to listen in.

"I know you didn't meet that goal of being married by thirty, either," I continue. "I'm truly sorry, babe. We just didn't get together in time." I glance at Marcus and Madeline, who are watching us like we're engaged in a tennis match. "Hey, did you guys know Jess is older than me?"

She brings her knee up to rest her leg over my lap, but with a force that grazes sensitive territory. I grab her thigh and realize that my grip is much higher than intended. I look down and then up at her, and she raises her eyebrows challengingly.

"Yeah, I've always liked my women a little older," I

manage. "They've got more experience handling difficult situations."

Jess's chest heaves slightly. Not because she's drawn to me, no, but because she's preparing to slowly destroy me. And I'm a sick bastard for enjoying this.

She launches into a story about me taking her to Disneyland for her birthday, knowing about her secret love of Mickey-shaped pretzels. What's unsettling is how she's incorporated real details, including my annual pass, which no one is supposed to know about, and my genuine affection for the Star Wars section of the park.

"And then," she continues, leaning into me like we're sharing an inside joke, "he bought me this ridiculous stuffed Chewbacca that's still on our bed, even though I tease him mercilessly about it."

I'm momentarily speechless because I do, in fact, own a stuffed Chewbacca. How does she know that?

More people join our table, and at some point, we switch to taking Vegas bomb shots because what happens in Vegas, right?

Our love story is now pulling a crowd, and a woman with a professional camera appears. I think it's someone from the NAB Show—I'm not sure—but she asks to take our photo for social media. Jess presses against my side, lays her head on my shoulder, and beams.

"You guys are so cute together," the photographer says. "How long have you been a couple?"

"Six months," we answer in unison, and for a second, it feels almost real.

"My boss is going to love your story," she says. We slide

right by that comment with more backstory on our pretend relationship.

As the night progresses, our stories become more elaborate. I find myself recounting how Jess hates roses but loves tropical flowers like plumeria and hibiscus, how she always steals the covers, and how she refuses to watch the end of sad movies. None of this is true—or at least, I don't think it is—but it rolls off my tongue with alarming authenticity.

Jess tells everyone about my supposedly secret love of cooking and how she fell for me when she found out I volunteer at an animal shelter. The first part isn't entirely untrue. I do love to cook. How she knows this is beyond me.

"To the happy couple!" someone toasts, and then another.

"They're all buying it," Jess whispers, her breath warm against my ear.

"We're pretty convincing," I agree as I tighten my arm around her waist.

Her blue eyes, slightly unfocused from the champagne, meet mine. "Maybe too convincing."

I don't know what possesses me, but I lean in and kiss her again, this time slower, more deliberate. The crowd around us cheers, but all I can focus on is how right it feels, how the curve of her body fits against mine, how the taste of her lips is rapidly becoming my favorite flavor.

"You know what you guys should do?" Marcus slurs, slamming down his glass. "You should get married! Right now! Vegas, baby!"

"That's the stupidest thing I've ever heard," Jess laughs, but her eyes don't leave mine.

"I don't know," I hear myself say. "Could be fun."

The crowd erupts in encouragement. Madeline has long since disappeared, giving up on any hope she had for us and the evening. The night has transformed into something unrecognizable from how it began.

"You're not serious," Jess says, but there's a dangerous glint in her eye.

The whiskey, Vegas bombs, and heat of her body against mine make me reckless. "Scared, Lexington?"

"You wish, Carmichael." She downs her champagne and stands, wobbling slightly. "Let's do it."

The crowd roars its approval, and as someone starts looking up the nearest chapel on their phone, I have the fleeting thought that this might be either the biggest PR disaster of my career or the best night of my life.

Maybe both.

five

. . .

Jess

COLD. Hard. Wet?

My eyes flutter open—and then immediately slam shut against the painful assault of sunlight. My mouth tastes like something died in it, and my head feels like it's being squeezed in a vise. When I finally force my eyelids apart, I'm greeted by the curved white porcelain of a bathtub. A very nice bathtub in what appears to be a very nice bathroom.

And I'm lying in it. In only my bra and panties.

"What the hell?" I croak, my voice raw, like I've been shouting. Or singing. Oh, God, was I singing?

I sit up too quickly and wince as pain ricochets through my skull. Something tickles my forehead, and I reach up to find a wedding veil tangled in my hair, the comb digging into my scalp.

My stomach lurches as fragments of the previous night flash through my mind. Champagne, lots of champagne. Shots. Lucas's arm around me. Madeline's face. More champagne. A crowd cheering.

I pull myself to standing, the bathroom spinning slightly, and step gingerly out of the tub. My clothes are scattered across the marble floor. My black pants are draped over the towel rack. One heel is on the counter, but the other is nowhere in sight. An empty champagne bottle sits on its side next to a—is that a garter? I haven't had a hangover like this since college.

After wrapping myself in a plush hotel robe hanging on the door, I venture out of the bathroom. I'm in a massive suite with floor-to-ceiling windows overlooking the Vegas strip. The place is scattered with evidence of a celebration: another empty bottle, a half-eaten strawberry, rose petals creating a trail to the bed.

As I follow them, dread builds with each step.

When I turn the corner, I find him: Lucas Carmichael, media spin master and eternal pain in my ass, sprawled face down on the king-sized bed. The sheets cover exactly none of him, giving me an unobstructed view of his perfectly toned backside. The baseball-player physique hasn't faded since college.

For a brief, clearly hangover-induced moment of insanity, I just stare. Not that I'm keeping score, but apparently, the man does squats. Jesus.

Then reality hits.

"WHAT. THE. FUCK."

Lucas twists and bolts upright, disoriented, his hair sticking out in every direction. He blinks at me, then down at himself, then back at me. Recognition dawns in his eyes, followed immediately by horror.

"Jesus Christ!" He grabs a pillow, covering himself, but

not before I get a complete view of everything he has to offer. And it's…impressive. Not that I care. "Why am I in your room?"

"This isn't my room!" I gesture wildly, and the movement sets off another wave of nausea. "I woke up in the bathtub! In my underwear! With this!" I point to the veil still hanging from my hair.

"Why are you…" he starts to say, but then he notices something on his left hand. He raises it slowly, staring at the simple gold band on his ring finger. "No. No, no, no."

I look down at my own hand. An identical band gleams back at me.

"This isn't happening," I whisper. "We didn't—"

"We couldn't have—"

We stare at each other, with panic mirrored in our faces. Lucas wraps the sheet around his waist and stands, scanning the room as if searching for an explanation.

"Wait. Whose suite is this?" he asks, moving toward the window. "This isn't my room. I was on the twelfth floor."

"I was on fourteen," I say, following him out to the living area, keeping a healthy distance.

As if on cue, we both spot the massive gift basket on the coffee table. A banner across it reads, "CONGRATULA-TIONS, MR. & MRS. CARMICHAEL."

"Mrs. Carmichael?" I echo, my voice rising to a pitch that makes my own head throb. "Oh, my God. I'm going to be sick."

"There!" Lucas points to a piece of paper on the bar. He crosses the room, careful to keep the sheet secured around him, and grabs it. "It's a marriage certificate."

"Let me see that." I snatch the document from him. "This can't be legal. We were completely wasted."

But there it is in black and white. My signature, wobbly but unmistakable. Lucas's, equally messy. Two witness signatures: Marcus Delgado and...

"Dylan Reeves?" I blink at the name. "Why does that sound familiar?"

"Documentary filmmaker," Lucas says, rubbing his temples. "Award-winning indie darling who, I think, just got a major deal with Wonderland Studios. I'm pretty sure he was at the bar last night."

"Why would he be a witness at our wedding?" I sink onto a bar stool, with the marriage certificate still in hand. "What else don't we remember?"

We're interrupted by the simultaneous buzzing of our phones, which are, miraculously, plugged in and charging on the counter. Lucas reaches his first and swipes it open. Then he freezes.

"Oh, shit."

"What?"

He turns the screen to me. It's open to Instagram, displaying a post from Dylan. The image shows Lucas and me at what is clearly a Vegas wedding chapel. I'm in my black suit from the conference, with a veil on my head and a bouquet in hand. Lucas is in his uniform blazer and jeans, and those fucking tennis shoes he loves so much, grinning like he's just won the lottery. We're gazing at each other with expressions that could only be described as besotted.

The caption reads:

Honored to witness true love unfold last night! Thrilled to announce that industry power duo @LucasCarmichael and @JessLexington will be the first newlywed couple featured in my upcoming *Real Power* documentary series! Their chemistry is undeniable. I can't wait to share their journey from rivals to partners! #RealPower #VegasWedding #ComingSoon

"What the actual…" I grab my own phone. Notifications flood the screen. I've got messages from family, friends, and colleagues, alerts from news outlets, and endless social media tags.

"We've gone viral," Lucas says, scrolling through his feed. "Everyone thinks we're—oh, God, my father is going to have a stroke."

"His documentary series?" I stare at Dylan's post again. "We agreed to be in his documentary?" It would be funny if it weren't my actual life imploding in real time.

Lucas paces, trailing the sheet behind him like a toga. "We need to fix this. Now."

"Agreed. We call our lawyers, get this annulled, issue statements explaining it was a drunken mistake—"

"Wait," Lucas interrupts, holding up a message. "Dylan says, 'The chemistry between you two last night was electric. I couldn't believe you've been secretly dating for six months. The viewers are going to love your story.'" He looks up at me. "Did we tell people we've been dating for six months?"

A memory surfaces. Lucas's arm around me, telling everyone about our "anniversary." Me, playing along, one-upping him with increasingly elaborate stories.

"I think we might have," I admit, "but how did Dylan get involved?" Another memory clicks into place. A photographer from the NAB Show. "The woman. With the camera. Was she working with Dylan?"

"I don't remember."

As we stare at each other, the gravity of the situation sinks in.

Lucas drops onto the couch, his head in his hands.

I bend to grab his button-down from the floor, and the hem of my robe flutters open. The cool morning air hits my skin, and when I glance down, I catch a glimpse of lace peeking through the gap.

When I straighten, I realize that Lucas isn't hiding in his hands anymore.

He's watching me.

His eyes trail from the gap in my robe down the length of my legs, pausing at my toes before climbing slowly back up to meet mine. There's a beat of silence, and his eyes flash with a glimpse of desire.

My stomach flips.

"Lucas," I say slowly, with dawning horror, "did we...you know..." I gesture at us and the bedroom.

"I don't think so? I mean, I was naked, but you were in the tub, and—"

"I think I would remember." I pull the robe tighter around myself. "I mean, I remember some things. The kissing. Your hands." I stop. Heat that has nothing to do with my hangover rises to my face. I know I would remember, and I see no evidence that indicates we did.

"Right." He clears his throat. "So, no sex. Just marriage. To each other."

"And a documentary we agreed to be in."

"I'll call my attorney when we get back to LA," he says. "Get this sorted out."

"Me, too."

An uncomfortable silence falls between us, broken only by the persistent buzzing of our phones. I look at him, really look at him: his messy hair, the stubble on his jaw, that familiar crease between his eyebrows that appears when he's stressed. For eight years, I've seen him as the opposition, the slick PR guy spinning stories to protect his clients from people like me. Now he's my husband.

"Lucas?"

"Yeah?"

"I'm going to need you to put on some pants before we figure out our next move."

For the first time since waking up, a hint of a smile crosses his face. "That's probably a good idea."

six

· · ·

Lucas

THE WONDERLAND STUDIOS lot is buzzing with its usual Monday morning energy: PAs rushing coffee orders, talent slipping into trailers, executives power-walking between meetings. No one gives me a second glance as I make my way to Grant's office. I feel like I should have a scarlet "V" for Vegas emblazoned on my chest or at least be trailing wedding confetti.

But no. Same nods from colleagues. Same life, except for the gold band burning a hole in my pocket. I couldn't bring myself to wear it, but throwing it away felt strangely wrong.

My phone vibrates with a text. Austin Lexington, Jess's younger brother. My former teammate and friend.

AUSTIN

Dude. DUDE. When were you going to tell me you were hooking up with my sister?

I wince. With all the chaos of the past twenty-four hours, including the rushed checkout from the hotel suite we didn't book, the wordless plane ride, with us seated nowhere near each other, and the tense "we'll call our lawyers" goodbye at LAX, I hadn't even thought about Austin.

LUCAS

It's not what it looks like. Call you later to explain. I'm sorry, man.

I slip the phone away as I reach Grant's office. His assistant waves me through with a knowing smile that makes my stomach clench. Grant is standing at the floor-to-ceiling windows overlooking the lot, hands clasped behind his back, exuding the casual power that's made him a legend before forty.

"The prodigal husband returns," he says without turning around.

"Grant, I can explain—"

Waving a dismissive hand, he finally turns to face me. "Lucas, sit down before you sprain something in your rush to apologize."

I sink into one of the leather chairs opposite his desk. "I'm sorry for embarrassing the studio. It was a drunken mistake, and I've already contacted my attorney. We'll have it annulled immediately."

Grant studies me for a beat too long. Then he sighs and takes his own seat. "How long have we known each other?"

"Five years, give or take."

"And in those five years, have I ever given you the impression that I give a damn what you do in your personal life?"

I blink. "No, but—"

"Is Jess Lexington pressuring the studio in her reporting?

Using your relationship for insider information? Causing any actual conflict of interest I should be aware of?"

"No, of course not. She's..." I stop, unsure how to describe whatever Jess and I are to each other. Rivals? Acquaintances? Temporary spouses?

Grant leans forward. "Frankly, Lucas, I've always suspected that something was brewing between you two. That kind of tension"—he makes an explosive gesture with his hands—"doesn't come from nowhere. Fine line between love and hate and all that."

Before I can respond, my phone buzzes on the table. "FATHER" flashes across the screen in all caps, and that one word hits me like a punch to the gut.

I brace myself. If I don't answer, it'll only get worse. And if I do...well, it won't be great, either.

The familiar twist tightens low in my stomach. Frustration. Resentment. Obligation.

Even now, with my own career, my own place, my own life, he still finds ways to insert himself. Always with expectations. Always with control.

I flash Grant an apologetic look. He gives me a small nod, a silent go-ahead.

I step out into the hallway and answer.

"Lucas." My father's voice is ice. "I expect you're already meeting with an attorney."

"Good morning to you, too, Dad."

"This is not a joke. You will annul this...indiscretion immediately. I've already called Bernard to handle the paperwork."

I pinch the bridge of my nose. Bernard, his ancient attorney, who still uses a flip phone and a fax machine. "I have my own lawyer."

"You will use Bernard. And you will issue a statement explaining that this was a misunderstanding, possibly orchestrated by that woman. Perhaps she had ulterior motives, given your position."

I feel heat creeping into my face. "She's not after my money, Dad. Her father owns the California Devils."

"The what?"

"It's a Major League Baseball team. Trust me, she doesn't need or want your money."

"Then they're after connections to my campaign. You'll suggest she took advantage—"

"Dad, stop." I'm surprised by the firmness in my voice. "I'm not blaming Jess for anything. This was mutual..." I stop myself before I say "stupidity." It doesn't feel exactly stupid.

A long pause.

"Lucas James Carmichael, the future of this family's legacy is at stake. Your sister's husband is up for re-election. I'm announcing my gubernatorial run in less than six months. And you're in the tabloids with some sports reporter—"

"Journalist," I correct automatically, my jaw already clenching.

"Whatever she is, she is not Madeline Bishop. Who, by the way, is devastated. Her father called me this morning. You will fix this. You will tell Madeline you are interested in her. You will do your duty to this family for once in your life."

The call disconnects, and as I stand there in the hallway, the silence is louder than anything he said.

My phone stays in my hand, but my fingers curl into a fist

around it. My jaw is tight, and my shoulders are tense. There's a throb in my temple and a burning at the base of my throat that I can't swallow away.

I'm almost thirty years old. I run communications for one of the most powerful studios in Hollywood. But after five minutes on the phone with him, I'm twelve again, with my back straight and my tie perfect, nodding through his monologue about legacy and image like it was gospel.

He didn't ask what I want. He never has. He doesn't care that I've built a career that I'm proud of and that I'm good at it. He doesn't care that I've done it on my own. All that matters to him is how I'm perceived, if I'm aligned, or if I can offer anything useful politically.

And now he wants me to call up Madeline, string her along for optics, and pretend she's what I want? That's not who I am. I might be his son, but I'm not him.

I have no interest in turning my personal life into a negotiation, no interest in pretending to care about someone for the sake of "family strategy." I've played the game long enough to know exactly what it costs, and I'm done footing the bill.

I take a deep breath, scrub a hand over my face, and steel myself before walking back in. Grant's watching me, his expression unreadable.

"I take it your father isn't happy?" he asks with one brow raised.

"No." I exhale slowly. "I've ruined his plans for a political merger between our family and one of his donors."

Grant nods slowly and then gestures to his laptop. "You know, Dylan Reeves has a first-look deal with us."

The abrupt subject change throws me. "I thought so."

"This show he's been developing about industry power dynamics, we're likely to bid on it when he's ready."

"Grant, listen—"

"The footage he posted of you and Jessica has already gone viral. The chemistry reads well on camera. Very authentic."

"It's not—"

"Let me guess," Grant continues, standing to pace. "Your father wants you to annul your marriage and blame your new wife, a respected journalist with significant industry connections, I might add, so you can marry the daughter of his donor." He stops to fix me with a pointed look. "How do you think that plays in the press?"

My stomach sinks. "Not well."

"Not well," he echoes. "And it puts this studio in the position of having our head of communications appear manipulative, dishonest, and, frankly, a bit of an ass."

He's right. As much as I hate to admit it, spinning this to blame Jess would be inexcusable, both personally and professionally.

"Dylan's documentary could be interesting," Grant says, returning to his seat, "and staying married, even temporarily, would certainly silence your father's pressure about Madeline."

I stare at him. "You can't be serious."

"Six months. Maybe a year at most. You present a united front, do the documentary, then have an amicable separation when the spotlight fades." He shrugs. "It's not uncommon in this town."

"You want me to stay married. To Jess Lexington. The woman who once published a three-thousand-word exposé on studios manipulating box office numbers."

"The very one." Grant smiles. "It was excellent reporting, by the way. Got us all to clean up our practices."

"She'll never agree to this."

"Maybe. Maybe not." He leans back in his chair. "But consider the benefits for her, too."

I think about how our marriage immediately protects her from relentless industry players like our friend Marcus—and the documentary exposure could boost her podcast significantly.

My mind races, attempting to process the surreal turn this meeting has taken. "You're suggesting I pitch this to her as a business arrangement?"

"I'm suggesting you consider all options before rushing to undo something that might actually solve several problems at once." Grant stands, signaling the end of our meeting. "Talk to Jess. See where her head is at."

I rise, feeling unsettled. "And if she says no?"

Grant clasps my shoulder. "Then you annul the marriage, weather the storm from your father and the press, and we all move on."

As I leave his office, my phone buzzes with a text from Jess.

JESS

My lawyer says we need to meet. Today.
How's 4pm? I'll send address shortly.

I stare at the message as Grant's proposal echoes in my

head. Six months of pretending to be married to the most infuriating woman I know. Six months of domestic proximity to someone who's made a career of challenging people like me. Six months of fighting this unwelcome attraction that's apparently visible enough for even Grant to notice.

It's ridiculous. Impossible. A disaster waiting to happen.

So, why am I already drafting a pros and cons list in my head?

LUCAS

I'll be there.

seven

. . .

Jess

"NO COMMENT MEANS NO COMMENT, Harvey. I don't care what TMZ is offering."

I end the call and toss my phone onto my desk, where it lands with a clatter among the organized chaos of notes, empty energy drink cans, and recording equipment. The glass-walled studio of *On the Red Carpet* normally feels like my sanctuary, the place where I'm in control, where I'm the one to ask the questions and shape the narrative.

Not today.

Today, I'm the story. And I hate it.

The door swings open without a knock, and Blair marches in, her designer bag swinging from her arm, her expression a mix of concern and barely contained excitement.

"Two days," she announces, dropping into the chair across from my desk. "Two days of unanswered texts and calls. I had to find out about your wedding from Instagram, Jessica Lexington. Instagram."

I cringe. "I'm sorry. It's been a bit chaotic."

"Oh, I bet it has." Blair leans forward, her eyes gleaming. "Now, spill it. What the hell is going on?"

"There's not much to tell," I say, fidgeting with my pen. "It was a mistake. A drunken Vegas mistake that's being handled."

"A mistake?" Blair arches a perfect eyebrow. "The photos Dylan posted look pretty convincing for a mistake."

Heat creeps into my cheeks. "That's the professional lighting in the chapel. And probably the eight glasses of champagne."

"Honey, that wasn't champagne lighting. That was lust lighting. I've known you since our Boston U days, and I've never seen you look at anyone the way you were looking at Lucas in those photos."

I groan, dropping my head into my hands, but not before a flicker of those images flashes behind my eyelids. His hand curled around my waist. The way he looked at me like I was the only person in the room. The way my smile—God, I was smiling—wasn't forced.

No. Nope. Champagne. Lighting. Chaos. All of it.

It's just physical. That's all. Lucas is objectively attractive in the most annoying way possible, all angles and confidence and that stupid knowing smirk. It doesn't mean anything. I don't even like him. I can barely tolerate him. So what if he smells like woodsy cologne and expensive decisions? So what if he has forearms that could break the internet?

It doesn't mean I want him.

"I mean, can you believe this happened?" I mumble into my hands. "Me? Married? To Lucas Carmichael, of all people? The guy whose entire job is spinning stories I'm trying to uncover?"

Blair studies me for a moment, clearly not buying it. "You know, you mention him an awful lot for someone you supposedly can't stand."

"Because he's constantly in my way!" I protest, perhaps too quickly. "Every time I'm working on a story about Wonderland, there he is with his perfect jawline and his media training, deflecting my questions and protecting the studio machine."

"Mm-hmm. His perfect jawline. Terrible."

I throw a pen at her, which she dodges effortlessly. "Stop it. This is serious. I'm meeting my attorney in two hours to figure out how to end this nightmare."

"How's your family taking the news? I assume Austin is thrilled that his former teammate is now his brother-in-law."

I roll my eyes. "Everyone's thrilled. Dad's so excited he's already planning a post-wedding reception at the stadium, never mind that he's never actually met Lucas—at least, as my boyfriend—and I've spent the last year telling him I'm not dating anyone."

"Your dad loves you."

"I know. He just wants me to be happy, and in his mind, marriage equals happiness." I sigh. "My older brother, Garrett, sent me this congratulatory text that somehow still managed to convey his judgment about my 'life choices.' As if choosing not to join the family business wasn't bad enough, now I've gone and married someone on a whim."

"And Austin?"

"Way too happy. Called me yesterday, going on about

how great it is that his teammate and his sister finally 'stopped dancing around each other' and how he's looking forward to having a friend at family holidays." I twist a strand of hair around my finger. "He did say he's going to kick Lucas's ass for hitting on his sister without his blessing, though."

Blair laughs. "At least that's appropriately brotherly."

"The point is," I continue, "everyone thinks this is some grand romance that's been brewing for years. My father, who usually spends his time worrying about bullpen stats, has suddenly taken an interest in my love life. It's...weird."

"So, what's the plan? Besides the annulment."

I straighten, shifting into problem-solving mode. "I'm meeting with my attorney at four. We'll file an annulment, issue a joint statement explaining that it was a mutual error in judgment, emphasize our continued professional respect for each other, and politely request privacy as we move forward."

"Very PR. Lucas would be proud."

I shoot her a glare.

"And the documentary?" Blair asks. "Dylan's been promoting it nonstop."

"We'll have to back out. Pay a penalty if necessary. I can't be followed around by cameras while pretending to be in love with Lucas Carmichael."

"Why not? You're both good actors—apparently good enough to convince an entire Vegas bar you've been together for six months."

"Because I'm a journalist, Blair. My credibility is everything. How can I maintain objectivity if I'm playing house with the head of communications at a major studio?"

Blair shrugs. "People have managed worse conflicts of interest in this town."

"Not me." I stand, gathering my notes and laptop. "I've worked too hard to be taken seriously. I'm not going to throw it away for some ridiculous reality show spectacle."

"Where are you meeting the attorney?"

"Wexler's office on Sunset. Lucas is meeting me there." I check my watch. "I've got a couple of things to knock out first, so I should get moving."

"Call me right after," Blair says, standing to give me a quick hug.

Lucas is waiting outside the building when I arrive, leaning against a concrete pillar in his signature navy blazer over a crisp white shirt, dark jeans, and those designer sneakers he's so precious about. His hair is impeccably styled, and sunglasses hide his eyes, the very picture of California professional casual. My heart does an annoying little skip that I immediately attribute to anxiety about the meeting.

"We need to file the annulment today," I say without preamble, approaching in a rush of words. "I've already drafted a joint statement emphasizing mutual respect and requesting privacy. We'll need to contact Dylan about backing out of the documentary. I'm happy to handle that call if you prefer. I think that if we move quickly, this whole thing will blow over in a week, two max."

Lucas removes his sunglasses slowly and looks at me with an unreadable expression. "Hello to you, too, wife."

"Don't call me that," I hiss, glancing around for potential eavesdroppers.

Still, the word zings through me, quick and warm. The worst part? I kind of like how it sounds coming from him.

"Right." His voice is oddly flat. "Let's get this over with."

Something about his demeanor unsettles me. He's usually more combative, but I don't have time to analyze it as we enter the building and take the elevator to the top floor in silence.

Victoria Wexler, my attorney, greets us warmly in her corner office with floor-to-ceiling windows overlooking the city. She's handled my contract negotiations and set up the paperwork to start my podcast, but I've never seen her look quite so intrigued.

"Jessica, Lucas, please have a seat." She gestures to the chairs across from her desk. "I've reviewed your case, and I have some important information to share before we proceed."

"We'd like to file for an annulment as soon as possible," I say, settling into my chair. "On whatever grounds will end this immediately."

"Yes, you mentioned that on the phone." Victoria opens a folder. "However, there's a complication I need to discuss with you first."

Lucas shifts beside me. "What kind of complication?"

Victoria looks at me. "Jessica, your marriage has triggered a trust provision established by your mother before she passed away."

I blink. "I'm sorry, what?"

"Your mother set up a trust for you as part of her estate

planning. It contains a significant inheritance from her personal investment portfolio and a board seat on the Reynolds Foundation for Journalism Ethics."

My mind reels. Mom has been gone for almost seventeen years. She was always passionate about the truth. The Reynolds Foundation is one of the most respected organizations supporting investigative reporting and ethics in media, and one of Mom's proudest moments was when she started serving on the board.

"I didn't know about any trust," I say slowly.

"Your parents kept it confidential. According to the documentation, they didn't want it to influence your life choices." Victoria smiles gently. "Your mother specifically noted that she didn't want you feeling pressured to marry for financial reasons, nor did she want potential partners pursuing you for the inheritance."

"So, what's the issue?" Lucas asks.

Victoria turns a document toward us. "The trust was structured to release when Jessica either married or turned thirty-five, whichever came first. Your Vegas wedding has activated the release clause."

I frown. "But if we annul—"

"If you annul or divorce within six months, the assets revert to a charitable foundation your mother established," Victoria explains. "You would still receive a modest distribution, but the bulk, approximately twelve million dollars in current valuation, would go to the foundation."

The room seems to tilt slightly.

"Twelve million dollars?" I repeat, my voice thinner than I want it to be.

"Including that board seat on the Reynolds Foundation," she adds, "which I know you've expressed admiration for in the past." She glances between us. "It's a position that could give you significant influence in shaping the future of journalism ethics."

I feel Lucas's eyes on me, but I can't look at him. I can't look at anything.

Twelve million dollars. A seat at the table I've dreamed of. And my mom...my mom built this. She built it for me. It's like she's reaching out from the grave, not just with a check but with a whisper: *I see you. I see the path you chose. I believe in it.*

I swallow hard, and my fingers curl into my lap. My chest is tight, not from the money but from the meaning underneath. The weight of what I thought I'd had to prove for all these years just lifted.

After she died, it was like the world around me calcified. Austin and I stayed close, since we were the two kids left at home who lost the same person and were trying to pretend we didn't. Dad was good, steady, warm. He made it through somehow. But Garrett left for college and never really came back in the same way. He got his share, I assume. He never said a word. I don't blame him.

Maybe Mom always knew I'd need something different. Not just money, not just freedom, but proof. That I mattered. That the choices I made by following her into journalism instead of sports, using my voice instead of my swing, weren't wrong.

"This trust," Lucas says, his voice careful, "requires her to stay married for at least six months?"

Victoria nods. "At that point, even if you divorce, the assets transfer permanently to Jessica."

And just like that, my heart riots in a swirl of gratitude, disbelief, and sheer panic.

Six months. With Lucas Carmichael.

Six months of pretending, of playing house with the one man who challenges me, contradicts me, drives me absolutely insane, and sees right through me.

"We need a moment," I tell Victoria, finally looking at Lucas. "Alone."

She graciously steps out and closes the door behind her.

"Did you know about this?" I demand as soon as we're alone.

"About your secret trust fund? No, Jess. Contrary to what you might think, I don't spend my free time investigating your financial situation."

I pace the office. "This is insane. We can't stay married."

"Why not?"

I stop and stare at him. "Because we're not actually in love? Because you work for a studio I regularly scrutinize? Because your father wants you to marry someone else for his political gain? Take your pick."

"Look," Lucas says, his voice surprisingly gentle, "I'm not suggesting we actually...you know. But if we played along for six months, you'd secure your inheritance, and I'd get my father off my back about Madeline."

"You sound like you've been thinking about this," I say suspiciously.

Lucas shifts in his chair. "I had a meeting with Grant this morning. He had some thoughts about the situation."

I groan, burying my head in my hands. "I can't believe Grant Hall knows about our marriage."

"Yeah. Just him. And a few million other people the world over."

Damn social media. Damn champagne.

I sit up, folding my arms. "And what did the great and powerful studio head have to say?"

Lucas hesitates. "He knows I've been dealing with some pressure from my father. About Madeline. Grant suggested the documentary might actually be good for both of us."

"So, your boss thinks we should stay married?"

"Six months," Lucas says, ignoring my sarcasm. "We do the documentary, make public appearances when necessary, and then part amicably. You get your inheritance and that board seat, I get some peace from my family situation, and we both get exposure from Dylan's project."

"This is absolutely crazy," I mutter, but I'm already running calculations in my head. Six months isn't that long. I could handle half a year of occasional appearances with Lucas. I see him at most of the events I attend already.

"We could live separately," I suggest. "Just meet up when we need to film or make appearances."

"That could work." Lucas nods. "Professional collaboration with a contractual end date."

I'm about to respond when both our phones buzz simultaneously.

I glance at the screen.

DYLAN

Excited to start filming! When can we schedule the moving-in footage? I want to capture the full "newlywed nesting" vibe. Let me know your availability!

I slowly look up and meet Lucas's eyes across the table. He's already staring at me with a mix of resignation and determination that mirrors my own.

"So much for living separately," I mutter.

"Six months," he confirms. "Then we go our separate ways. And we can discuss where we'll live."

"Agreed. And no actual...relationship stuff."

A corner of his mouth twitches. "Wouldn't dream of it, Scoop. I know it'll be hard for you to keep your hands to yourself when we live together, but try to show some restraint."

My mouth drops open. "I'd rather go back to Vegas and let that seventy-year-old Elvis impersonator kiss me on the mouth."

Unbothered, Lucas shrugs. "Your loss. But while we're on the topic, maybe we also agree there are no outside parties."

I squint. "Meaning?"

"We don't date other people. Can't risk a cheating scandal getting attached to our fairytale romance."

It's logical, smart, totally reasonable, yet the thought of Lucas Carmichael dating someone else during these six months sparks a pain in my chest that I don't have the time, or emotional bandwidth, to unpack.

"Fine," I say with a huff. "No dating."

I push off the table and walk to his end, where I lean my hip against the edge with my arms crossed. He shifts in his seat to face me more fully, his knee bumping mine lightly as he moves. Neither of us apologizes.

Then Lucas stands, slowly, purposefully, and just like that, we're facing each other head on, close enough that I can feel the heat rolling off him.

I extend my hand between us. "Deal."

He steps in, just enough that our shoes nearly touch, and slides his much larger hand into mine. His palm is warm and solid, and the roughness of his calloused fingertips surprises me. He doesn't shake, just holds. Steady. Strong.

Then his thumb starts to move in slow, rhythmic strokes across the back of my hand, like he's trying to hypnotize me into forgetting how much I claim to hate him.

My brain forgets a lot of things in that moment.

Lucas's smirk is infuriating. "Let's make some magic, Mrs. Carmichael."

I pull my hand back, hoping to break whatever spell he just cast, but my fingers still tingle, like his touch left a signature I can't quite scrub off.

Six months. That's all.

Then this whole thing will be behind us.

eight

· · ·

Lucas

THE CRACK of a bat connecting with a ball. The smell of grass baking in the afternoon sun. The familiar weight of a well-worn glove. Saturday afternoons at Cheviot Hills Park are sacred and the one time each week when I'm not Lucas Carmichael, Head of Communications, or Lucas Carmichael, the Senator's Son, or even, as of this past weekend, Lucas Carmichael, Accidental Husband. I'm just number seventeen for the Spin Doctors, our beer league team made up mostly of my old USC teammates.

"So, you're fucking married?" Alex Chen drops onto the bench in our dugout, even though he's not technically on the team. He hands me a bottle of cold beer, already dripping with condensation, from the cooler.

"Yeah, but only you and Grant know the backstory." I take a long swig. "The fewer people who know, the better this is for everyone."

I grab a bat from the corner and walk outside the fenced area to take a few practice swings. The late afternoon sun casts long shadows across the field, and for a moment, I can almost pretend life hasn't gotten incredibly complicated.

Alex follows, and he leans against the fence. As head of comedy development at Wonderland, he has an eye for absurdity, which, unfortunately, means my life is currently premium entertainment for him. We bonded five years ago over our shared obsession with Disneyland, spending more early mornings riding Space Mountain before work than either of us would care to admit. He's a fixture at our Sunday games, despite his complete inability to hit a curveball.

With his perfectly tailored jeans, worn even at a baseball field, designer sunglasses, and an enigmatic smile that's charmed industry execs and bartenders of all genders alike, Alex carries himself with the easy confidence of someone who knows exactly who he is. It's why he's my most trusted confidant, along with the fact that he has zero tolerance for bullshit, including mine.

"Please tell me you recorded your father's reaction," Alex says, his eyes gleaming with mischief behind his sunglasses. "I bet his head exploded."

Alex knows all about the the Carmichael dynasty, my father pushing me toward politics, and me sprinting in the exact opposite direction.

"Oh, it was fun," I deadpan, taking another practice swing. The motion grounds me, the satisfying pull of muscle helping to keep my temper in check. "But he thinks we're getting everything annulled."

Alex arches a brow. "And you didn't correct him?"

I shrug. "Timing matters."

It's not that I'm scared of my father. Not anymore. It's

just, I know how he works. He's a strategist. A manipulator. If I give him this information now, he'll start circling the wagons and calling Madeline, his donors, his PR team, anything to find an angle, a way to spin it, fix it, or control it.

But if I wait and make it clear that this marriage is real, established, and already tied to a dozen media cycles and public goodwill. Well, then he can't touch it. Can't spin it. He has to live with it.

"He's smart, though, too," I add, "so convincing him it's real will be key. The fact that I've refused every conservative debutante and donor's daughter he's pushed on me for the last decade? He'll be suspicious either way."

Alex grins. "So, you're playing the long game."

"Exactly," I say, lining up another swing. "This time, I want the win to be checkmate."

"Unless Jess can be your excuse?" Alex suggests, tilting his head.

"What do you mean?"

"Maybe you've always rejected his pairings because you've been in love with Jess all this time."

The words land harder than they should. There's this half-second pause in my chest, like my heart missed a step and is scrambling to catch up. In love with Jess? No. That's not what this is. It's proximity. History. A shared past and a ridiculous present. It's chemistry, sure, but we've always had that. Doesn't mean it's anything more.

Does it?

I scoff, shaking my head. "Don't be ridiculous."

Alex raises a brow.

"I mean, come on," I add. "It's Jess. We spend half our time trying not to strangle each other."

Alex shrugs. "Sounds like foreplay."

I roll my eyes, but I'm already walking away because, if I stay in this conversation any longer, I might start asking myself questions I'm not ready to answer.

"Hey batter, batter, swing batter! They're waiting for you in the box!"

The low, husky quality of her voice flows through me like a shot of whiskey mixed with warm honey. It's familiar, soothing, yet unexpected. It heats my blood and somehow steadies me at the same time.

I turn to see Jess standing just outside the fence along the third baseline. She's in cut-off shorts that showcase her long, toned legs and a fitted tank that reveals the benefits of her early morning surfing habit. Her blonde hair is pulled back in a ponytail, and oversized sunglasses hide her eyes. Somehow, she makes baseball casual look like a magazine spread.

My mind immediately, traitorously, flashes to how it would feel to wrap that ponytail around my fist.

Alex isn't wrong. She does have a certain magnetic effect, the kind that people can't look away from. Like lightning strikes. Or car crashes.

"What are you doing here?" I ask, unable to keep the surprise from my voice.

"Austin's here," she says, gesturing to where her brother is laughing with some of the guys near the bench: Austin Lexington, the Tampa Bay Thunder's star pitcher, currently sidelined in rehab after Tommy John surgery.

"I saw him before the game," I say, gripping the bat a little tighter. "He congratulated me. Slapped me on the back and said, 'Welcome to the family.'" I smirk.

The guilt's been sitting like a stone in my gut ever since.

We made plans to grab a beer later this week and catch up. It's a conversation I'm absolutely *not* looking forward to. Austin's a good guy, one of the best, and he deserves more than half-truths and a PR-friendly version of whatever this is with his sister.

Jess leans against the fence, her smile syrupy-sweet and weaponized. "Plus, I couldn't miss watching my husband pretend he's still in college, trying to live out his lost dreams of making it to the MLB."

I smirk as I step up to the plate. "Scoop, if you wanted to stare at me wielding my bat, all you had to do was ask."

Her glare could strip paint off the fence. Worth it.

I tap my bat on either side of the plate and settle into my stance. This is just a rec league game, but something about her voice, her taunts, hits that deep, competitive nerve.

The pitcher, a former USC teammate, winds up and throws.

I swing hard.

And miss completely.

"Strike one, Senator!" Jess yells from behind the fence, using the nickname she knows I despise.

The next three pitches are low, and then I take another swing and miss. I'm either getting walked or striking out if I can't hit this last pitch.

"Hey, batter, batter, batter! Sa-wing batter!" Jess calls out, channeling her inner Ferris Bueller. "He's got a pocketful of kryptonite!"

I don't know if it's her heckling or my dysfunctional need to prove her wrong, but something shifts in my focus. The next pitch seems to move in slow motion. I connect with the ball perfectly, and the vibration travels up my arms as the ball soars toward the outfield and clears the fence with room to spare.

Home run.

As I round the bases, I catch Jess staring at the ball's trajectory, her mouth slightly open. When I reach third base, I give her an exaggerated wink.

"Close your mouth, wife. You can congratulate me later."

"Pig!" she shouts, but there's a reluctant smile tugging at her lips.

And just like that, I'm relaxed and enjoying myself for the first time since Vegas.

"What's that smile for?" Alex asks when I return to the dugout.

"What? I can't be happy about a home run?"

"Sure, except you didn't start smiling until you rounded third," he points out, his eyebrows raised.

"Whatever. Don't you have a script to read or something?"

"I don't think you're going to have any issues convincing your family this is all real," he says, nodding toward Jess, who's now chatting with Austin.

"Well, if everything goes well, I may not even have to introduce them to her at all. We're only doing this for six months. I can avoid my family for that long."

"You do realize that you'll have to bring her to the Carmichael Foundation Gala this summer?" Alex says, checking his phone calendar. "No doubt, your mother already has your tux dry-cleaned and your name on the program."

Fuck. He's right. How did I forget about this? Oh yeah, I was busy getting accidentally married.

After the game, which the Spin Doctors won five to three, thank you very much, I find Jess waiting by my car, scrolling through her phone.

"Nice swing," she admits. "Austin says I might be your good luck charm, since this is the first game of yours I've ever watched and you won."

"Is that why you showed up? To provide a public service?"

"That and we should talk about tomorrow. Dylan texted again, and he wants to shoot at your place. Something about better natural light for the cameras."

"Of course he does." I give her a look. "And this couldn't have been a phone call?"

She shrugs. "I was meeting Blair for lunch nearby anyway. Figured I'd stop by and see if the rumors about your baseball skills were exaggerated." A smile plays at the corner of her mouth. "Turns out, they were only slightly exaggerated."

I laugh. "Well, since you're here, want to grab dinner and sort out the details?"

"Is Lucas Carmichael asking me on a date?" she teases, pressing a hand to her chest in mock shock.

"It's not a date if it's with your wife," I shoot back, grinning. "It's cohabitation logistics."

She groans. "That phrase is almost worse."

I open the passenger door of my car to let her in, but before she can take a seat, I ask, "So, for real, you want to move into my place? It has two bedrooms, and it's five minutes from the studio. It might be the easier move."

She tilts her head. "I was kind of hoping we could fake the whole thing. You know, shoot a few clips, stage some boxes, call it a day."

"You want to fake living together for six months? Dylan's not that easily fooled."

"Ugh. Fine," she says. "But I'm not actually moving in. I'll bring a few boxes of my things to make it appear so, and I'll crash in the guest room on days when Dylan's filming or the illusion needs to be maintained. But I'm not leaving my place completely. I like my coffee maker. And my bath towels."

"Noted. But for the record," I say with a smirk, "I have very nice towels."

She rolls her eyes as she glides into the front seat. "I'll believe it when I see them."

"So, it's settled, then?" I hold the door open, dipping my head to see her better.

She sighs like she's agreeing to something far more dramatic than it is. "Fine. We stage the apartment, I half-move in, and we tell Dylan to bring his stupid lighting setup."

I nod. "Perfect. Domestic bliss, here we come."

"Which means I get to pick where we eat. Happy wife and all that."

"Let me guess—Porto's Bakery? You still obsessed with those potato balls?"

Her eyebrows shoot up. "How did you know that?"

I don't tell her that I remember her bringing a box to Blair's agency opening nearly a year ago, insisting they were "better than any fancy catering." I'm not entirely sure why I filed away that detail.

"Lucky guess," I say instead, rounding the car and getting into the driver's seat.

The eye roll she gives me could register on the Richter scale, and before I drive away, I catch Alex watching us with an amused expression.

He mouths, *Totally buying it*, and gives me a thumbs up.

The annoying thing is, I'm not entirely sure what's real and what's performance anymore. But as Jess starts arguing with me about how the designated hitter rule ruined baseball before I've even started the car, I realize I'm not dreading the next six months nearly as much as I should be.

That might be the most worrying development yet.

nine

. . .

Jess

LUCAS'S APARTMENT is nothing like I imagined. I'm not sure what I expected. Maybe sleek, soulless bachelor minimalism or the pretentious mid-century modern furniture favored by studio execs who want to seem cultured. Instead, I'm standing in a surprisingly warm space with floor-to-ceiling bookshelves, comfortable-looking furniture, and—are those Disneyland posters?

"Is that original concept art from the Haunted Mansion?" I ask, moving closer to examine a framed piece on the wall.

Lucas shifts uncomfortably. "It's from a limited gallery release."

"Oh my God, you really are a Disney adult." I laugh, remembering my fabricated story in Vegas. "I just made up that stuff about you taking me to Disneyland because I thought it would be funny to suggest the head of communications at Wonderland Studios secretly loves their biggest competitor."

"I'm not a *Disney adult*," he says, the air quotes practically visible. "I appreciate the creative and engineering feats of the original park. It's iconic Americana."

"You obviously have an annual pass and throw up peace signs in front of the castle. That's textbook Disney adult behavior." I point to the collection of photos on a nearby bookshelf.

"I've never thrown up a peace sign," he mutters, but there's a hint of color in his cheeks.

I set down one of the boxes I've brought over and continue exploring. The kitchen is unexpectedly well equipped, with professional-grade cookware and an impressive knife collection.

"You actually cook?" I ask, running my finger along the edge of a granite countertop.

"Is that so hard to believe?"

"I figured you survived on restaurant meals and whatever your PR minions bring you during crisis mode."

"My PR minions, as you call them, know better than to interrupt me, even for food," he jokes. His voice softens slightly. "It helps me decompress."

I file that information away, oddly fascinated by this glimpse into his real life. A Lucas who cooks to unwind is not something I was prepared for.

We move down the hall and into the bedroom, and I try not to look too closely at the king-sized bed with its simple navy duvet or the surprisingly well-used books on the nightstand. He has actual paperbacks, not just status-symbol coffee table decor.

I glance at the bed, and a flicker of awareness zips through me before I shut it down. Hard.

"Uh, where's the guest room?" I ask.

Lucas gestures to a door just off the hall. "Down there. It's small, but it's yours for as long as you're playing wife."

I nod. "Perfect. That's all I need. I just have the essentials, and I'll be here when Dylan needs the footage."

He raises an eyebrow. "So, no late-night newlywed cuddling?"

"Not unless you want me to murder you on camera," I reply sweetly.

He grins. "So, only off camera?

"Ground rules," I say, needing to refocus. "For the sake of appearing authentic."

Lucas nods, suddenly all business. "Right. I assume hand-holding is fine. Arms around shoulders or waist if the situation calls for it."

"Kissing only if absolutely necessary," I add. "And only closed mouth, like we did in Vegas before things escalated."

The memory of our kiss in the casino hangs between us for a beat too long.

"What's in the rest of these boxes?" he says, bringing us both back to the present.

"Just stuff to make it look convincing. Clothes, some books, a few framed photos."

He peers into the box on top and pulls out a faded black T-shirt with Pearl Jam's logo across the front. "No way. Ten was one of the best albums of the nineties."

I reach for the shirt reflexively. "It was my mom's."

Something in my voice must give me away, because his expression shifts.

"Sorry," he says quickly. "I didn't mean to—"

"It's fine." I fold the shirt carefully and smooth a nonexistent wrinkle from the fabric. "She loved them. Used to play their records while she worked on stories at the kitchen table."

"You mentioned she was a journalist, too?"

"Yeah. Investigative. Loved to break stories." I hesitate. "She died when I was fourteen. Breast cancer."

He goes quiet for a beat.

"I'm sorry," he says, and this time, his voice holds something warmer, gentler, than I've heard before.

"It was a long time ago."

"Still," he says softly. "My dad gives me hell about my career choices, but at least he's around to do it. I can't imagine losing a parent that young."

It catches me off guard, this version of Lucas. Not cocky. Not defensive. More caring.

We're having a moment, an actual human moment, when a sharp knock at the door jolts us both back to reality.

"Showtime," Lucas mutters.

Dylan Reeves bursts in with the energy of someone who's had way too many espressos and hasn't slept since Sundance. He's wearing black skinny jeans, scuffed boots, and a graphic tee under a worn Army surplus jacket, also known as filmmaker camouflage. A pair of round tortoiseshell glasses has slid down the bridge of his nose, and his dark curls are pulled into a messy half-bun that somehow looks intentional. He's got a vintage camera bag slung crossbody like a satchel of genius.

He's trailed by a surprisingly large crew for what's supposed to be an "intimate" documentary. There are camera operators, sound people, a lighting tech, and what appears to be a stylist in all black, carrying a garment bag and three different shades of setting powder.

"There they are! America's new favorite power couple!" Dylan beams, clasping his hands together. "We're just going to capture some natural moments of you two unpacking and settling in together. Just be yourselves!"

Be ourselves. Right. Myself would be back at my apartment, scrolling through tips from sources, not pretending to move in with Hollywood's most infuriating spin doctor.

Lucas and I awkwardly begin unpacking boxes. I arrange a few books on a shelf while he makes space in his closet for clothes I'll never actually wear here. Dylan hovers nearby, his smile fading as he watches.

"Ok, let's try something else," he says finally. "Lucas, why don't you show Jess where to put her toiletries in the bathroom?"

We comply, moving to the master bathroom, where I place my toothbrush into the holder next to his, careful not to let them touch.

"You two are standing like there's an invisible force field between you," Dylan says. "I need you to be closer. You just got married! You should be in the honeymoon phase!"

Before I can protest, he physically guides Lucas to stand behind me at the mirror, repositioning us like we're mannequins in a store window. Lucas's hands land on my waist, and I stiffen at the contact, instinctively pulling my shoulders back before I remember I'm supposed to like him.

His touch is warm through the thin fabric of my shirt, and for a second, I forget we're being watched. I forget the cameras. I forget the crew. Then I shake the thoughts from my head. This is just acting. A job. Six months.

"Perfect!" Dylan calls, backing toward the door. "Just stay like that for a moment."

In the mirror, I catch Lucas's gaze. It's uncertain, guarded, but there's a flicker of vulnerability that presses against the edges of my resolve, tight and sudden in my chest.

We're the definition of contrast: his dark hair and tailored frame towering behind me, my lighter, softer silhouette against his. Somehow, though, we fit, with my back to his chest and the sculpted ridges of his pecks pressing gently into my shoulder blades each time he inhales.

I feel his breath where it hits the loose hair at the nape of my neck, warm and maddening. His thumbs flex slightly on my waist, just enough to send awareness rippling across my skin.

His gaze drops from mine, trailing down my reflection. I watch the way his throat bobs with a swallow, the way his lashes lower like he's trying not to look but is failing miserably.

Every nerve in my body is on high alert. I can feel the moment wrapping around us like a warm, tight blanket.

"Sorry about this," he murmurs, his voice low, the breath of it grazing my ear.

"Just part of the deal," I whisper back, trying—and failing—to ignore the flutter blooming in my stomach.

"Great chemistry!" Dylan calls from the doorway. "Now let's move to the living room for some questions, ok?"

The sound of a chair scraping snaps us both out of it. We

step apart like we've been burned, and the absence of his hands is somehow louder than the moment itself.

We separate quickly, like teenagers caught doing something they weren't supposed to, and follow Dylan out into the living room.

The crew has arranged the living room into an interview setup. Lucas and I sit on the couch, a careful space between us, until Dylan gestures emphatically for us to move closer. Lucas drapes his arm along the back of the couch behind me, not quite touching but close enough that I can feel the warmth radiating from him.

"So, tell me about when you two first met," Dylan says, settling into a chair across from us.

"College baseball game," Lucas answers smoothly. "Jess was there covering a celebrity player for some gossip publication."

"I was also there to see my brother play," I interject, unable to help myself. "And then Lucas insulted me."

Lucas shifts beside me. "And you fired back with your own insults."

"It wasn't you I insulted," I mutter.

Dylan laughs. "So, it wasn't love at first sight?"

Lucas's gaze lands on me a beat before he answers. "Not exactly, but she did make an impression."

His tone is soft, but there's a flicker in his expression that makes my stomach do a little twist. Ok, fine. Gooey is the word.

"And Lucas certainly made an impression, too," I counter sweetly, batting my lashes just enough to make him suspicious.

"When did you realize there was something more between you?"

Lucas and I glance at each other. Nope. We did not plan for this.

"I think it was when Grant and Sophia went public with their relationship last fall," Lucas says smoothly. "Jess was professional in keeping it exclusive until he was ready to share, and she asked such insightful questions that went beyond the usual PR fluff. I remember thinking how refreshing her approach was, even if it made my job harder."

A little too polished, but points for effort.

"Probably at an industry panel on media ethics last fall," I say. "He was the only communications exec who admitted that studios sometimes cross lines. Of course, he immediately spun it into how Wonderland was different, which was complete BS." I flash him a grin. "But for a brief moment, there was actual honesty there."

"So, you were drawn to each other's professional integrity?" Dylan prompts.

"I was drawn to how passionate she is," Lucas says, his arm drifting lower to brush my shoulder. "Even when she's stubbornly wrong about something."

I smile sweetly and lean into him just a little harder. "And I appreciated how he could articulate his position, even when it's carefully calculated spin designed to protect the studio machine."

Without breaking eye contact, Lucas slides his hand down to cover mine and pats it like I'm a toddler who's just spelled her name right.

I retaliate by pinching the inside of his thigh. Hard. He jerks slightly and lets out a muffled yelp.

"Everything ok?" Dylan asks.

"Perfect," we answer in unison.

Lucas, not to be outdone, subtly jabs his elbow into my side. I grit my teeth and dig the point of my nail into his knuckle. His smile never wavers, and neither does mine. We're both on the verge of either cracking up or starting an actual physical fight. Possibly both.

"But what made you decide to get married in Vegas?" Dylan asks.

"Temporary insanity," I say.

"The culmination of years of chemistry," Lucas says at the exact same time.

We stare at each other, still locked in that too-sweet, too-sharp smile.

And even though we're surrounded by lights, lenses, and a full production crew, somehow, it feels like we're the only two people in the room.

"What my wife means," Lucas says as he wraps his arm around me, his fingers digging slightly into my shoulder, "is that we'd been dancing around our feelings for so long that when we finally admitted them, we didn't want to wait."

"And what my husband means," I say, my hand digging into his thigh with a smile that doesn't quite reach my eyes, "is that after years of pretending we didn't care, we finally stopped lying to ourselves and maybe skipped a few steps along the way."

By the time Dylan finally calls it a day two hours later, any warm feelings from our earlier moment have completely evaporated. The second the door closes behind the crew, I move to the opposite end of the room.

"Well, that was a disaster," I say.

"You couldn't resist taking shots at my career, could you?"

"Me? You practically called me stubborn and wrong on camera!"

We glare at each other from across the living room that's supposed to be our shared home for the next six months. Right now, six hours feels impossible.

"This is never going to work," I mutter.

"It has to," Lucas says, running a hand through his hair in frustration. "For both our sakes."

The worst part is, he's right. And the fact that I can acknowledge that might be the only hope we have of surviving this charade.

That and separate bathrooms.

ten

. . .

Lucas

"SO, when, exactly, were you planning to tell me you had a thing for my sister?"

Austin drops this question casually as he sets down his beer on the high-top table at Barney's Beanery. We're in a back corner where no one is likely to recognize either of us: him as a famous baseball star or me as the newly viral half of Hollywood's most unexpected marriage.

"It wasn't exactly planned," I say, focusing intently on the menu I've seen a hundred times before.

"No shit." Austin laughs, leaning back in his chair. "Vegas wedding? Surprisingly off-brand for you, Mr. Always-Has-A-Strategy."

Unlike his sister, Austin has an easygoing nature that makes it impossible not to like him. We were good friends and teammates at USC. He was always quick with a joke in the dugout, but deadly serious on the mound. That same duality is present now as he studies me with eyes that are eerily similar to Jess's.

"Look," I say, setting the menu down. "It's complicated."

"Try me."

I hesitate, calculating how much to reveal. Jess and I agreed to keep the truth between us, Grant, and our attorneys, but Austin is different. He's family—her family—and if we're going to pull this off, I need him on our side.

Still, I can't risk putting Jess's inheritance in jeopardy if word gets out, especially if her trust has conditions her siblings could or could not have.

"We've had feelings for each other for a while," I begin, surprised at how easily the half-truth rolls off my tongue. "Been getting closer over the past few months."

"Bullshit. She was bitching about you shutting down her questions at that Wonderland press junket three weeks ago."

I can't help but smile. "That's kind of our thing. Professional antagonism, personal attraction."

Austin looks skeptical but motions for me to continue.

"The alcohol probably accelerated the monogamy plans," I concede, "but I'm not mad about it."

I take a long pull of my beer. "I've always admired her professionally. Even when she's making my job harder, she's doing it because she cares about the truth."

This, at least, is completely honest. Despite our constant professional clashing, I've never questioned Jess's integrity.

"And personally?" Austin presses.

"You really want to hear this?"

"Not particularly, but as her brother, I feel obligated to assess your intentions."

I lean forward and lower my voice, despite the privacy of our corner. "The first time I saw her in that stadium tunnel, I was instantly attracted to her. It wasn't just physical, though, obviously—" I catch Austin's warning look. "Right, not going there. But she had this fire, this absolute certainty about what she was doing and why it mattered."

"And then?"

"And then it went south fast. We both said things and had our professional pride wounded. But I couldn't stop thinking about her for weeks afterward." I stare into my beer, surprised by the ring of truth in what was supposed to be a cover story. "And I guess, apparently, for all this time."

Austin studies me for a long moment. "You're either a better actor than I gave you credit for, or there's some truth in there."

"Does it matter? We're married now."

"It matters to me because she's my sister." He leans forward. "Jess doesn't let people in easily. Not since Mom died."

"She mentioned that," I say quietly. "About your mom."

Austin looks surprised. "She told you about Mom? Voluntarily?"

I nod, remembering how carefully she'd folded the Pearl Jam T-shirt, how her voice had softened when she'd shared how her mother had been a journalist, too.

"Huh." Austin sits back. "She doesn't talk about Mom with just anyone."

"I'm not just anyone. I'm her husband." The word still feels foreign on my tongue, like a language I'm learning to speak.

"That's on paper. I'm talking about in here." He taps his chest. "Jess puts on a tough act, the fearless journalist who doesn't flinch from asking the hard questions, but you know what she does after every major story breaks?"

I shake my head.

"She calls me and asks if she did the right thing. If the story was worth whatever fallout it caused." Austin picks at the label on his beer bottle. "She cares so much about the impact of her work that she loses sleep over it, but she'll never let the subject of her reporting see that doubt."

That catches me off guard.

The Jess I know, or thought I knew, is all confident swagger and unflinching determination. The idea of her second-guessing herself doesn't fit the image she projects.

"Why are you telling me this?"

"Because if this is real, and the jury's still out on that, you need to know who you married. Not just the public version."

He fixes me with a level gaze. "And if it's not real, if this is some weird PR stunt or whatever, then I'm warning you now, don't break her heart."

My throat goes a little dry. For the first time, it hits me: she's Jess Lexington-Carmichael now.

She has my name.

It was just a legal formality, a check box on some paperwork, but suddenly, it feels bigger than that.

He's trusting me. She's trusting me. And I'm not sure what the hell to do with that.

"Break *her* heart? She's more likely to break mine." I say.

Austin just gives me a knowing look. "You'd be surprised."

We spend the next hour catching up on safer topics like his rehab progress, mutual teammates from USC, and the current baseball season, before he checks his watch and announces he has a physical therapy appointment.

"It was good seeing you, man," he says as we part ways outside. "Weird circumstances, but good."

"You, too. Your slider looked deadly before the injury. You'll get it back."

"That's the plan." Austin hesitates. "And Lucas? Whatever's really going on with you and Jess? Just be careful with each other, ok?"

I nod, giving him a tight smile before heading for my car. The conversation has left me off-balance with too many half-truths and too many feelings I'm not ready to face.

My phone buzzes just as I slide behind the wheel. "MOM" flashes on the screen.

With my dad, every call feels like an obligation, a test, a power play I didn't agree to but will somehow still lose.

But my mom? She's different.

She's the reason I haven't cut ties completely. She's the tether that pulls me back in, even when I swear I'm done.

I take a breath and answer. "Hi, Mom."

"Lucas, darling." Her voice is warm and composed, polished like silver but not cold. It's a voice that has comforted foreign dignitaries and family friends alike. "I was just checking in about the gala. Your father mentioned you hadn't RSVP'd yet."

Of course he did.

The Carmichael Foundation Gala. Black tie, donor schmoozing, political networking disguised as charity.

"I'll be there," I say, starting my car.

"Wonderful. When do you think you'll be up to visit? A

few days before, perhaps? The Bishops will be there, of course, and Madeline has been asking about you."

Of course she has. Despite my unplanned Vegas elopement, my father is clearly still pushing the Carmichael-Bishop merger.

"Actually, Mom, I'll be bringing someone with me."

A beat of silence. "Oh? Instead of Madeline?"

"Yes. My wife."

The word slips out before I realize it, and something shifts in my chest. My wife. Jess. Jessica Carmichael. The name has a rhythm to it I hadn't noticed before.

My mother is silent long enough that I check to see if the call dropped.

"Mom?"

"Your wife," she repeats carefully. "I thought your father said you were arranging an annulment."

"Nope," I say. A beat of silence follows.

"I see." Her tone is unreadable. "Lucas, are you happy?"

The question catches me off guard. My mother has always been the perfect political spouse. She's supportive, elegant, and unfailingly appropriate, but she's always been my biggest supporter, even when I've made decisions that go against my father's wishes.

"I am," I answer, surprised to find I'm not entirely lying. "Jess is... She challenges me. Makes me think. She's brilliant and fearless and completely herself, no matter the consequences."

"You sound like you admire her very much."

"I do." I pause, realizing I'm revealing more than I intended. "She's not who Dad would have chosen for me."

"No," my mother agrees softly, "but I've never cared about that as much as he does. I've only ever wanted my children to be happy and healthy. If Jess makes you happy, then I'm truly happy for you, and I can't wait to meet her."

There's a sincerity in her voice that makes a lump form in my throat. "Thanks, Mom."

"I'll let your father know—"

"No," I cut in quickly. "Let it be a surprise. I'll handle any backlash."

After another moment of conversation and promises to send details about our travel plans, we hang up. As I sit there, a wave of something like panic washes over me.

Christ. I'm lying to everyone.

The guilt hits harder than expected. I've spent my career crafting narratives, but those were for movies and talent, not my family, not people I care about. Not Austin, who shared his sister's vulnerabilities with me out of genuine concern. Not my mother, who sounded truly happy for me.

Worse, I'm starting to believe my own spin. The truth is, parts of what I told Austin weren't fabricated at all. I was instantly attracted to Jess eight years ago. I did think about her for weeks afterward. And when I called her my wife just now...

"It's just proximity," I mutter as I start the car. "A chemical reaction. Nothing more."

eleven

. . .

Jess

"LET ME GET THIS STRAIGHT," Brandon says, leaning against my kitchen counter with an expression of pure disbelief. "You...are now...Mrs. Jessica Carmichael?"

I flip him off without looking up from the box I'm packing. "Don't call me that."

"Which part? Jessica or Mrs. Carmichael?" Brandon's grin is infuriating. As a stuntman, he's built to take physical punishment, which is the only reason I haven't thrown something at him yet.

"Both. Either. And it's Lexington-Carmichael." I shove books into the box with more force than necessary. "Are you going to help or just provide color commentary?"

"Definitely commentary," he says, helping himself to a beer from my fridge. "This is premium entertainment."

My apartment has become command central for what Blair is secretly calling "Operation Marriage Plot." After three days of shuttling between here and Lucas's place for Dylan's filming schedule, I realized I needed to actually move in to maintain the illusion. This is why Blair, Brandon, and Stella are allegedly helping me pack, though they're mostly interrogating me about my sudden marital status.

Brandon, my across-the-hall-neighbor-turned-accidental-best-friend, is lounging on the couch with a half-eaten bag of pretzels. As a stuntman, he's one of those guys you've seen in a hundred action movies but wouldn't recognize on the street, and he's also possibly the chillest person I've ever met. He helped me carry up a broken bookshelf three years ago, and now he has a permanent spot in my life.

Stella, on the other hand, is delicately wrapping a framed photo in bubble wrap like it's one of the crown jewels. She's the youngest of us, all soft edges and sunshine. She started out as Blair's intern at The Wynn Agency and followed Blair when she opened up her own agency, Tangerine Talent. Somehow, she's become everyone's little sister. Technically, she lives on the other side of the complex, but she's always at my or Brandon's apartment, usually with snacks and support.

"I still can't believe it," Stella says, squinting at the photo before adding more wrap. "Isn't this the same Lucas you once described as having the emotional depth of a spoon?"

Blair snorts. "Or the one she called the human equivalent of an email that starts with 'Per my last note.'"

"My personal favorite," Brandon adds, "was when she said his press statements were so sanitized they could be used as disinfectant."

"Or when she signed him up for *Manifesting for Men*," Blair adds. "That was inspired."

Stella gasps. "Did you really?"

"I also sent him a digital subscription to *Goat Yoga*

Monthly," I mutter. "Are you guys keeping a catalog of every insult I've ever used?" I ask, exasperated.

"Only the really creative ones," Blair says, patting my shoulder. "It's just, you have to admit, this is a complete one-eighty from everything you've ever said about him."

I take a deep breath. This is the hardest part, lying to my friends. I glance at Blair; she's the only one who knows the truth.

Journalism is about truth; it's what I've built my career and reputation on. But here I am, constructing an elaborate fiction for the people closest to me.

"Sometimes, the line between hate and not-hate is thinner than you'd think," I say carefully.

Brandon raises an eyebrow. "And that line just disappeared in Vegas?"

"When you know, you know," I offer weakly.

"Bullshit," Brandon coughs into his fist.

I throw a pillow at him. "No one asked you, Grimaldi."

"Hey, I'm just saying what we're all thinking." He catches the pillow effortlessly. "The Jess I know would never marry her nemesis."

He's right, of course. Brandon has lived across the hall from me for three years. He's been witness to my rants about Lucas.

"Well, maybe you don't know me as well as you think," I retort, but my words lack conviction.

Stella, ever the peacemaker, intervenes. "Whatever the reason, we support you. Right, guys?"

"Always," Blair agrees immediately. "Even when you marry the 'enemy.'"

"He's not the enemy," I say, and I'm surprised to find I mean it. "He's just on the other side of the professional fence."

A knock at the door saves me from further explanation. Brandon, closest to the entrance, swings it open to reveal Sophia, stunning as always in skinny jeans and an oversized sweater.

"Hey, superstar." Brandon greets her with a hug. "You're early."

"Meeting got pushed up," Sophia explains, stepping into the apartment. When she spots me surrounded by boxes, her eyes widen. "Jess! I heard the news. Congratulations?"

The question mark at the end is subtle but unmistakable.

"Thanks," I say, accepting her quick embrace. Sophia and I became close over the last year when her house flooded and she moved in with Grant Hall, head of Wonderland Studios and Lucas's boss. I tortured her in the beginning. Lucas wouldn't share anything with me, and I was suspicious that something was going on. Turns out I was right, but it didn't happen in the way I thought. And I never could have imagined teaming up with Lucas to help Grant with a public declaration about his feelings for Sophia on my podcast.

"Marriage looks good on you," she says, studying my face. "You're glowing."

I quickly correct her. "That's stress sweat. Moving is hell."

"Speaking of," Brandon says, checking his watch, "we should head out if we're going to make that meeting with the stunt coordinator."

Sophia nods. "I hate to rush out, but duty calls. We're

prepping for that action sequence in Wonderland's new spy franchise." She eyes the boxes. "So, you are moving into his place?"

"Yes, until we can find our own place together," I reply. "And it's closer to the studio for him."

"And further from everything for you," Blair points out. "A true sign of love."

I resist the urge to roll my eyes.

"That reminds me," Stella says, perking up. "If you're mostly staying at Lucas's now, would you mind if I used your apartment occasionally? The tenant across from me is doing renovations, and the noise is driving me crazy. I can't concentrate on scripts."

"You want to use my place as a reading room?" I ask.

"Just sometimes! I'd water your plants, grab your mail." She bites her lip. "And your place is closer to a certain someone in the building."

Brandon makes a face. "Not that tech bro? The one with the messenger bag and the cold brew addiction?"

"He has a name, Brandon. It's Mason." Stella's cheeks flush. "And he's not a tech bro. He develops apps for nonprofit organizations."

"Same difference," Brandon mutters.

"Sure, use the place whenever," I tell Stella. "I'm paying rent either way, and most of my stuff is staying here. Lucas and I haven't exactly figured out the long-term logistics yet."

And there it is, the first truly honest thing I've said all afternoon. We haven't figured anything out beyond surviving the next six months of this charade.

Later, after everyone has left and I'm alone with my half-packed boxes, I pour myself a glass of wine and stand at my living room window. The sun is setting over the city, casting long shadows across the buildings.

"This is just a story," I whisper to myself, "like any other story with an embargo date. Six months from now, the truth comes out, and everything goes back to normal."

I'm making a deal with the universe, or maybe just with my own conscience. I, Jessica Lexington, who has built a career on exposing truths, am living a lie. But it's a necessary lie, a temporary one, like going undercover for a story.

The problem is, undercover agents sometimes go rogue, and the line between pretend and reality gets blurrier every day I spend with Lucas.

My phone vibrates with a text. Speak of the devil.

LUCAS

Dylan wants to film us having dinner with friends next weekend. Says it'll make good B-roll for the "support system" segment. Any chance your friends are free that Saturday?

I stare at the message. Looks like I'm dragging my friends deeper into this fabrication.

JESS

I'll ask. Blair and Stella for sure. Brandon if he's not working.

LUCAS

Alex too. Maybe Grant and Sophia if they're free.

JESS

Quite the dinner party for two people who
barely tolerate each other.

LUCAS

We're married, remember? Try to look like
you enjoy my company.

JESS

That will be an Emmy-worthy performance.

LUCAS

Funny. I've seen how you look at me when
you think no one's watching.

My breath catches. What does that mean? Before I can overthink it or craft a suitably cutting response, another text comes through.

LUCAS

Don't forget I'll pick you up from work
tomorrow at 7 for the Survivor premiere.

Great. More lying to people I care about. I set down my phone, pick up my wine glass again, and take a long sip.

"Just a story," I repeat to myself, "with an embargo date."

But as I turn back to my packing, I can't shake the feeling that this particular story might be getting away from me, and the journalist in me knows those are always the most dangerous kind.

twelve

. . .

Lucas

"THREE MINUTES UNTIL SHOWTIME," I murmur, leaning so close to Jess that my lips brush her ear. The cameras mounted in the town car are capturing every moment, and I need her to remember that we're being watched. "Smile like you love me, Scoop."

I catch the slight shiver that runs through her body as my breath hits her skin. Interesting.

"I am smiling," she whispers back, her lips barely moving. "And if you call me Scoop one more time, I will stab you with my stiletto when we get home."

The threat is delivered with such honeyed sweetness that our documentary crew probably thinks she's whispering sweet nothings. I pull back just enough to see her professional smile, perfect makeup, and hair swept up to expose the elegant line of her neck. She's stunning.

And she smells amazing. She reminds me of ocean breezes and summer nights. It's distracting in ways I can't afford right now.

I reach for her hand and lace our fingers together with practiced ease. "Ready for tonight?"

"Born ready," she says, giving my hand a squeeze that's just shy of painful. "The sound bites I get tonight will be a perfect companion to the interview we have with Edie and Sophia."

"I know." I resist the urge to rub my thumb across her knuckles. "Grant's thrilled you got the exclusive. *Survivor* is tracking to be Wonderland's biggest opening this year."

"And Sophia's going to crush it," Jess adds, with genuine enthusiasm breaking through her professional mask. "She deserves this moment."

"She does." I pause, noticing how the documentary cameraman is zooming in on our joined hands resting on the seat between us. "Speaking of moments, how are the invites for the dinner party going?"

"Good. Blair's bringing the wine. Stella's handling dessert." She tilts her head, studying me. "You nervous to have all those people invade your space?"

It's a fair question. My apartment, now technically *our* apartment, has never hosted that many people at once. Having both our friend groups collide feels strangely intimate, more real than this charade deserves to be.

"Just wondering if Brandon and Alex will manage to be in the same room without competing over who can do the most dangerous stunt."

Jess laughs, and it sounds almost genuine. "My money's on Brandon."

"Traitor."

The car slows as we approach the theater, and Jess's grip on my hand tightens.

She hasn't said much since we started our drive. Not because she's nervous, exactly, but likely because she's preparing: for the spotlight, for the questions, for the fact that tonight, she's not just a journalist; she's also the story. We're the story. Tonight, the cameras are aimed at her from both sides.

"Hey," I say quietly, leaning in. "You've got this."

She turns to me, and for a second, vulnerability flickers in her eyes, and maybe a little gratitude. I reach up and gently tuck a loose strand of hair behind her ear. My fingers skim her cheek, lingering there for a heartbeat too long as my thumb sweeps softly across her skin.

Jess nods once, lips parting like she wants to say something, but then the car door opens, and the moment dissolves into a wall of flashing lights and high-pitched shouts.

She steps out first, and for a second, I forget to follow.

Slipping the coat from her shoulders, she hands it to an assistant at the curb, and then she's completely, devastatingly revealed.

Her dress is the color of midnight, a deep navy that hugs every curve like it was sewn onto her body. The neckline dips just enough to make my mouth dry, and the fabric glides over her hips like liquid. With her hair swept back and her bold red lips, she is the perfect mix of cool and confident. She's not just stunning. She's undeniable.

I swallow hard and step out after her, adjusting my suit like it might somehow make me worthy to stand next to her.

Every touch between us now is calculated. A hand at her

waist. A brush of fingers along her back. Close enough to look intimate. Careful enough to maintain the line. It's exhausting.

"Lucas! Jess! Over here!" The paparazzi shout from all directions, desperate for shots of Hollywood's surprising new power couple.

Further ahead, I spot Grant and Sophia. He's effortlessly perfect in his suit, and she looks like a damn Oscar statuette in gold. Grant gives me a subtle nod of approval, maybe even pride. Sophia catches Jess's eye and mouths, *You two look amazing.*

Jess beams, and something catches in my chest.

We're halfway down the carpet when I see Marcus circling like a shark that's scented blood. His eyes lock on Jess with that same smarmy, predatory gleam I remember from Vegas, and something hot and possessive flashes through me.

"Incoming at two o'clock," I murmur. "Marcus alert."

She goes still for half a second. "Great."

Marcus intercepts us with practiced smoothness. Wearing expensive cologne and a slick smile, he exudes the kind of charm that's too practiced to be real. "Jess! Absolutely radiant tonight." His eyes drag down and back up her body, and my jaw ticks. "Marriage clearly agrees with you."

"Marcus," she says evenly. "Hope you enjoy the movie tonight."

"Lucas." He nods, but his smile never reaches his eyes. "Mind if I steal your wife for a moment? Wanted to discuss some upcoming opportunities."

Before I can respond, he's already reaching for her elbow.

Nope.

I slide my arm around her waist and tug her subtly closer. "Actually," I say, pressing a kiss to her temple and letting it linger just long enough to send a message, "we're on a pretty tight schedule tonight. But I'm sure she'd be happy to set something up later this week. Just reach out to her office."

Jess leans into me like we rehearsed it. "Absolutely. My assistant can find time in my calendar."

Marcus's smile tightens. "Of course. Wouldn't want to separate the newlyweds."

As he walks away, Jess tilts her face up to mine.

"My hero," she murmurs sarcastically, but there's something soft in her expression, something unspoken that lands like a punch to the chest. Something that tells me I just might be.

"Just doing my husbandly duties," I reply, letting my hand fall from her waist as I reach for hers and intertwine our fingers.

Except, it's not just about being her fake husband. I'd keep her safe from the likes of Marcus whether we were married or not, on camera or off. No woman should have to deal with that shit. Especially not her.

The rest of the evening flows with surprising ease. Jess conducts her interview with Edie Lang brilliantly, asking thoughtful questions that have the Oscar winner visibly impressed. I handle a minor scheduling crisis for Grant, ensure the key critics get their face time, and even manage to enjoy the film.

All night, Jess and I orbit each other with practiced awareness. A touch here, a smile there, knowing glances across the room that anyone watching would read as authentic connection.

The town car is silent on the drive home, with both of us conscious of the cameras still rolling. The tension that dissipated during the event builds again in the enclosed space.

"You were amazing tonight," I say because it's true and because it's what a supportive husband would say.

"So were you." Her smile is picture-perfect. "Especially with Marcus."

"Just protecting what's mine."

"Now I'm yours?" The edge in her voice is subtle but unmistakable.

I raise an eyebrow. "Would you have preferred I let him paw at you all evening?"

"I can handle Marcus."

"I know you can." I keep my voice even, aware of the cameras. "But you shouldn't have to."

She doesn't answer, but I feel her lean against my shoulder. She's pretending to be affectionate for the cameras, but beneath the façade, she's distant.

The moment we're inside the apartment, with the door closed behind us and the cameras finally gone, Jess kicks off her heels with a fury that suggests she might like to aim them at my head.

"What the hell was that with Marcus?" she demands, unpinning her hair with sharp, angry movements.

"What was what?" I loosen my tie, trying to maintain my composure.

"That caveman routine. The territorial marking." She gestures wildly. "The temple kiss!"

"I was playing the part," I counter, though, even to my own ears, the excuse sounds hollow. "Marcus was crossing lines. Again."

"I told you, I can handle Marcus."

I step forward, and my voice is low and tight as I say, "You shouldn't have to."

She opens her mouth to argue again, but then she freezes.

I'm standing right in front of her now. Close. Closer than I should be.

And we both feel it. The space between us is practically electric. The only thing louder than our argument is the pounding of my heart in my ears. Her eyes flick down, just once, to my mouth. My fists clench at my sides to stop myself from reaching for her.

"I would've stepped in for any woman being harassed like that," I say, my voice rough. "But for you?" I shake my head. "There's no version of me that stands there and lets that happen."

Her breath hitches, and her eyes lock on mine. For a second, I swear we're both about to cross a line we can't uncross.

"This isn't real, Lucas," she says finally, her voice quieter. "You don't actually have to protect me."

"I know that," I snap, running a hand through my hair in frustration. "But nobody else does. And if were going to convince others, including my father, who can smell bullshit from miles away, that this marriage is legitimate, it needs to look and feel real."

Jess sinks onto the couch, suddenly looking exhausted. "You think we can't pull it off?"

"I think tonight proved we can be good at this," I admit, and the truth surprises even me.

She looks up at me, and for once, there's no mask, no performance, just Jess looking as confused as I feel.

"What are we doing, Lucas?" she asks softly.

I wish I had an answer. Instead, I loosen my tie further and head to my bedroom.

"Getting really good at lying," I call back, not turning to see her reaction. "Better get some sleep. We've got a dinner party to plan."

As I close my bathroom door, I catch my reflection in the mirror, where I see my flushed cheeks, bright eyes, and slightly disheveled hair. I look like a man coming undone.

Five months and two weeks to go. God help us both.

thirteen

. . .

Jess

"IS it weird that you two already move around each other like you've been married for years?" Sophia asks, watching as Lucas takes the wine glass from my hand and refills it without breaking his conversation with Grant.

I nearly choke on my sip. "Professional synchronicity," I manage. "Years of orbiting each other in press rooms."

"Mm-hmm." Her knowing smile is unbearable.

The dinner party is in full swing in Lucas's apartment—our apartment, I guess—filled with the warm buzz of conversation and laughter. The documentary cameras are discreetly positioned in corners, catching "authentic moments of the newlyweds' first dinner party," as Dylan put it.

Blair and Wyatt are deep in conversation with Stella. Brandon is animatedly describing some death-defying stunt to Alex and his date, a tall gallery owner who looks both horrified and fascinated. Then there's Austin, my brother, watching me with that unsettling attentiveness he's had since we were kids. He knows me too well, which makes him dangerous to this whole charade.

"So, how did you two end up agreeing to this documentary in the first place?" Grant asks, drawing me back to the conversation circle. "Dylan mentioned you signed the release forms that same night as the wedding."

Lucas looks at me, and a silent communication passes between us.

"Well," I say, "we were obviously not in our most rational state."

"But," Lucas smoothly picks up, his hand finding the small of my back, "we'd both admired Dylan's work for years. His documentary on the fall of print media was incredible."

"And *Real Power* does have the potential to showcase genuine partnerships in the industry," I add.

"Right." Lucas nods. "As opposed to the manufactured couples Hollywood usually promotes."

The irony nearly makes me laugh. We are literally the definition of a manufactured couple.

"Plus, Dylan can be very persuasive," I continue. "He spun the 'rivals to lovers' thing as a metaphor—finally, a merger between spin and substance."

Grant raises his glass. "To unlikely partnerships that work better than anyone expected."

Everyone drinks, and Lucas's hand slides around my waist, pulling me closer against his side. The gesture is so natural that it frightens me. We've been doing this kind of thing all night: casual touches, finishing each other's sentences, and anticipating each other's needs. The scariest part is how easy it's becoming.

"You two are nauseating," Austin says when he corners me in the kitchen later. "I can barely recognize my sister under all that domestic bliss."

I'm arranging dessert plates, carefully keeping my back to the nearest camera. "Don't be dramatic."

"You handed him your olives without a word, and he disposed of them without breaking his conversation with Wyatt."

"That's just good hosting."

Austin leans against the counter and says in a lowered voice, "Look, when I talked to Lucas, I was pretty sure this was some kind of elaborate PR stunt, but tonight..."

My heart rate spikes. "Tonight, what?"

"You look happy, Jess." His expression softens. "Like, genuinely happy. And from the way he looks at you when you're not watching, it's obvious he was telling me the truth when he said he's liked you since he first saw you at USC."

My ears ring with this confession, and I focus intently on the dessert arrangement as I casually ask, "What do you mean?"

"It's the same look he had eight years ago when you showed up at that baseball game."

My head snaps up. "What are you talking about?"

Austin grins. "Come on, sis. The guy was checking you out until he made that crack about reporters being vultures and you insulted his father. Then it all went downhill from there."

"That's—" I struggle to find words. "That's ridiculous."

"Is it? Because, from where I'm standing, you two fighting

your attraction for eight years and then drunkenly getting married in Vegas seems about right."

I throw a napkin at him. "I'm revoking your invitation to all future dinner parties."

His laugh is warm and familiar, reminding me of surf sessions and late-night conversations on the beach after Mom died. Our older brother Garrett was away at college, trying to hold it together from a distance, but Austin and I were the ones still at home, actually talking about her and trying to pretend we were fine. We were just kids, but grief made us teammates in a way even baseball never could.

"By the way, when are we getting in the water? Your husband mentioned you've been slacking on your surf time."

I'm not sure how to digest all of this information, so I just roll my eyes.

"She would have liked him," Austin says quietly.

"You think?" I ask, surprised by how much I want the answer to be yes.

"Yeah. He doesn't let you get away with your bullshit, but he clearly respects you." Austin's smile turns melancholy. "That's all she ever wanted for us, to find people who could see past our sharp edges to what's underneath."

I swallow against the unexpected tightness in my throat. "Next Sunday," I say. "Zuma Beach, six o'clock. Bring your A-game."

"Always do." He hesitates. "Mom would be proud of you, Jess. The stories you chase, the podcast, your fierce drive for the truth, all of it."

"She'd be proud of you, too," I manage, grateful when Blair appears in the doorway.

"Dessert emergency out here," she announces. "Brandon's threatening to tell the story about Stella's first Hollywood party."

The rest of the evening flows with surprising ease. Brandon does share the Stella story (involving a well-known director, a misunderstanding about sushi, and an unfortunate allergic reaction), but only after she tells them about his mishap on the set of a superhero movie.

Alex regales everyone with tales of Lucas's secret Disneyland obsession, complete with photographic evidence of him wearing Mickey ears, which earns him a death glare from my "husband" that would terrify anyone who didn't know him well.

"I think that's going in the documentary for sure," Dylan's assistant announces from behind her camera, and Lucas groans.

"If they include that, I'm adding the footage of Jess singing karaoke at the Wonderland holiday party last year," he threatens.

"You wouldn't dare," I gasp. "I was doing my Stevie Nicks impression. It was art."

"It was something," Grant deadpans, and everyone erupts in laughter.

I catch Lucas's eye from across the room, and he gives me a wink that sends an unwelcome warmth through my chest. For a moment, I forget this is all pretend. For a moment, it feels like we're just a couple hosting friends, sharing inside jokes, and building memories.

It's dangerously close to perfect.

Hours later, after the last guests have left and the documentary crew has finally packed up their equipment, Lucas and I stand side by side in the kitchen, loading the dishwasher in comfortable silence.

"That went well," he says, handing me a wine glass.

His fingers brush mine as I take it, and a little jolt shoots up my arm. I tell myself it's nothing. Static electricity. Kitchen humidity. Definitely not the warmth of his skin or how close he's standing.

"Surprisingly well," I say, trying to focus on loading plates instead of the stupid flutter in my stomach. "Alex is hilarious."

"Your friend Brandon is a menace," Lucas replies, but there's a smile tugging at his mouth. "I can't believe he did that impression of me at the press conference."

"It was spot-on." Laughing, I grab another plate from the counter. "The hair thing and everything."

"I do not do a hair thing."

"You absolutely do a hair thing," I say, mimicking the way he runs his hand through his hair when he's stressed.

He rolls his eyes, but I don't miss the way his lips twitch at the corners.

"At least I don't twirl my hair when I'm thinking hard, like someone I could mention."

"I don't—" I stop, catching myself mid-twirl. "Ok, fine. Touché."

We continue passing forks, stacking plates, and trading glass after glass, and every time our hands make contact, it feels like the air shifts, like we're caught in some kind of slow-burn gravitational pull.

It's ridiculous. We're doing dishes. But his hands are so

much bigger than mine, rough in all the right places, and unnecessarily gentle with every single glass. I reach for the silverware tray at the same time he does, and our fingers tangle. For a second, neither of us moves.

The moment stretches. My pulse kicks up. I look at his hand around mine, then up at his face and find him already watching me. The apartment is silent.

Suddenly, I can't remember how we got from "temporary insanity" in Vegas to this quiet domestic dance that somehow feels comfortable.

"Austin believes this is real," I blurt out.

Lucas pauses, dish towel in hand. "I think we've managed to convince all of our friends."

"We've gotten good at this." I lean against the counter, suddenly aware of how close we're standing.

"Too good," he agrees, his voice lower.

"All those touches, the inside jokes." I should step back. I should make a joke, break this tension, retreat to my room. Instead, I find myself swaying slightly forward. "Lucas," I whisper, not sure if it's a question or a warning.

His gaze drops to my lips and returns to my eyes. "For the documentary," he says, his voice rough. "We should probably practice. To make it look natural."

"Right," I agree too quickly. "Practice. For authenticity."

He cups my face with one hand, and I can feel the slight tremor in his fingers. Or maybe that's me, trembling at his touch. His thumb brushes my cheek, and my eyes flutter closed.

"Just for the cameras," I whisper.

"Just for the cameras," he echoes, and then his lips are on mine.

Unlike our frantic kiss in Vegas or our performative pecks for the documentary, this is slow, deliberate. His lips are soft but insistent, and I find myself responding with an intensity that should alarm me. My hands slide up his chest to his shoulders, and his arm wraps around my waist, pulling me closer.

He tastes like the chocolate dessert we served, the expensive bourbon Grant brought, and something else entirely that's just...Lucas. My mind goes blissfully blank, with all the complications and consequences fading into background noise, as he deepens the kiss.

When we finally break apart, we're both breathing heavily. His pupils are dilated, and his hair is wrecked from where my fingers have been. I must look equally affected because something like satisfaction flickers in his eyes.

Reality crashes back, cold and sobering. I step back, breaking his hold.

"That should look convincing enough," I say, my voice only slightly unsteady. "Good practice."

A series of emotions crosses his face, too quickly to interpret, before he settles on a neutral expression. "Definitely convincing."

"I should..." I gesture vaguely toward my bedroom.

He nods. "Me, too."

"Right," I echo. "Goodnight, Lucas."

"Goodnight, Jess."

I make it to my room before I allow myself to touch my

lips, which still tingle from his kiss. "Just practice," I remind myself firmly. "Nothing more."

But as I crawl into bed, I can't help replaying the kiss in my mind, analyzing every moment, every sensation.

Practice has never felt so explosive.

fourteen

. . .

Lucas

THURSDAY EVENING TRAFFIC is a special kind of hell, especially after a day of putting out PR fires. Some rising star from our newest drama series decided to trash-talk the show's writing on a podcast, and damage control consumed my entire afternoon. But that was better than obsessing about the kiss that has distracted me all week.

By the time I unlock the door to the apartment, my shoulders are tight with tension, and my patience is threadbare. All I want is silence, a drink, and maybe a mindless baseball game on TV.

What I get is Jess, curled up on my couch in my old USC baseball hoodie. The worn gray fabric swims on her smaller frame. She's focused intently on her laptop, with her blonde hair piled messily on top of her head and her legs tucked beneath her. The sight stops me in my tracks.

She glances up, and her expression shifts from concentration to something almost like guilt.

"Hey," she says, tugging at the bottom of the sweatshirt.

"I was cold, and this was in the laundry room. Hope it's ok that I borrowed it."

I should be annoyed. That hoodie is practically a sacred relic of my college days. It's faded in all the right places, softened by countless washes, with a small tear in the cuff where I caught it on a fence while jumping over to see a late-night concert. But instead of irritation, something warm unfurls in my chest at the sight of her wearing it.

"It's fine," I manage, setting down my briefcase. "Looks better on you anyway."

Her eyebrows shoot up at the compliment, but she doesn't comment on it. "Rough day? Your right eye is doing that twitchy thing."

I press my fingers against my temple. "How do you even know about that?"

"I've been watching you handle press for years, Senator. The eye twitch is the only tell that you're about five minutes from losing your cool." She closes her laptop. "What happened?"

"Liam Chen from *Afterlight* decided to publicly roast his own show's writing. Called it 'derivative' and 'pandering to the lowest common denominator.'"

"Ouch." She winces. "Though he's not entirely wrong."

I shoot her a look.

"What? The dialogue is clunky in places." She holds up her hands defensively. "But I would never say that on the record."

"And that's why you're a better professional than Liam," I mutter, loosening my tie and heading for the kitchen. "Want a drink?"

"Sure. Dylan's crew is coming by at eight, by the way."

I freeze, with the bottle of whiskey halfway to the counter. "What? Why?"

"Individual testimonials," she says, making air quotes. "Solo confessionals to 'deepen the narrative of our relationship.'"

"Great. Just what I need after today."

"If it helps, they'll film us separately. I go first, then you." She unfolds herself from the couch and pads into the kitchen. The hoodie hangs to mid-thigh over her leggings. "They said we should be honest about our feelings. Apparently, the footage from the dinner party was 'too perfect.'"

"Too perfect?"

"Dylan thinks we're holding back. Says the audience needs to see our vulnerabilities." She rolls her eyes. "His words, not mine."

I pour two fingers of whiskey into glasses and slide one toward her. "What are you planning to say?"

"No idea." She takes a sip and then immediately winces. "God, I don't know how you drink this stuff straight."

"It's an acquired taste."

"It's masochistic."

We share a small smile, and for a moment, the tension of the day eases. This has been happening more often lately, these flickers of something real cutting through the performance. We haven't talked about the kiss. By mutual, unspoken agreement, it's filed under "practice," even though I think about it more than I should. Like now, watching her lips press against the glass. Her mouth. The shape of it. The way her tongue darts out to swipe a drop from the rim.

She pushes the tumbler back toward me. "Take it. I'm done pretending that stuff is drinkable."

I should pick up my own glass. I don't. Instead, I take hers, and I drink from the exact spot her lips just touched, slow and deliberate. Her gaze snags on mine and stays. The whiskey burns going down, but the heat that settles between us is something else entirely. Her expression shifts—just barely, but I catch it, her awareness, the weight of the moment, how still everything suddenly feels. For a beat, neither of us says anything.

"Hey," she says finally, her voice just a little unsteady, "can I ask about the fundraiser?"

I take another swallow, this time grateful for the shift.

"Sure."

"The documentary crew wanted to—"

"They're not invited," I cut in firmly. "My father would turn it into a campaign opportunity, and I'm not giving him that platform."

She studies me closely. "You really don't like your father, do you?"

It's a deceptively simple question with a complicated answer. I lean against the counter, choosing my words carefully.

"My father has spent his entire life calculating what will benefit Logan Carmichael. Every decision, every relationship, every public stance is filtered through that lens. Including his family." I stare into my glass. "He wanted me to follow him into politics. Cultivate the right connections, marry the right woman, build the perfect dynasty. When I chose USC over Stanford and baseball and PR over political science, it was the first major disappointment I delivered. And I've been adding to the list ever since."

She's quiet for a moment. "What about your mom?"

The mention of my mother softens something in me automatically. "She's amazing. Brilliant, compassionate, genuinely dedicated to education reform. She was a teacher before my father's political career took off."

"I remember reading about her foundation," Jess says.

I nod, unsurprised that she knows this. "That's her passion project. She's helped hundreds of kids get to college." Pride warms my voice. "She's the real deal, Jess. Not a typical political wife at all."

"She sounds wonderful," Jess says, and there's a wistfulness in her tone that makes me curious.

"What about your dad?" I ask. "Besides the baseball team, I don't know much about him."

She shifts to lean on the counter beside me. "Dad took over the Devils when I was ten. He's baseball-obsessed, but in a good way. After Mom died, he threw himself into the team and into making sure Garrett, Austin, and I were ok. He's uncomplicated. What you see is what you get."

"Tell me more about your mom?" I ask gently, remembering her reaction to the Pearl Jam shirt.

Something shifts in her expression, and there's a soft vulnerability I rarely see. "She was a force. A brilliant journalist with an unshakable moral compass. She always said that the truth isn't just what happens. It's what matters."

"Sounds like someone I know," I say quietly.

She smiles, but it's tinged with sadness. "Everyone says

I'm just like her. Same stubbornness, same drive. She would have been a star if she hadn't gotten sick."

"Is that why you're so committed to journalism? Carrying on her legacy?"

Jess looks startled by the question, as if no one has ever asked her this directly. "Partly. But also because I believe in it. In getting the story right, in holding people accountable." She pauses. "Maybe it's naïve, but I still think the truth matters."

"It's not naïve," I say. "It's admirable."

She looks genuinely surprised by the compliment. "Even when I'm making your job harder?"

"Especially then." I offer her a small smile. "You keep me honest."

We fall into a comfortable silence, something that would have seemed impossible weeks ago. I find myself wanting to know more about what makes Jessica Lexington tick, why someone as beautiful and brilliant as she is remains single, and what she might want beyond her career.

"Can I ask you something personal?" I venture.

She looks wary but nods.

"Why haven't you..." I hesitate, not sure how to phrase this delicately. "I mean, you've never mentioned relationships. Before this." I gesture vaguely between us.

"It's complicated."

"We've got time."

With a sigh, Jess crosses her arms in front of her. "I learned early on that most guys like me because of my connection to baseball. Or I'm a pretty face they think they can control and who will look good on their arm." She stares at some point over my shoulder. "But I also learned quickly that most men don't like strong women."

"Dumb men," I acknowledge.

"Plus, my career has always come first. I've worked so hard to be taken seriously, to not be seen as just 'the baseball owner's daughter.' Relationships seemed like a distraction at best, a liability at worst." She shrugs.

The honesty in her answer catches me off guard. "I get that," I say eventually. "More than you might think."

"Yeah? What's your excuse?"

It's my turn to be put on the spot. "Besides my father's relentless attempts to pair me with politically advantageous partners?"

"Besides that," she says with a small smile.

I take a breath. "I watched too many political marriages growing up. People who started with genuine feelings but ended up as business partners at best, adversaries at worst. Public smiles, private resentments."

"Your parents?"

I shake my head. "Not exactly. My father is complex. He does love my mother, in his self-centered way. He's always tried to be a good family man, at least in his own mind."

"But?"

I choose my next words carefully. "But his definition of good has always been flexible, especially when it comes to his campaigns."

Jess's expression shifts slightly. There's a flicker of something unreadable. Understanding, maybe, or something closer to disappointment?

"Ah," she says quietly.

I don't ask what she means by that, but I wonder what's playing across her mind right now. Stories she's told about other politicians? The scandals she's uncovered? Is she slotting my family into one of her mental files, wondering if there's more to dig into?

"Yeah." I drain my glass. "So, between that example and growing up in the public eye, relationships always felt like performances rather than real connections." I gesture around the apartment. "Kind of like our current situation."

She laughs softly. "Can't argue with that."

The doorbell rings, jolting us from the moment. Jess glances at her watch.

"That's Dylan. Right on time."

I nod, oddly disappointed that our conversation is being cut short. "I'll make myself scarce while you do your confessional."

She stands, smoothing down the hoodie. "Thanks for the drink. And the talk."

"Anytime."

As she heads for the door, I call after her, "Jess?"

She turns, her eyebrows raised in question.

"One more thing about the fundraiser. My father will probably say something insulting. Just ignore him. He's not worth getting upset over."

She offers a small smile. "Don't worry, Carmichael. I can handle difficult men."

"I know you can." I hold her gaze a moment longer than necessary. "But you shouldn't have to."

She gives a knowing nod before she turns to let Dylan in.

I retreat to my bedroom, but not before hearing her greet the crew with genuine warmth.

I change out of my work clothes, trying not to think about how right Jess looked in my hoodie or how much of myself I just revealed to a woman who, until recently, I considered a professional adversary. And who, with every passing moment, feels more and more like my wife.

fifteen

. . .

Jess

THE PACIFIC GLITTERS like scattered diamonds in the early morning light as I trudge up the beach with my surfboard tucked under my arm and salt water dripping from my wetsuit. My muscles burn with the pleasant fatigue that only comes from battling waves for two hours straight.

Austin jogs up beside me, looking annoyingly fresh despite our early surf session. At twenty-six, my younger brother is the picture of athletic prime. Or he would be, if not for the surgical scar on his elbow.

"Admit it." Grinning, he shakes water from his hair like an oversized golden retriever. "You missed this."

"The surfing or your insufferable gloating when you catch more waves than me?" Being in the water together has always been our safe space, our shared language since the days after Mom died.

"Both." He bumps my shoulder. "You're rusty. Too many mornings in bed with that husband of yours instead of paddling out."

I hope the flush in my cheeks can be attributed to exertion rather than the sudden image of mornings in bed with Lucas.

"Dad's making his famous pancakes. Garrett is there, too. Come have breakfast?"

I hesitate. Family breakfast means questions about Lucas, about our marriage—questions I'm not prepared to answer without carefully constructed half-truths.

"Dad's been asking about you," Austin adds, his expression softening. "He misses you."

Guilt tugs at me. I've been avoiding my family since Vegas, using work and the documentary as excuses. "Ok, but I can't stay long. I've got—"

"Stuff with Lucas, I know." Austin tosses his board into the back of his Jeep. "The newlywed bubble. I'll get you back home before he can miss you."

I climb into the passenger seat, peeling back my wetsuit to let my skin breathe. "How's the arm feeling?"

Austin flexes his elbow carefully. "Better. Doc says I'm ahead of schedule, but I'm still looking at another four months of rehab before I can even think about throwing again."

"Must be driving you crazy being sidelined."

"You have no idea." He starts the car, and the familiar rumble of the engine is comforting in its consistency. "Tampa's off to a strong start this season, and I'm stuck doing resistance bands and watching from the couch."

His frustration is palpable. Austin's been the golden boy of baseball since he could hold a bat. He was a high school phenom, college all-star, and first-round draft pick. Being injured is foreign territory for him.

"At least you're using the time wisely," I say. "Taking those sports management classes, right?"

He nods. "Yeah, figured I should have a backup plan. Not everyone gets to play until they're forty."

"Smart." I study his profile as he drives, noticing the subtle changes since he moved to Florida three years ago. He's more confident, more mature, but still with that easy optimism that's always been his defining quality. "You seeing anyone? Dad mentioned something about a model from South Beach."

Austin laughs. "That was nothing. Just some PR setup the team arranged."

"No one special, then?"

"Nah." He flicks on his turn signal. "I'm not in a rush. When it happens, I want it to be real, you know? Not just convenient or expected."

"My brother the romantic," I tease.

"Mock all you want, but I've seen what the real thing looks like." He gives me a pointed look. "With Mom and Dad. And now with you and Lucas."

My stomach twists with guilt. "Austin—"

"It's cool if you don't want to talk about it," he says, misinterpreting my hesitation. "I just never expected you to be the one to fall head over heels first."

I stare out the window at the passing coastline. "Life's full of surprises."

"That, it is." There's something wistful in his tone that makes me glance back at him.

"What about you? What are you looking for?"

He thinks for a moment. "Someone who challenges me, who sees me as Austin, not just the baseball player. Someone with depth, you know? And passion for something that matters."

"Sounds like you've given this some thought."

"I've had a lot of time to think lately." He taps his injured arm. "Sitting on the sidelines gives you perspective."

"Well, when you find her, make sure she's worthy of you," I say, surprised by the protective surge I feel. "You deserve someone exceptional."

Austin laughs. "Look at you, getting all big sister on me. I seem to remember you telling every girl I liked in high school that I had terrible gas problems."

"I was doing them a service. Full disclosure and all that."

We're both laughing as we pull into our father's driveway. The Spanish-style mansion is exactly as it's been since we moved here after Mom died, immaculately maintained but somehow frozen in time, like it was built for a version of our family that never existed.

Dad greets us in the kitchen, spatula in hand, looking surprisingly vibrant in his Devils baseball cap and "World's Best Grandpa" apron (a gift from Garrett when his daughter was born last year).

"There she is!" he booms, enveloping me in a hug that smells of maple syrup and the same aftershave he's worn for thirty years. "Mrs. Carmichael finally graces us with her presence."

"Dad," I warn, but I can't help smiling. At sixty-two, Sam Lexington is still a force—former college baseball star turned business mogul turned team owner, with a laugh that fills every room.

"What? I can't tease my daughter about her whirlwind romance?" He flips a pancake with practiced ease. "When are you bringing that husband of yours to a game? I've got a luxury box with your names on it."

"Soon," I promise vaguely. "We've been swamped with the documentary and work."

"Ah, yes, the documentary." He shakes his head. "My journalist daughter, suddenly the subject instead of the storyteller."

Garrett walks in with a cup of coffee in one hand and a baby monitor in the other. My older brother has always been the most serious of us, following Dad into the business side of baseball while Austin played and I rebelled.

"The prodigal sister returns," he says, but his smile is warm as he kisses my cheek. "How's married life?"

"Surprisingly complicated," I answer truthfully.

"All the best things are," Dad says, sliding pancakes onto plates. "Your mother used to say that marriage is like baseball. It's long stretches of routine punctuated by moments of pure magic and terror."

"Sounds about right," Garrett agrees, glancing at the baby monitor where his daughter occasionally makes soft sleeping sounds.

"Where's Kristy this weekend?" I ask, nodding toward the monitor.

"Visiting her mom," he says. "She'll be back tomorrow."

We settle around the kitchen island, falling into the comfortable rhythm of family breakfast.

"Hey, Dad? Can I ask you something?"

He looks up, curious. "Of course."

"The trust from Mom," I say slowly. "Why didn't you ever mention it?"

Dad's expression softens. "Because it wasn't mine to explain. Those were your mother's wishes. I didn't want to influence your choices, Jess. She set it up with the lawyers before she died, and she was very clear that she wanted you to make your own path, but she also wanted to give you something meaningful. When the time was right."

I nod, swallowing past the unexpected lump in my throat. "So, you knew about the marriage clause?"

"I did," he says quietly. "But I also knew how fiercely independent you are. If I told you, I worried you'd see it as manipulation, and that's the last thing your mother would've wanted."

"What about you guys?" I glance between Austin and Garrett. "Did Mom leave you anything?"

Garrett leans back in his chair. "Same rules. Found out when Kristy and I married. Came with a stake in the team. Just minority shares, but still. I think she knew I'd be the one to follow in Dad's footsteps."

I turn to Austin. "And you?"

He lifts a brow. "I'm not married, so technically, I wouldn't know, right?"

Garrett and I exchange a glance, suddenly aware that we've said too much. We look at Dad to rescue us.

Austin speaks up. "Ok, wow. You all suck at poker faces."

I open my mouth to respond, but he waves a hand. "It's fine. I'm not mad. I always knew she had something lined up for all of us. I stumbled across some paperwork once. Nothing I could make sense of, but it had our names on it."

He pauses, and his voice becomes softer. "I guess I'll have to wait and see what she has planned for me."

She knew us. All of us. Somehow, she'd carved out these wildly specific paths for each of her kids, trusting that we'd grow into exactly who she believed we could be.

Garrett clears his throat and shifts the mood, asking Austin how rehab's going. Just like that, we all slip back into the familiar rhythms of teasing, storytelling, and avoiding eye contact when it gets too real.

Austin shares physical therapy war stories. I deflect questions about Lucas with carefully curated anecdotes from our dinner party. Garrett updates us on the team's performance and his daughter's first steps.

As we're clearing dishes, Dad pulls me aside while Austin and Garrett debate pitcher stats in the other room.

"Walk with me?" he asks, and I follow him out to the terrace, overlooking the ocean.

We stand in silence for a moment, watching waves crash against the shore. It's a view that never gets old.

"You know," Dad says finally, "I wasn't sure about this Lucas fellow at first. Seemed sudden, out of character for my methodical daughter."

I tense, preparing for interrogation.

"But I see how you light up when you talk about him," he continues. "Even when you're complaining about his work habits. It reminds me of how your mother used to talk about me."

The comparison steals my breath. "Dad—"

"I know, I know. You hate the sentimentality." He smiles, crinkling the lines around his eyes. "But let me impart some fatherly wisdom, if I may."

I nod, my throat suddenly tight.

"Love isn't what you expect it to be, Jess. It's not the fairy tales or the romance novels. It's finding the person who makes the hard things easier and the good things better. The person who sees all your jagged edges and sharp corners and isn't intimidated by them."

My phone buzzes in my pocket.

LUCAS

Dylan wants more B-roll of us being "domestically authentic." Whatever that means. How soon can you get home?

Home. When did Lucas's apartment become home?

"That him?" Dad asks, noticing my expression.

"Yeah." I tuck the phone away. "Documentary stuff."

Dad studies me. "You know, your mother would have liked him."

"Austin said the same thing."

"Smart kid, your brother." He wraps an arm around my shoulders. "She always wanted you children to find partners who challenged you, who made you better versions of yourselves."

I think about Lucas, how he pushes back when I push, how he sees through my defenses, how he listened when he asked about mom.

"I should go," I say, surprising myself with the urgency I feel. "Lucas is waiting."

Dad's smile is knowing. "Of course."

Austin and I say goodbye, and as we head toward his Jeep, excitement settles in my chest. There's a pull, a longing to be back in Lucas's apartment, with its Disneyland posters and perfectly arranged kitchen.

JESS

On my way. Need anything?

LUCAS

Just you.

The smile creeps across my face before I get sidetracked by trying to dissect what he means.

"What's got you grinning so big?" Austin asks.

"Nothing," I reply, but I'm still smiling as I slide into my seat. "Just Lucas being Lucas."

As we drive away, my father's words echo in my mind: *The person who makes the hard things easier and the good things better.*

But this is a six-month arrangement with a clear end date. So, why does the thought of that ending make my chest ache?

sixteen

. . .

Lucas

BY THE TIME I walk through the front door, the silence in our apartment feels like a gift I didn't know I needed. No cameras tracking my movements. No Dylan directing our "authentic" interactions. No carefully orchestrated playing house for the documentary. Just blessed, beautiful silence.

I drop my keys in the bowl by the door. It's one Jess bought last week because she was "tired of watching me lose my keys like some kind of stereotypical sitcom husband." The memory of her rolling those blue eyes makes something warm unfurl in my chest.

The apartment is dark except for the city lights filtering through the windows, painting geometric shadows across the hardwood floors. For the first time in what feels like forever, we're not scheduled to perform for anyone tonight.

I loosen the top buttons on my shirt and roll up my sleeves, heading straight for the kitchen. After a day of managing other people's narratives, I need something real, something tangible.

Cooking has always been my reset button. It's the one thing that makes my brain go quiet when everything else is chaos. There's something almost meditative about it. The order, the rhythm. Chop. Sauté. Stir. Season. It's the complete opposite of spin. No strategy required. Just food, focus, and the immediate satisfaction of creating something with my hands.

I pull ingredients from the fridge, including chicken breasts, lemons, a block of parmesan that cost more than it should have, and a handful of herbs from the planter Jess insisted would die within a week but has somehow survived our mutual neglect. By the time I've got water boiling for pasta and a skillet warming for the chicken, the knot of tension between my shoulders begins to ease.

I hear the front door open and close, and the faint scent of her fills the air. Jess's heels click softly against the hardwood, moving toward the kitchen with a rhythm I've grown embarrassingly familiar with. I don't turn around, but I can feel her presence like a shift in atmospheric pressure.

"Is this for more B-roll?" Her voice carries that edge of dry humor that used to irritate me but now just makes me want to smile. "Did Dylan hide cameras in the potted plants?"

I glance over my shoulder. She's leaning against the doorframe in dark jeans and a crisp blouse, her blonde hair pulled back in a sleek ponytail that swings when she tilts her head. That ponytail does things to me. It makes me think about wrapping it around my fist, using it to gently tug her head back so I can...

I clear my throat and focus on the chicken.

"No cameras," I say. "No audience. No Dylan. Just dinner."

"Just dinner?" She raises an eyebrow, dropping her bag on the counter and sliding onto one of the barstools. "What's the special occasion? Did we hit some documentary milestone I'm not aware of?"

"Can't a man cook for his wife without an ulterior motive?" I slide a glass of white wine across the counter to her.

"A man, sure. You?" She takes the wine with a smirk. "There's always a strategy."

"No strategy tonight. Just thought we deserved a meal that wasn't takeout or performed for an audience." I turn back to the stove, oddly self-conscious now. "First time cooking just for us, that's all."

She's quiet for a moment, and when she speaks again, her voice has softened. "Well, it smells amazing. I'm intrigued."

"You should be. My pasta is legendary."

"Among who, exactly?" She sips her wine, watching me over the rim of the glass.

"The entire USC baseball team house. Six guys, one kitchen, and a strict rotation. You learn fast or you starve."

Her lips twitch. "I bet you were team captain of cooking duty, too."

"Actually, I was banned for two weeks after the Great Pasta Fire of 2013." I slice a lemon into paper-thin rounds, enjoying her surprised expression. "Actual flames. Fire truck. Very embarrassing."

She lets out a real laugh, not the carefully calculated

chuckle she uses for the cameras. "No way. Tell me every-thing immediately."

"Not much to tell. Turned my back for two minutes, and suddenly, the fettuccine was an inferno. My roommates didn't let me live it down for months."

"And now here you are, making..." She peers into the pan. "Lemon chicken pasta? Quite the redemption arc."

"I'm what they call multi-talented." I wink as I drain the pasta and toss it with lemon juice, butter, and parmesan, aware of her eyes following my movements. There's some-thing intimate about cooking for someone, especially when that someone is Jess, who still manages to surprise me daily despite having lived in my space for a month now.

"You want to help or just heckle from the sidelines?" I ask, nudging a cutting board in her direction.

She swirls her wine thoughtfully. "I'm a phenomenal heckler. Award-winning, really."

"I know you are." I roll my eyes and hand her a bunch of parsley. "Chop. Finely."

"So bossy," she mutters, but she slides off the stool and joins me at the counter, taking the knife with a confidence that doesn't quite match her technique.

I move behind her, unable to resist the urge to correct her. "Not like that. You'll cut your finger off, and I'm not in the mood to drive to the ER."

"I know how to use a knife," she protests, but she doesn't pull away when I place my hands over hers.

"Like this," I say, adjusting her grip. My chest brushes against her back as I guide her hands, showing her how to anchor the herbs. Her ponytail tickles my cheek, and it takes every ounce of self-control not to wrap it around my fingers. "Use your knuckles to guide the blade. There."

She nods, suddenly silent. I'm acutely aware of how close we're standing. I catch the faint scent of her shampoo, the warmth of her body just inches from mine. My hands linger over hers, longer than necessary.

For a few suspended heartbeats, we just exist. Close. Quiet. Breathing the same air. The city noise fades, and all I can hear is the soft sound of her breath catching slightly.

Her fingers tense beneath mine. "This feels like a lot of pressure for parsley," she finally says, her voice slightly quieter than before.

I should step away. Let the moment pass. But I don't. Not right away.

Eventually, I pull back, putting space between us with a practiced calm I don't really feel.

Together, we finish plating the meal and eat on the couch like the uncivilized heathens we apparently are, passing a single bowl back and forth between us. It's oddly intimate, more so than the carefully choreographed moments we perform for Dylan's cameras. Jess steals the bigger pieces of chicken with surgical precision, and I pretend not to notice.

"This is actually good," she admits, twirling pasta around her fork. "No fire trucks required."

"Your confidence in me is overwhelming."

"I maintain a healthy skepticism about all things. It's what makes me an excellent journalist."

"And a difficult wife," I counter, but there's no heat in it.

She grins. "You knew what you were getting into."

Did I? I wonder, watching her tuck a loose strand of hair

behind her ear. When we made this arrangement, I thought I was signing up for six months of strategic alliance with a professional adversary. I didn't expect this. Whatever this is. Comfortable silence, easy banter, feeling like I've known her all my life—and also not at all.

"What?" she asks, catching me staring.

I shake my head, trying to find safer ground. "Nothing. Just...you're not what I expected."

"No?" She tilts her head, sending that ponytail swinging hypnotically. "What did you expect?"

"I don't know. Someone colder, maybe. More calculating." I shrug, suddenly feeling like I'm navigating a minefield. "The journalist who made three different studio heads cry in one press tour."

"That was a good day," she says with a small amount of pride. "They deserved it."

"I'm sure they did."

She sets her fork down, her expression turning serious. "What else?"

"What else, what?"

"What else did you expect? About me." There's a vulnerability in her question that feels tempting, like we're venturing into territory beyond our carefully negotiated boundaries.

"I didn't expect to like you," I admit, and my honesty surprises even me. "I didn't expect any of this to feel..."

"Real?" she finishes.

"Yeah."

She nods slowly, and a smile spreads across her face as

something genuine reaches her eyes. "You're not what I expected, either, Carmichael."

"No?"

"Not even close."

The tension between us shifts into something electric, something that has nothing to do with our arrangement and everything to do with the woman sitting across from me, a woman who's brilliant, frustrating, and impossibly compelling.

Suddenly, I'm forced to acknowledge the truth I've been avoiding for weeks: somewhere along the way, I've started falling for my fake wife in a way that feels alarmingly, inconveniently real.

seventeen

. . .

Jess

IT'S ALMOST midnight by the time I finally crawl into bed. The apartment is quiet. Lucas retreated to his room about an hour ago, claiming he had emails to catch up on. I said something snarky about corporate masochism, but really, I was relieved to have a little solitude.

Not because I didn't enjoy dinner. The opposite, actually. I enjoyed it too much. It felt too real, like we were breaking rules we'd silently agreed to maintain.

Now the lights are off, the AC is humming, and I'm settling into that delicious place between almost asleep and dreaming when I feel it.

Something brushes my leg. Light. Tickling. Crawling.

I kick off the covers and sit up so fast I nearly punch myself in the face. My heart jackhammers against my ribs as I jump from the bed and slam my hand on the light switch so my eyes can scan the room like I'm searching for an assassin.

There it is. On my comforter. In my bed.

Eight legs. Too many eyes. Way too calm for my liking.

"Oh, HELL no."

I trip over my own feet and launch myself across the room like I'm auditioning for a one-woman Cirque du Soleil show. I grab the closest weapon—my slipper—and shout at the spider like it's personally threatened me. Because, well, it has.

"Do NOT come any closer. I will destroy your entire bloodline, I swear to God!"

The door bursts open with enough force to rattle the windows. "Jess?!"

Lucas skids into the room, out of breath, chest bare, wearing nothing but black boxer briefs and pure panic. The light spotlights him, showcasing those broad shoulders and defined muscles narrowing to a trim waist. I've seen him in swim trunks at Grant's pool parties before, but this is different. This is intimate. This is bedroom territory.

"Are you ok? What happened?" His voice is rough with alarm, and his eyes frantically search the room for danger.

I'm pointing at my bed with my makeshift weapon. "SPIDER."

He blinks. Once. Twice. "You screamed like you were being murdered because of a spider?"

"A large spider," I clarify, still breathless, trying desperately to keep my eyes above his neck. "With *opinions*."

He follows my gaze and sees it. Then he calmly walks over, grabs a tissue from my nightstand, and handles it like it's no big deal. Which, to be fair, it isn't, but I refuse to be shamed.

"You face down some of Hollywood's most powerful players in interviews on the regular," he says, his mouth quirking into that half-smile that does things to my insides, "but this is your weakness?"

I cross my arms, realizing too late that I'm in a thin tank top and sleep shorts that suddenly feel much shorter than they did five minutes ago. And Lucas is standing way too close, wearing only form-fitting boxer briefs that hide precisely nothing. My skin suddenly does that tingly thing that makes the hair on my arms stand up.

"I wasn't expecting a house guest with fangs," I manage, aiming for nonchalance but missing by about a mile.

"That's what you call me now?" His mouth twitches, and his eyes crinkle at the corners. "I'm hurt."

I swat at him with my slipper. "Very funny. You can go now."

But neither of us moves.

The air shifts.

His gaze drifts down over my bare legs, up to the curve of my hip, and to the rise of my chest where the tank dips just slightly. I watch his throat work as he swallows, and something tightens low in my stomach. The cotton of my tank top suddenly feels too thin, and my nipples harden under his gaze in a way that's impossible to hide.

My eyes betray me and do the same inventory on him. He's all lean muscle and golden skin, with a scattered trail of dark hair narrowing down his abdomen and disappearing beneath the waistband of his boxers. I can see the clear outline of him through the thin fabric, and my mouth goes dry.

When I finally drag my eyes back up to his face, his

pupils have dilated, turning his eyes nearly black. Neither of us says anything.

Not with words.

His hands flex at his sides like he's physically restraining himself from reaching for me. I find myself swaying forward slightly, magnetized.

"Thanks for the save," I say, my voice a little too breathy, a little too quiet.

"Anytime." The single word comes out rough, almost a growl.

The tension stretches between us, elastic and charged. For a heartbeat, I think he might close the distance and take the two steps that would bring his body against mine, his hands in my hair, his mouth on me.

He backs out slowly instead, giving me one last lingering look before pulling the door closed.

I sink onto the edge of the bed, my heart pounding like I just sprinted a mile. My skin feels too tight, too sensitive, every nerve ending alive and humming with awareness.

God help me.

I am so screwed.

I fall back against the pillows and press my hands against my eyes as if I can physically push the image of him out of my brain. It doesn't work. All I can see is the way his muscles shifted as he moved, the clear definition of his abdomen, the way the boxer briefs clung to the curve of his ass when he turned to leave.

This is ridiculous. I'm a grown woman, not some horny teenager. I've seen half-naked men before. I've interviewed actors fresh from set and dated reasonably attractive men.

None of them made me feel like I might actually combust from wanting.

But Lucas, dammit. Lucas, with his perfect face, surprising cooking skills, and the way he looks at me sometimes like I'm the only person in the world worth listening to.

I grab my pillow and press it over my face, groaning into it.

This wasn't supposed to happen. We had an arrangement: a clean, professional, mutually beneficial business arrangement with an expiration date. No messy feelings. No inconvenient desires. Just fake marriage, mutual advantage, clean split.

But there's nothing clean about the thoughts running through my mind right now, thoughts involving Lucas's hands, Lucas's mouth, Lucas pressing me into this mattress until I forget my own name.

The ache between my thighs becomes impossible to ignore. As I squeeze my eyes shut, my hand trails down my body almost of its own accord. If I'm going to be tortured by thoughts of Lucas anyway, I might as well find some relief. I slip my hand beneath the waistband of my sleep shorts, and my fingers find the slick heat that betrays exactly how much he affects me.

I imagine those strong hands roaming every inch of my skin, remember the way his muscles moved beneath his shirt as he cooked for me this evening and the way his bare body came to my rescue just now. My breathing grows ragged as I picture him above me, those piercing eyes dark with want, his voice rough as he whispers my name. A small whimper escapes my lips before I can stop it, and I press my free hand firmly over my mouth, terrified that he might hear through the thin wall between our rooms.

I work myself faster, chasing the release that builds low in my belly, all the while imagining Lucas's mouth replacing my fingers, his tongue doing impossibly skilled things that make my back arch off the bed. When I finally come, it's his name I barely manage to muffle against my palm, and the satisfaction is both perfect and completely inadequate at the same time. As good as that was, I know it would be infinitely better with him.

I toss the pillow aside and stare at the ceiling, trying to regulate my breathing. It's just physical attraction, I tell myself. Proximity and convenience. We're both reasonably attractive people living in close quarters. Of course there's tension. It doesn't have to mean anything.

Except it does. It means something because it's not just his body I'm drawn to. It's the way his eyes crinkle when he laughs. The focused intensity on his face when he's working. How he listens when I talk about my mom, my career, or anything else that matters to me. The careful way he handled the spider, respecting my irrational fear without making me feel small for having it.

I roll onto my side and stare at the door he just walked through, wishing it would open again. Wishing he'd come back. Wishing a lot of things I have no business wishing.

There are still five months left in our arrangement—five months until I secure my inheritance and we go our separate ways like we planned. Thank God he's going away this weekend. I need a break.

I slip out of bed and pad to the bathroom, where I splash

cold water on my face. The woman in the mirror looks flushed, and her eyes are too bright, like she's running a fever. In a way, I suppose I am.

I've caught feelings for my fake husband.

And as I crawl back into bed, I realize with perfect clarity that I'm in far deeper trouble than any spider could ever pose. While Lucas might have rescued me from eight legs and too many eyes, there's no one who can rescue me from this.

Least of all myself.

eighteen

. . .

Lucas

THE FIRST THING I see when I pull up is a custom banner stretched across the white stucco balcony that reads: "MANMORIAL 2025 – TAKEN MEN, BEACHFRONT VIEWS, ZERO FILTERS."

I laugh out loud. Of course Jake had a banner made. Of course it's in all caps.

The house itself is ridiculous—in the best way. Four stories of Southern California style luxury carved into the cliffs of La Jolla, overlooking the Pacific. Ocean views from every window, a rooftop hot tub, and enough space to host a minor awards show. Jake really outdid himself this year. Then again, extravagance is basically the Manmorial brand.

Apparently, this whole thing began when Jake and Wyatt pulled together a guys' weekend in law school. When Jake got engaged, the trip doubled as his bachelor party, and from there, it evolved. Now it's attached-men-only. No drama. No bachelor antics. Just a curated, bro-approved bonding weekend for the committed elite. The group's smaller. The tequila's more expensive. And the jokes? Appear to be dad-worthy.

Jake, the host and human exclamation point behind this entire production, is an entertainment lawyer I've worked with for years. He reps a ton of talent we negotiate with at Wonderland, so we've crossed paths plenty of times at premieres, galas, and contract signings. We're not exactly friends, but we're not strangers, either. He knows how to throw a party and how to work a deal.

He's waiting at the door, barefoot, holding a tray of tequila shots like he's welcoming guests to a wedding reception.

"Welcome to paradise, Carmichael," he says. "You made it. Thought Jess was gonna chain you to the kitchen island and make you alphabetize the spice rack or something."

He doesn't even blink at the puzzled look on my face. Clearly, he's had a head start on those shots.

"Look who finally showed up!" Grant calls from the kitchen. "Is it true you had to make a last-minute press statement on behalf of marriage itself?"

"Sorry," I say, dropping my bag. "I had to convince Dylan that filming Jess brushing her teeth wasn't essential B-roll. He's slipping into full reality-show-producer mode."

"Well, welcome," Grant says. "Come on in." He has his phone in hand, his head buried in what are likely early numbers for the opening weekend of *Survivor*.

"Manmorial Weekend," I repeat as I settle onto the couch. "I still can't believe this is a real thing."

"It's not," Grant deadpans. "It's a lifestyle."

Jake raises his shot glass. "To tradition."

"To delusion," I mutter, but I clink with them anyway. "So, how are the numbers looking?"

"We're on track to hit $120 million this weekend, maybe more," Grant says, beaming. This is Sophia's first film as a producer, and she's also playing the lead role. It's also the film that brought her and Grant together in more ways than one.

"That's good to hear, man. Congrats." I shake his hand and head over to take a seat on the couch. "How's everything with you and Lauren?" I ask Jake.

He hesitates, just for a second. Then the smile returns, and it's bright, practiced, and way too shiny.

"Good. She's just been busy."

Grant reappears with a beer for himself and one for Jake. "Busy filming audition reels for *Real Housewives*, probably."

Jake rolls his eyes. "She's networking."

Lauren is a presence: beautiful, social, and allergic to subtlety. I've only seen her when she's at events with Jake. She's always polished, always working the room like it owes her something. Last year, she nearly caused a press frenzy at a studio fundraiser when she loudly suggested that Grant should get back together with his ex and co-parenting partner, right in front of Sophia. Nobody's said it outright, but it's common knowledge that Lauren enjoys the proximity to power more than the quiet behind closed doors.

Jake's always defended her, always brushed it off.

But now? It looks like there might be trouble in paradise.

"She's networking with producers by asking them to follow her on Instagram mid-brunch," Grant mutters.

Jake waves him off. "Look, I get it. She's a lot. But she's trying."

Wyatt glances over at him but says nothing. Jake picks at the label on his beer bottle, peeling it back slowly.

"It's all fine," he says.

Which is code for definitely not fine.

"You know," Jake says, pointing his beer at me. "We almost didn't invite you."

"Gee, thanks."

"Not because of you," he clarifies. "Because of Jess."

My eyebrows lift. "What about her?"

"She's scary," Jake says immediately. "In a hot way. Like a Bond villain you root for. But if you'd told me even six months ago that you two would end up married?"

"Same," I say.

Jake leans forward slightly. "So, how's it going? Really."

I think back to a few nights ago when I heard a moan come from her room after I rescued her from the killer spider on her bed. When she screamed, I almost went into cardiac arrest from worry. I got so caught up in getting to her that I didn't even realize I had no clothes on. She didn't, either. You can't call what she was wearing proper clothing. It took every ounce of willpower and determination I had to walk away.

I wondered if I should go back in there, but then I heard her moan. I've never strained so hard to listen beyond my bedroom walls. I slid my hand beneath the waistband of my boxer briefs and wrapped it around my cock, stroking slowly as I imagined her doing the same. I imagined her thinking of me while she used her hands to satisfy the same urges I felt for her. When I finished, I heard her in the bathroom at the same time I was in mine, cleaning up my mess.

I open my mouth to deliver one of my practiced

responses—*we're adjusting well; the documentary's keeping us busy; it's been surprisingly fun*—but none of them feel quite right.

"She challenges me," I say instead, "in a way I didn't know I needed."

Grant whistles low. "Funny thing about love."

"She also stole the good towels for her bathroom and labeled the fridge shelves by food group," I add. "So, don't worry. We're still locked in a cold war of petty domination."

Jake grins. "Marriage is balance."

"So, no Brandon?" I ask, doing my best to change the subject.

"He's ineligible as a single dude," Jake says, "although I would've voted for an exception. I finally saw the *Road House* remake and he was fantastic in the fight scenes. I want to know who he trained with."

You wouldn't know it to look at him, but Jake can put a guy on the ground in under ten seconds. His body is built like a blueprint for a fighter, with broad shoulders, lean waist, and arms that stretch every T-shirt he owns without trying. He's got dark skin that always looks sun-warmed, even in winter, and hazel eyes that seem too light for how grounded he is, almost like they're letting in more of the world than the rest of us can handle. His hair's always cut close, clean and simple, like everything else about him. There's a scar on his eyebrow from some sparring match he refuses to talk about, and a kind of stillness in him that makes people lean in when he speaks. Most folks assume he's just the nice guy with the good suits and the calm voice. They have no idea he could drop a man twice his size without breaking a sweat. Hell, even I forget sometimes.

We sit in silence for a few moments, watching the waves crash just beyond the deck.

Jake leans back in his chair. "So, when did you know?"

"Know what?"

"That she was the one."

It's a simple question, and it should have a simple answer. I should say something charming. Something neutral. Something vague enough to keep the myth intact.

Instead, I pause.

"I think it was when I realized she never flinches," I say. "She says what she means. Stands by it. Doesn't care if it makes people uncomfortable."

Wyatt nods. "That'll do it."

"She challenges me," I add. "Not in a competitive way. More like she sees through all the noise. Including mine."

Wyatt raises his glass. "To women who keep us honest."

We all drink.

Somewhere back in L.A., the women are having their own girls' night—at least Blair, Jess, Sophia, and Stella are. Lauren didn't go. She never does. Too busy, too uninterested, or maybe just never really clicked with them, which, depending on who you ask, is part of the problem.

Eventually, the conversation shifts to baseball, work drama, and the playlist Wyatt insists is vibe-certified, but I stay quiet for a while, because what I said was true. Jess sees through the noise. She calls me on my bullshit before I can even hear it myself, and for some reason, I keep letting her.

I wonder what Jess is doing right now.

If she's laughing with Stella and Blair over wine, or already curled up in bed in that tiny shorts set.

And the noise around me fades. Just long enough for me to realize: I miss her.

Which is stupid. I've only been gone a few hours. But it already feels like it's been weeks.

nineteen

. . .

Jess

BLAIR PICKS me up in her matte black G Wagon, sipping a green juice that smells vaguely like lawn trimmings and witchcraft.

"You're wearing real yoga clothes," I say, sliding into the passenger seat.

"You're not," she replies, eyeing my ancient USC baseball tee, tied at the waist, and biker shorts that have seen better days. "Did you bring a mat?"

"I brought an attitude," I say, tossing my bag in the back. "That should count."

She laughs as she begins to drive. "I'm told we're going to love Natalie. Stella swears she's part life coach, part wellness witch, all abs."

"High bar."

"It's a Monday morning yoga class in Silver Lake," Blair says. "The bar is buried beneath a pile of emotional unavailability and oat milk foam."

The drive is just the two of us, and it's filled with gossip, laughter, and just enough complaining about men to officially check off the bonding portion of the day. We spent most of the weekend at her and Wyatt's house in Santa Monica, just the girls, lounging on the patio, sipping cocktails, and soaking in ocean air like it could cure everything. I'd been the one to suggest it, not because I needed a social night, but because I really didn't want to be alone in Lucas's apartment. Or my own.

Lucas left on Friday for La Jolla to celebrate Manmorial Weekend. The infamous "attached men only" beach trip Wyatt and Jake started back in their college days. I've heard all about it from Blair, but this is the first time that Lucas has been invited, the first time he's technically counted.

He mentioned it casually and then suggested that I gather the girls together for our own weekend of fun activities. Fake husbands aren't supposed to be this thoughtful. It messes with the boundaries and makes the pretending feel a little too real.

We pull up to a sleek little studio storefront with a name that sounds like an indie perfume brand, and I spot Sophia waving through the glass, looking unfairly fresh-faced for someone who was drinking negronis with me until midnight.

Inside, Stella's already set the mats out in perfect rows. The water bottles are labeled and aligned like she's trying to win an Olympic gold medal in hosting.

She beams when she sees us.

"Ok, so this is Natalie," she says, gesturing to the stunning brunette at the front of the room. "She's a literal goddess and my new favorite person."

Natalie turns toward us with a smile that's warm,

genuine, and somehow both calming and intimidating. She looks like she could talk you into a headstand or a major life change without raising her voice.

"Hi! I'm so excited you're all here. I've heard amazing things," she says, her voice smooth but not rehearsed.

"You've heard amazing things?" I ask, skeptical.

"I have! You must be Jess, the badass podcaster," she says as she takes my hands in hers. "And you must be Blair, Stella's boss." She gives Blair a wink.

"We've already been introduced," Sophia offers cheerfully, "but Jess is the one who just got married and is working with Dylan on the *Real Power* documentary."

"Wait," Natalie says, blinking. "You're married to Lucas Carmichael?"

I slowly descend to my mat. "Depends. Do you have a strong opinion about PR execs with unnervingly symmetrical faces?"

Natalie laughs. "No, but I do have a strong opinion about your husband being hot."

Blair hoots, and I groan. "You can keep that opinion," I say. "I hear it enough on Instagram."

Natalie shrugs, totally unbothered. "Married men are safe to thirst after. No stakes."

I shoot her a look, smiling despite myself, but something twists in my stomach quick and subtle, like the snap of a rubber band. It's stupid. She's not wrong, and it's not like I actually want to claim him. Still, the idea of anyone else thirsting after Lucas makes me feel off.

I brush it away, but the ping of possessiveness lingers longer than I want to admit.

Class begins with a flow that feels easy until I realize it's just the warm-up. Half an hour in, I'm dripping sweat and attempting a twisted triangle pose that should be illegal in polite society.

Beside me, Blair mutters, "If I die here, delete my browser history."

Sophia's already in full zen mode, effortlessly following Natalie's cues like she's auditioning for a luxury wellness retreat commercial. Stella, of course, looks like she belongs on the cover of the wellness retreat's magazine. When we hit savasana, she sighs contentedly and whispers, "Told you. Natalie is magic."

After class, we file out slowly, our limbs loose and our spirits slightly higher. Natalie joins us at the smoothie bar attached to the studio, and we gather around a tiny reclaimed-wood table, sipping things with spirulina and chia seeds like we understand what those are.

Blair's phone lights up with a FaceTime from Wyatt, and she answers with a grin. "Hey, babe."

He's in the passenger seat, his hair wind-tousled from the drive. "Hey, gorgeous. Just left San Diego. We're headed home." He flashes her a crooked smile and then flips the camera around quickly. "Jake's driving, Grant's still nursing a hangover."

"Not a hangover!" Grant shouts from somewhere offscreen. "Just deeply reflective."

Sophia's movie *Survivor* surpassed the $120 million mark this weekend, so I'm sure he was celebrating, and rightfully so. He bet big on a first-time producer in Sophia, and it paid off.

Wyatt laughs and turns the camera back to himself. "Can't wait to see you tonight." He blows her a kiss before the call ends, and all of us groan at the sweetness of it.

As Blair tucks her phone away, Natalie leans in with casual curiosity. "Ok, who was the hot guy driving with the movie star hairline?"

Blair chuckles. "Jake. Wyatt's best friend. And also married."

Natalie nods appreciatively. "Even better. I can add him to my no-stakes lusting scrapbook. Lucas." She points at me with a wink. "Harry Styles, that hot priest on TikTok, and now Jake."

We all laugh as we take a shot of what I'm sure is grass plucked from the patch of lawn in front of the studio. It's disgusting.

Stella nudges me with her elbow. "Hey, has Brandon posted anything lately? He said he was going to Cabo for a few days, but I haven't seen any stories."

"Cabo?" I ask, surprised. "He didn't say anything to me."

She shrugs, too casually. "He was bummed that he didn't get an invite to the guys' weekend. So, that's usually where he goes when he wants to reset. Or, you know, ruin someone's faith in dating apps."

"Concerned?"

"No!" she says a little too quickly. "I just wish I were as fluent in dating as he is. That man could give a masterclass."

I look at her sideways. "You do realize he once ghosted someone because they said they liked musicals, right?"

"I mean, I get it," Stella says. "Some people are *too* into *Wicked*."

Natalie arches a brow. "Wait. Who's Brandon?"

"Friend of ours," Blair says. "Stuntman. Gorgeous. Unavailable. A walking cautionary tale, basically."

"Stella and Jess's neighbor," Sophia adds with a knowing smile.

"Ah, I think I remember you mentioning him before. The neighbor." Natalie leans back toward me. "So, you and your husband. How long were you together before you got married?"

The table goes quiet. I keep my tone light. "We've known each other for years. Worked closely together on many things. One day, we decided to go all in."

It's not a lie. It's just not the whole truth.

Natalie nods, seemingly satisfied. "He seems like the kind of guy who'd do anything for his people."

My chest tightens for a second. "Yeah," I say. "He really is."

We talk and sip until we've turned into the table that's too loud, too happy, and a little bit obnoxious, the kind that makes you want to join or run screaming, depending on your current therapy status.

When we finally say our goodbyes, Natalie hugs each of us and says, "Next week, I'm teaching candlelit yoga on the roof. You're all coming."

It's not a question.

Back in the car, Blair plays DJ while I scroll through texts, and my heart stutters when I see the one from Lucas.

LUCAS

Home. No rush, just wanted you to know.

LUCAS

PS: I left something for you on the kitchen island.

Curiosity hums through me the whole ride back. When I step into the house, the space is quiet and warm. Sunlight spills across the kitchen floor in soft gold streaks, like the house is exhaling after a long weekend.

Lucas appears from the hallway at the same time I drop my bag, his hair still damp like he's just showered. He's barefoot and in a faded tee and well-worn shorts that hit just above the knee, showing off his thick athletic thighs and tan skin. It's entirely too distracting. He looks casual and comfortable, like someone I want to come home to.

It's ridiculous. He was only gone three nights, but at the sight of him now, standing there with that easy grin, something loosens in my chest.

"Hey," he says, his voice low and warm.

"Hey," I reply, trying not to sound as breathless as I feel. "Did you win at whatever Manmorial competition you were dragged into?"

"Cornhole champ," he says smugly. "Not to brag, but Jake cried."

I laugh as I walk to the island. "Please tell me there's video."

He laughs, and the sound hits low in my stomach, making it flutter and twist into a deep ache. I'm not sure when I started liking the sound of his laugh, but I do. When I reach the island, I see it: a small package on the counter, wrapped in brown kraft paper and tied with a simple navy ribbon.

"What is this?"

"Open it," he says casually, but I swear there's a hint of excitement in his eyes.

I pause. Gifts aren't really a thing in my world, not unless they're corporate swag or half-hearted PR gestures. I can't remember the last time someone gave me something just because. Part of me braces for a joke, a gag, something ridiculous that'll make me roll my eyes, because, if it is real, if it's thoughtful, I'm not sure what to do with that.

I tug the ribbon loose and slowly unwrap the paper.

Inside is a charm bracelet. There's a microphone, a tiny, folded newspaper, and three round silver discs, each engraved with a word: "Voice," "Vision," "Power." The last charm is a little scroll that reads: "OTRC – 3 YRS."

My heart catches, the kind of stutter-step that steals your breath before you even realize you've lost it. I stare at it, completely still. He remembered. Not just the name of my podcast. Not just the anniversary. But the way I talk about it. What it means to me.

"Lucas…"

"I saw it when I was picking something up for Grant. The charms felt like you."

I swallow hard. My eyes sting, and I have to look away for a second to regain my balance. Because this? This isn't part of the deal. This is real. Personal. Disarming.

I run my fingers over the metal. "No one's ever bought me something like this."

He shrugs. "Well, I'm honored to be the first."

I don't know what to say. Which is rare.

There's a beat of silence, warm, full, and charged. I feel it in my chest. In the space between us. In the way he's looking at me like I matter. Like he sees through all the noise and still chooses to stand here anyway.

Before I can stop myself, I reach for him.

My arms wrap around his waist, and I press my face into his chest. The fabric is soft beneath my cheek. He remembered. Something small, maybe, but it means everything. Now I'm standing here, hugging the one man I've called my sworn enemy for years. Somehow, he's become the person I want to share things with.

His arms slide around me like they've been waiting for the invitation. One hand settles at the base of my spine, and the other slides smoothly up my back. Neither of us lets go. Not right away.

"You hungry?" he asks finally.

"Starving."

"Good. I made us your favorite pasta to celebrate."

"You cooked for me again?"

"Don't look so surprised," he deadpans. "Here, let me put that on you."

I watch as he takes the bracelet from my hand and latches it around my wrist. His hand holds on to mine for a beat, and I look up at him, realizing there's nothing fake happening here anymore.

He drops my hand and flashes his most charming smile. "Let's go eat."

twenty

. . .

Lucas

IT'S BEEN two weeks since I gave Jess the bracelet.

Two weeks since she looked at me like I was something more than a PR partner. Like I was someone who mattered to her.

Two weeks since she hugged me without cameras, without fanfare, just soft and close, her head against my chest like she belonged there.

She's in my space now. In my head. In that quiet corner of me that I've spent years keeping locked down. The part that wants things I don't usually let myself want.

I haven't been able to shake it.

I'm in my office at Wonderland Studios, where I'm trying to focus and pretend my inbox isn't eating me alive. My phone pings for the fourth time in as many minutes. I don't have to look to know it's from legal, asking if I've reviewed the third draft of our *Pink Slip* holding statement.

I have.

I just hate it.

I scroll to the bottom of the Word doc on my laptop and rework the ending for the fifth time. I need something that doesn't sound like a studio executive was held hostage by a publicist and forced to read cue cards with a gun to his head off-screen. It has to sound human.

Levi Peterson didn't kill anyone. With a blood alcohol level that is protected by HIPAA laws and a damn-near heroic claim of avoiding a neighborhood cat, he swerved into a tree and was mildly concussed. The internet has already meme-ified him into some kind of pet-protecting vigilante.

Unfortunately, there's a video now, not of the crash but of him stumbling out of the car and muttering, "It's always fucking cats." It's not ideal.

But now, instead of keeping this story to myself like I did when it broke back in Vegas, I find that I'd like to work through it with Jess. She's infiltrating my home, my thoughts, and now, it looks like, my workplace, too.

LUCAS

Any chance you can record today's podcast episode over here? The Levi coverage is turning into a mess. Would be good to align.

JESS

You mean you want me to not torch your studio this time? I guess. Studio? 30 minutes?

I forward the most recent internal update to her inbox. If we're going to thread this needle, I'd rather do it face to face. She's the only reporter I trust to handle this with integrity—and the only one who could blow it all up if she's not given the full picture.

My assistant catches me in the hallway. "Legal is waiting on the Levi update."

"Tell them it's coming by noon."

Thirty minutes later, I walk into the conference room, and Jess is already there, perched on the edge of a chair with her laptop open and a cold brew balanced on one knee. She's in one of those outfits that make her look like she didn't try at all, yet still, somehow, radiates presence: tight jeans, oversized tee, and with her hair up with a pencil stabbed through the bun.

She doesn't look up as she types. "You're late."

"You're early," I counter, setting the coffee and pastries between us. "You always show up early when you think I'm going to lie."

"I was nearby," she replies still focused on her laptop. "Interview with someone from the costuming team for *Survivor*. Also, your intern downstairs offered to park my car."

I pause. "We don't have interns who valet."

"Then I just gave my keys to a stranger in a *Dazed and Confused* T-shirt."

I freeze, halfway to sitting down, and she bursts into laughter.

"Kidding. Relax, Senator."

"I hate it when you call me that," I mutter, opening the donut box.

She pauses for a beat longer than usual, then says, "Guess I'll have to find a new nickname for you."

She reaches for a cruller. "You get what you need from legal?" she asks, taking the glazed donut like it was custom made for her.

"I got something," I say. "Whether it's usable remains to be seen."

Jess moves around the desk and walks straight into my space. She leans in beside me, with one hand on the back of my chair and the other resting on the desk near mine. Our fingers brush. Just briefly. Just enough.

Her perfume wraps around me, and it's that light, subtle scent of florals. Her hair catches the sunlight streaming through the tall office windows, causing it to glow gold at the ends like she's lit from the inside out. Her eyes skim the screen with laser precision, narrowed in concentration, and when she tilts her head to ask a question, her cheek is barely a breath from mine.

"You added the part about his charitable work with the pet shelter," she says in a low voice. "That's a good call."

"Figured it softens the cat thing," I manage. My voice comes out rougher than I expect. Too much awareness. Too much heat for a weekday morning. She doesn't seem to notice. Or maybe she does, and she's just better at hiding it.

She scrolls through the draft, her fingertips moving fast, but I can't focus on a single line of text. Not when her arm keeps brushing mine. Not when I can feel the heat of her body so close that it's messing with my brain.

God help me, I like working with her. I like this version of us. We're sharp but aligned, collaborative without constantly trying to one-up each other. It took a few weeks—ok, two months—but we've found a rhythm. And I'm not entirely convinced it's just because of the cameras.

"It does. And you cut the part where the studio 'remains steadfast in its commitment to employee wellness.'"

"I couldn't say it with a straight face."

She laughs again. "Look at you. Evolving."

I sigh and look up at her. "I need this episode to walk a fine line. We're not spinning. We're clarifying. Your podcast is already on the trades' radar, and if your narrative contradicts ours, the media will eat us alive."

"And if it aligns," she says, "people will believe it. Because I'm not the studio. I'm the voice they trust."

Exactly. She's my best shot at getting the right tone into the public space, and she knows it.

"So, what's the problem?" she asks.

I open my phone and show her the headline that just dropped: "LEVI PETERSON'S TEAM SAYS 'COLD MEDS & FATIGUE' TO BLAME FOR CRASH."

Jess reads it twice and then closes her eyes. "Oh, come on."

"His personal publicist gave a statement without clearing

it through us. Now it sounds like we're contradicting ourselves."

"And if I run with the studio-approved version, I look like I'm helping you cover it up."

I nod. "That's why I want to do this together. We co-author the tone. You call it straight. I'll stay in my lane."

For a moment, she studies me like she's deciding whether to believe that. Then she opens her laptop again and starts typing.

"Alright. Let's fix it."

We settle into our usual back-and-forth, refining talking points and fact-checking timelines. She records an intro blurb for her podcast while I check off calls to talent management and the studio's insurance lead.

She asks for a statement to include in the bonus content, and I give her one I already know will run longer than we agreed to.

"I'm adding context," I say when she gives me a look.

"You're adding caveats."

"Same thing."

"Not even close."

I lean back in my chair and watch her. She's in her zone now, pulling quotes, tagging timestamps, adjusting her voice tone between cuts. I don't feel defensive anymore when she pokes holes in my version of the truth. I just want to make sure we're building something accurate. Respectful. Fair.

We've done dozens of press moments and podcast tie-ins, but now there's an added element that didn't exist before. I realize I'm not just impressed with her hustle. I admire her clarity, her integrity, her ability to call out bullshit while still caring about people. Somehow, we're on the same side, and it doesn't feel like giving up ground. It feels like alignment.

It's almost five by the time we wrap. Jess closes her laptop with a satisfied sigh and tosses the empty donut box in the trash. "Your team's getting better," she says, grabbing her bag.

"You mean I'm getting better."

She shrugs, already halfway to the door. "Or I'm rubbing off on you."

I follow her into the hallway, matching her pace. The elevator dings and opens, but before she can step inside, I speak up. "I do have one question."

"Shoot."

"The fundraiser. You still good with it?" She pauses, turning to face me fully, surprise flickering across her face.

"You mean emotionally or logistically?"

"Both." The elevator doors close without us, but neither of us moves to call it back.

"I told you I'd go," she says simply. "I meant it."

I nod but find myself pressing further. "It's a lot. Press, guests, my family. And my father will be there."

Her eyes narrow slightly at the mention of him, but her voice remains steady. "I'm not worried."

"You're sure? The doc crew won't be there, so you don't have to be on if you don't want to deal with him."

"Lucas." Her voice softens, and she takes a small step closer. "Don't worry about me. We're on the same side now."

"That's exactly why I'm worried," I say quietly. "You're a lot more dangerous now."

She raises an eyebrow, and a slow smirk spreads across her face. "Good thing you're married to me, then."

"Don't remind me," I mutter, but I'm fighting a smile.

She laughs as she calls another elevator, and when the doors slide shut with her inside, I'm left alone in the hallway with a thousand unspoken thoughts and a growing certainty that I am completely, irreversibly fucked.

twenty-one

Jess

THE HALLWAY IS quiet except for my keys jingling in the lock when I twist them to open the door. I'm back at my place for the first time in almost a month, stopping by to grab a few things before the trip to Lucas's parents' house for the fundraiser. Clothes. Shoes. A dress that says "cool and collected daughter-in-law," not "accidental Vegas bride."

The scent of eucalyptus and rose hits me immediately, and I know that's Stella's doing. One of her intention candles flickers gently on the coffee table, casting the whole living room in a soft amber glow.

She's curled up on the couch in one of my sweatshirts, her knees tucked under her, with a laptop balanced on her thighs and a bowl of popcorn nestled beside her.

"Oh, hey!" she chirps when she sees me. "You're back! I didn't know I'd see you tonight."

"Just a pit stop." I drop my bag by the entry table and toe off my boots. "We leave for Lucas's parents' place in the morning, and I forgot the dress I need.

I head toward my room, but she calls out before I disappear. "Hey, do you—do you have a sec?"

Something in her voice gives me pause.

I glance over my shoulder. "What's up?"

She bites her bottom lip, hesitant. "Can you sit for a minute? I...I kind of need to ask you something. About marriage."

That earns a blink. "Wow, ok. Give me two minutes to grab my dress, and I'm all yours."

When I return, she's already cleared the popcorn and made tea because of course she has.

I settle onto the couch beside her. "Alright, shoot."

She fidgets with the string of her hoodie. "So, this is going to sound dumb, but when you and Lucas got married, even though it was like, wild and fast, I kind of thought, ok, maybe this is what happens when people are in love. Like, when you know, you know, right?"

I stare at her. "Stella. You do remember that we were both wildly drunk in Vegas, right?"

She nods quickly. "Yes! Yes. I mean, I get that. And I know you've explained that it's more complicated. But I guess what I'm wondering is, how do you actually know when it's real?"

Ah. There it is.

I take a breath. "Are we still talking about me?"

Stella blushes. "Maybe."

"Does this have anything to do with Mason-from-the-elevator?"

Her eyes widen. "No. Maybe. I just, I don't know. Every time I see him, I feel ridiculous."

I lean back, folding my arms. "Let me guess. He's hot. He smells good. He once held the door for you and said, 'After you,' and your soul left your body."

She covers her face. "I'm never telling you anything again."

I bite back a laugh. "Stella. Girl."

"I know," she moans, hiding her face behind a couch pillow. "I know it's ridiculous. But I've built up this entire fantasy in my head. We run into each other while I'm carrying groceries, and he helps me with the door. Then we're talking and laughing, and the next thing you know, we're watching rom-com movies together on his couch, and he's brushing my hair behind my ear like—"

"Like a Hallmark character who just came back from three years abroad?"

"Exactly!" She drops the pillow. "But in real life, he doesn't know my name and probably thinks I'm a teenager."

"You're a grown-ass woman, who happens to be an excellent talent agent."

"Yeah, but I give off 'first-job energy.' And he definitely gives off 'has a home espresso machine' energy."

I laugh. "It's ok. We've all been there. But listen. Wanting someone to notice you is not the same thing as knowing they're right for you."

"But how do you know?" she whispers.

I think about Lucas, about the way he looks at me when my guard is down and the way I feel when I'm around him: seen, challenged, steady and unsteady all at once.

"You know," I say carefully, "when you feel like yourself

around them. Not just the shiny parts you show the world, but the weird, scared, messy parts, too."

She nods slowly. "That's what I want."

I lean back into the couch, sipping my wine. "You know who actually sets the bar crazy high?"

"Who?"

"Brandon."

Stella quirks an eyebrow. "Brandon?"

I nod. "Yeah. Think about it." I gesture vaguely toward the kitchen like he might walk in at any second. "He always remembers our coffee orders, even the obnoxious ones with oat milk and extra foam and sugar-free vanilla."

Stella nods slowly. "That's true."

"And he texts the group chat exactly when we need it, whether it's a pep talk before a big meeting or some meme about emotionally unavailable men from *The Bachelor*."

"Also true."

"And when your car died in North Hollywood last month? He didn't even hesitate. Just showed up."

She's quiet, thinking. "That's just Brandon, though. He's everyone's go-to person. Like, platonic ride-or-die. I don't think he even knows how *not* to show up."

"Exactly," I say. "That's the point. He does all that because that's who he is, not because he wants anything from us. That kind of thoughtfulness and effort shouldn't feel rare. That's the bar. Bare minimum, honestly."

Stella nods again, more slowly this time, her eyes a little unfocused. "Yeah. That makes sense."

I watch her for a second, letting the silence stretch. "So, if

Mason isn't even *trying* to meet that bar, is he really worth your time?"

She opens her mouth and then hesitates. "I don't know. I mean, I hear you, and you're probably right. But I'd like the chance to find out. I haven't even had one real conversation with the guy. What if he is that type of person and I just don't know it yet?"

"I guess time will tell."

She looks at me and smiles. "Honestly, Lucas has set a pretty amazing bar being with you."

I pause. "With me?"

She nods like it's obvious. "Yeah. He's always looking out for you. Like, at your dinner party? He made your plate with all your favorite stuff and didn't even ask. He just *knew*. The Porto potato balls, the cheese you like, those weird little crackers."

I blink, caught off guard.

"And he always makes sure you get the exclusives before he tips anyone else off. He backed you up in the press release about Sophia when it could've caused a whole storm."

I don't say anything.

I've always seen the competition. The quick-witted banter. The sharp edges. The rivalry that feels like gasoline and sparks. But there were moments. Little ones.

The way he makes sure I have water on red carpets. The way he stepped in with Marcus that night in Vegas. The bracelet he gave me with the engraved charm of my show's name. Now, with Stella laying it out so plainly, it clicks.

He has been showing up for all of us—and for me, even when I wasn't looking.

I glance at the time on my phone and jolt a little. "Shit. I gotta go. Lucas is probably wondering if I fell into a hole."

Stella grins. "Tell him I said hi. And that I expect a full Sacramento debrief the second you're back."

I stand from the couch and grab the garment bag I left near the door. "Deal. And for the record?"

She raises an eyebrow.

"You are a catch, Stella. Don't settle and don't sell yourself short. You deserve the fairytale Hallmark story of your delusions!"

She laughs. "I won't hold my breath."

"Maybe you should!"

I head out with a laugh and a grin that stays with me all the way to my car, along with the growing realization that I am happy.

twenty-two

. . .

Lucas

THE DRIVE UP to Sacramento is quiet in the way that Jess and I have learned to make comfortable. Her shoes are off, and her feet are tucked beneath her as we listen to the playlist, which alternates between '90s grunge and today's Top 40. She's scrolling through emails, occasionally muttering something under her breath about click-through rates, and I keep stealing glances at her when I think she's not looking.

She catches me once.

"What?" she says, arching an eyebrow but not looking up from her phone.

"Nothing," I say. "You're just...being nice."

Her lips quirk like she's trying not to smile, but she doesn't look away. "You say that like it surprises you."

I don't answer. But maybe it does.

When we turn onto my parents' street, the air in the car changes. The weight of what's waiting tightens across my shoulders like muscle memory. The tidy colonial houses feel too symmetrical, too polished. Jess doesn't say anything, but I know she feels it, too. She leans forward slightly in her seat as we pull into the driveway, her eyes scanning the neighborhood.

"Nice place," she says in a casual but observant voice.

"My dad picked it because three former governors lived on this street."

Jess turns toward me, her brow raised. "Of course he did."

I kill the engine and rest my hands on the steering wheel, letting the silence stretch for another beat. "Just remember," I say finally, "I'm not like them. Not like him."

Jess's expression softens, and she reaches out to touch my arm. "I know."

The front door opens before we even make it to the porch, and my mother steps out, composed and radiant in her usual, understated way. She hugs me tightly, long enough that I feel something inside me loosen. Then she turns to Jess and offers the kind of warm, practiced smile that's managed fundraisers, foundations, and decades of high-stakes dinners.

"And you must be Jessica," she says, pulling Jess in with ease. "I'm Katherine, but please, call me Kate."

"And you can call me Jess," Jess replies, hugging her back. "It's so nice to meet you. Thank you for having us."

Once we're inside, Mom leads us upstairs, chattering warmly about how thrilled she is that we came up early.

"I told Lance and Lucy not to bombard you right away," she says as we reach the landing. "Figured you two might want a moment to settle in before the inquisition begins."

She opens the door to my old bedroom, now updated to

guest-room status. The baseball posters and dorm-style desk are gone, replaced by built-in bookshelves, a queen-sized bed with a navy duvet, and clean, neutral decor. But there's still a photo of my USC team on the nightstand and a few worn spines of books I never took with me.

Jess steps inside and gives the room a once-over. "This is nice," she says politely, her voice easy but curious.

"Let me know if you need anything," my mom says, giving Jess's hand a gentle squeeze before heading back down the hall. "We're starting dinner in about half an hour."

And just like that, we're alone.

Jess eyes the bed the second the door clicks shut. I follow her gaze. One bed. Queen-sized. No sofa. There is an armchair in the corner, but I'm not sure my spine could survive one night, let alone two.

"Ok," she says, then turns slowly to face me. "Well."

"I can sleep on the floor," I offer immediately, already glancing at the armchair and knowing full well it's a death sentence.

She doesn't even blink. "Don't be ridiculous. The bed's huge. We're adults."

My body disagrees. Loudly. But I nod. "Yeah. Ok."

Jess crosses the room and drops her bag on the chair with dramatic finality. "Besides," she adds, opening the zipper, "I snore, hog the covers, and talk in my sleep. I'm basically the nightmare version of a sleepover."

"Perfect," I say, dropping my own bag next to hers. "I grind my teeth, sleep shirtless, and have night terrors about bad press statements."

She snorts. "You sleep shirtless, huh?"

I glance up, just in time to see her trying not to look at my chest. "Just setting expectations."

She lifts her chin. "Great. Then I'll set one, too. If you steal the blankets, I'll go full ice queen. I have zero hesitation about weaponizing cold feet."

"Noted."

The smile she gives me is quick, sharp, and dangerous, and for a beat too long, we both stand there, pretending the bed is just furniture, pretending it doesn't matter that we'll be inches apart, all night, pretending that we don't feel the shift between us every time the other one moves.

Jess finally breaks the moment, brushing past me, toward the bathroom, with a tossed, "I'm going to powder my nose."

And just like that, we're moving again.

The tension lingers as we head downstairs, and I lace my fingers through hers. Lance is already there, pouring a glass of wine. At twenty-seven, my younger brother still has the unlined face and easy smile of someone whose path has been largely uncomplicated. He followed my father into politics without complaint and currently serves as a legislative aide while he builds connections for his inevitable run for office.

"There they are!" he exclaims, setting down the wine bottle to greet us. "The Vegas rebels."

"Lance," I warn, but there's no heat in it. Despite our different choices, we've always maintained a solid relationship. He's a true believer in my father's political vision, but he's never judged me for walking away from it.

"What? It's not every day a Carmichael elopes without consulting the family PR team first." With a grin, he offers

Jess a glass of wine. "How are you finding married life, Jess? Has my brother alphabetized all your clothes yet?"

"Only my shoes," she replies without missing a beat. "He's working his way up to my sweaters."

Lance laughs with genuine delight. "I like her already, Lucas."

My sister, Lucy, joins us, with her husband, Robert, trailing behind. At thirty-two, she's the most politically savvy of us all, having married a state assemblyman and masterfully managing both his career and planning for a picture-perfect family of four, eventually. Her smile is warm but assessing as she studies Jess.

"So, you're the journalist who managed to capture my commitment-phobic brother," she says, accepting a glass of wine from Lance. "I've followed your work. That exposé on gender pay disparities in production companies last year was excellent."

Jess looks genuinely surprised. "You read that?"

"Of course. Just because I'm surrounded by politics, it doesn't mean I don't care about substantive issues." Lucy's smile turns mischievous. "Besides, it drives my husband's more conservative donors crazy when I quote progressive journalists at fundraisers."

"Lucy's always been the secret rebel," I explain to Jess. "She just hides it better than I do."

"Someone has to work from the inside," Lucy responds with a shrug. "Not all of us can escape to Hollywood."

There's no accusation in her tone, just the acknowledgment of our different approaches to the Carmichael legacy.

Lucy is as trapped in my father's political machine as I once was, but she's found ways to maintain her own identity within it. It's a balancing act I've always admired, even if I couldn't sustain it myself.

My mother enters, carrying a steaming dish that fills the room with the rich scent of her cioppino, the San Francisco seafood stew she makes for special occasions. "Dinner's ready, everyone. Lucas, would you open another bottle of the cabernet?"

As we take our seats, I notice how naturally Jess falls into conversation with my family. She asks Lance about his work in the legislature, drawing him out beyond the usual talking points. With Lucy, she discusses the challenges of building a career while navigating family expectations. She even gets Robert, normally the quietest person at any Carmichael gathering, to enthusiastically explain a conservation bill he's helping to draft.

"So, Jess," Lucy says, dipping into her dish, "what's it like working with Lucas?"

"We don't exactly work together," I clarify. "More like our professional paths cross occasionally."

"And when they do, Lucas is honestly brilliant," Jess says, her voice warming with genuine admiration. "Just last month, there was this crisis with one of Wonderland's biggest stars, and his actions could have tanked an entire production."

I shift in my seat, not used to being the subject of Jess's praise.

"Everyone was panicking," she says, leaning forward slightly, "but Lucas just handled it. No drama, no public meltdown. He crafted this strategy that protected the studio without throwing the actor under the bus. I've seen PR disasters play out a hundred different ways, and trust me, what Lucas did was extraordinary."

"She's exaggerating," I say as warmth spreads across my face.

"I'm not," Jess insists, turning to face me directly. "You're the best at what you do, Lucas. Everyone in the industry knows it."

The way she's looking at me with such open admiration sends heat coursing through my body. I'm used to calculated compliments in this house, praise with political purpose. This is different.

After dinner, coffee is served in the living room, and the atmosphere softens even more. My mom nudges me gently as Jess laughs at something Lucy said.

"She's wonderful," my mom whispers. "Genuine. Not what I expected."

"What did you expect?"

"Well, your father mentioned that she was a journalist. I assumed this was strategic. But she's real."

Before I can answer, Jess appears beside me and slips her hand into mine like it's second nature. The rest of the evening passes in a blur of conversations and my constant awareness of her.

When we finally return to my room, the tension that's been building all night crackles between us. Jess slips off her heels with a sigh.

"God, these are torture devices," she groans, flexing her feet.

I unbutton my shirt, trying not to stare as she reaches up to remove her earrings. "You were amazing tonight."

"We were amazing," she corrects, meeting my gaze. "Award-winning performances out there."

"Yeah." I swallow, watching as she unpins her hair, letting it fall in waves around her shoulders.

At this moment, I want to stop pretending, even to myself, because whatever this is between us, it hasn't felt like a performance in days. I should be more cautious. I should keep my distance. But she's standing there in the dim light, in my space, and all I can think is how much I want to touch her, how every day with her chips away my ability to stay away from her.

"Except it wasn't all an act. Not for me."

I close the distance between us in two steps, drawn to her like gravity. My hands find her waist, anchoring me, and draw her closer with a certainty that surprises us both.

"Not even close," I murmur, brushing a strand of hair from her face. My fingers trail along her cheek, and as she leans into my touch, her eyes flutter closed for a heartbeat.

When they open again, there's a heat there that matches the fire burning through my veins. She rises on her tiptoes, bringing her face closer to mine. "For the cameras?" she asks, but there are no cameras here. No audience. No documentary crew.

"No," I tell her, my voice low, my hand curling at the small of her back. "Not for the cameras."

Her lips part slightly, and I watch as something shifts in her expression and the last wall between us crumbles.

"Then what are we doing?" she asks softly.

I don't hesitate. "I have no idea. But I don't want to stop."

"Neither do I," she whispers as her hand slides up to the back of my neck.

The pull between us is magnetic, inevitable. I capture her lips with mine, and everything else falls away.

twenty-three

. . .

Jess

HIS LIPS CRASH AGAINST MINE, demanding and insistent in a way that sends electricity racing through my entire body. This is Lucas unleashed, and he's commanding, intentional, and utterly hot.

Before I can process what's happening, he's backing me against the wall, with one hand tangling in my hair while the other grips my hip with possessive urgency. The controlled PR executive I've known all these months has vanished, replaced by something primal and hungry that makes my knees weak.

"I've wanted to do this for weeks," he growls against my mouth, nipping at my bottom lip in a way that draws a gasp from my throat.

"What took you so long?" I challenge, even as my pulse races wildly.

His answer is to press his body fully against mine, pinning me to the wall with delicious pressure. The hard planes of his chest against my softer curves send heat pooling between my thighs. This commanding side of Lucas is unexpected and embarrassingly arousing.

His hands are everywhere, sliding beneath the hem of my dress and skimming up my thighs with deliberate slowness that makes me squirm against him. When his fingers graze the edge of my underwear, I nearly whimper.

"Tell me what you want, Jess," he demands, his voice rough with desire as his lips trail down my neck.

The question momentarily startles me. I'm used to leading interviews, not answering questions. But there's something intoxicating about relinquishing control to him, just for tonight.

"You," I manage, my voice breathier than I've ever heard it. "All of you."

He smiles against my skin, and I can feel the curve of his lips as he sucks lightly at the junction of my neck and shoulder. "That wasn't specific enough, Mrs. Lexington-Carmichael."

The formal address, combined with his thumbs now circling just shy of where I need them most, sends a shudder through me.

"Not fair," I gasp.

"I never claimed to play fair," he murmurs, his hands sliding higher, pushing the fabric of my dress up as they move. When his thumbs brush the undersides of my breasts, I arch into his touch.

"Touch me," I demand, grabbing his wrist and guiding his hand to my breast. "Properly."

His eyes darken at my directness, and a flash of approval crosses his features before he complies, cupping my breast through the thin fabric of my bra. His thumb circles my nipple until it hardens beneath his touch, and I can't stop the moan that escapes me.

"God, the sounds you make," he groans, his control visibly fraying. "I've imagined this so many times, but nothing compares to the reality of you."

His confession sends a thrill through me that has nothing to do with physical pleasure. Lucas Carmichael, master of careful words and measured responses, admitting he's fantasized about me? It's a heady power all its own.

I tug at his shirt, suddenly desperate to feel his skin against mine. "Too many clothes."

He steps back just enough to pull his shirt over his head in one fluid motion, and I take the opportunity to remove my dress, letting it pool at my feet. His eyes track the movement, and there's an urgency in them as they take in the black lace of my bra and matching underwear.

"Christ, Jess," he breathes, the reverence in his voice making me feel more powerful than any byline ever has.

I reach for him, running my hands over the defined planes of his chest, feeling the rapid beat of his heart beneath my palm. "Not so bad yourself, Mr. Carmichael."

A flash of satisfaction crosses his face before he captures my mouth again, and his tongue slides against mine in a dance that mimics what I desperately want him to do elsewhere. His hands grip my thighs, lifting me slightly as he presses between my legs, the hard length of him evident through his pants.

I wrap my legs around his waist, using the leverage to

grind against him, relishing his sharp intake of breath. Two can play at this game.

"You taste incredible," he murmurs against my jaw before trailing kisses down my neck to my collarbone. "I wonder if you taste this good everywhere."

I tangle my fingers in his hair and tug slightly to bring his gaze up to mine. "Why don't you find out?" I arch an eyebrow in challenge.

The groan that escapes him is deeply satisfying. In one smooth motion, he drops my legs and sinks to his knees before me. He looks up with such raw desire that I nearly come undone on the spot.

"Is that an invitation, Mrs. Lexington-Carmichael?" he asks as his hands slide up my thighs with torturous slowness.

"It's a demand," I correct, my voice husky with want.

His smile is pure wickedness as his fingers hook into the waistband of my underwear and slowly drag the lace down my legs. I step out of them, expecting him to toss them aside. Instead, he deliberately folds them and tucks them into his pocket.

"Souvenir?" I ask, amused despite the heat building inside me.

He responds by putting his mouth on me, hot and insistent, and coherent thought becomes impossible. His tongue traces my center with devastating precision, finding the bundle of nerves that makes my knees buckle. Only his strong hands gripping my thighs keep me upright as pleasure courses through me.

I look down at him. Lucas Carmichael is on his knees before me, his eyes closed in concentration as he tastes me, and the sight is nearly as arousing as the sensation itself. My fingers tighten in his hair, guiding him where I need him most.

"There," I gasp as his tongue flicks against my clit. "Right there."

He hums in acknowledgment, and the vibration adds another layer to the pleasure building inside me. One of his hands leaves my thigh, and I feel his finger circling my entrance before slowly pushing inside and curling to hit a spot that makes stars explode behind my eyelids.

I'm making sounds I've never heard myself make—desperate, needy noises that would embarrass me if I weren't so utterly lost in sensation. My hips move of their own accord, seeking more of his mouth, his fingers, anything he'll give me.

"Lucas," I breathe, not even caring that it sounds like pleading. "I'm close."

He responds by adding a second finger alongside the first and sucking gently on my clit. The dual sensation pushes me right to the edge, and my entire body tenses as pleasure coils tighter and tighter at the base of my spine.

When I shatter, it's with his name on my lips. My body arches against the wall as waves of ecstasy crash over me. He works me through it, his touch gentling but not stopping until I'm trembling from oversensitivity.

Only then does he pull away, pressing a kiss to my inner thigh before looking up at me with an expression of such raw hunger that it steals my breath. I expect him to stand, to seek his own release, but instead, he rests his forehead against my hip, his breathing ragged.

"You have no idea how beautiful you are when you come," he says, his voice strained.

I reach down to pull him up, intent on returning the pleasure he's given me, but he shakes his head.

"Too late," he admits as a flush spreads across his cheekbones. "Just watching you, hearing you. I couldn't help myself."

The realization that he found his release simply from pleasuring me, without even being touched, sends a fresh wave of heat through my body. There's something profoundly intimate about it—and more vulnerable than anything I expected from the always-composed Lucas Carmichael.

"That's the hottest thing I've ever heard," I tell him honestly.

Laughing, he rises to his feet and scoops me up in one fluid motion. "Next time I'll show more restraint."

"Next time?" I arch an eyebrow as he carries me to the bed.

"Unless you have objections, Mrs. Lexington-Carmichael?" There's a hint of vulnerability beneath his confident tone.

I should have objections. This complicates our arrangement beyond measure. But with my body still humming from his touch and the promise of more nights like this, I can't bring myself to care about the consequences.

"None whatsoever, Mr. Carmichael," I murmur as he lays me gently on the bed.

He disappears briefly before returning with a warm washcloth to clean us both up. The tenderness of the gesture contrasts sharply with the intensity of moments before, revealing yet another layer to this man I thought I had figured out.

As he slides into bed beside me, pulling me against his chest, I realize how perfectly I fit against him, how his heartbeat seems to sync with mine.

"What are you thinking?" he asks, his fingers tracing lazy patterns on my shoulder.

"That you're full of surprises, " I say honestly.

He laughs softly and presses a kiss to the top of my head. "Get some sleep, Jess. We've got a long weekend ahead of us."

As sleep begins to claim me, I can't help but wonder if this is what it could be like all the time. Not just explosive passion, but genuine connection. Not just six months of pretending, but something that outlasts contracts and arrangements.

twenty-four

. . .

Lucas

I WAKE to the feeling of warm skin against mine, Jess's body curled into my side, and her blonde hair splayed across my chest. For a moment, I just breathe her in. The lingering trace of her perfume is something uniquely her that I'm already becoming addicted to.

Memories of last night flood back, sending heat through my veins. The way she responded to me. The sounds she made when I touched her just right. The surprising vulnerability in her eyes when she came apart.

I should be panicking. This wasn't part of our arrangement. This crossed every line we'd carefully drawn. But watching her sleep, her features softened and unguarded, I can't bring myself to regret it.

Jess stirs, and her eyes flutter open. For a heartbeat, confusion clouds her face before recognition dawns, and she smiles a sleepy, unfiltered smile that hits me square in the chest.

"Morning," she murmurs, her voice raspy with sleep.

"Morning," I reply as my fingers trace lazy patterns on her bare shoulder. "Sleep ok?"

"Mmm, fantastic." Her smile turns teasing as she stretches, causing the sheet to slip dangerously low.

I pull her closer and press a kiss to her forehead before I can second-guess the gesture. "We should probably get downstairs soon. My mother's making her famous breakfast casserole."

Jess groans, burying her face against my neck. "Do we have to? I'm not sure I can look your mom in the eye after what we did in your childhood bedroom."

"Come on. Let's shower." I start to pull the sheets off of her, and her eyes darken momentarily before she shakes her head.

"Not unless you want to explain to your family why we're both an hour late to breakfast."

"Fine. Rain check, then."

I watch as she gathers her clothes and disappears into the bathroom with one last glance over her shoulder.

Then I head into the hallway bath. There, under the spray of the shower, I try to make sense of what's happening between us. When did Jess Lexington, the journalist who's been the bane of my professional existence for years, become the woman I can't stop thinking about?

I grow hard at the memory of her body pressed against mine, and I wrap my hands around my cock, stroking it to the thought of touching her again tonight. Jesus, we haven't even slept together, and I'm already addicted to her. It doesn't take long before I find my release and know it's done little to curb my desire.

After the shower, I quickly dress and head downstairs, where I find my mother standing at the stove, peeking into the oven while Lance nurses a cup of coffee at the counter. Lucy and her husband are already seated at the table, deep in conversation about some political fundraiser they're organizing next month.

And there, at the head of the table, sits my father.

Logan Carmichael is still an imposing figure at sixty-four: silver-haired, broad-shouldered, with the practiced smile of a career politician and eyes that miss nothing. He's studying the morning paper, but his attention shifts immediately when I enter the room.

"The newlywed emerges," he announces, his voice carrying that familiar cadence perfected over decades of campaign speeches. "I was beginning to think you'd sleep through my return."

"Dad," I acknowledge, pouring myself a coffee. "Thought you weren't getting back until later."

"The meeting wrapped early." His eyes assess me with the calculating precision I've known all my life. "You look rested."

I can't help the smile that tugs at my lips. "I am."

My mother glances over her shoulder, her expression warming. "Lucas, sweetheart, there you are. Where's Jess?"

"Getting ready," I answer as I take a seat across from Lucy. "She'll be down soon."

"She made quite an impression last night," my mother says, pulling the casserole out of the oven. "She knew so much about all of us, even your brother and sister."

"That's Jess," I say, feeling an unexpected surge of pride. "She does her research."

"I suppose that's useful in her line of work," my father comments. His tone is neutral but loaded with unspoken judgment. "Entertainment journalism, is it?"

"She hosts one of the most respected industry podcasts in Los Angeles," I reply, keeping my voice even. "She's built it from nothing into a powerhouse."

My father's eyebrows lift slightly with an air of skepticism. "Hmm. A podcast. Isn't that what everyone's doing these days?"

Jess walks in, completely unbothered. "Maybe. But not everyone interviews Oscar winners, breaks exclusives, or gets invited to speak on industry panels. I do."

She says it calmly, almost casually, like she's listing the ingredients of a salad, not rattling off receipts that could silence a room.

Standing there in fitted jeans and a simple white blouse that somehow makes her eyes look even bluer, her hair is pulled back in a loose ponytail, she looks fresh and confident —and so goddamn beautiful that my heart actually skips.

My father rises, a professional smile firmly in place as he crosses to her. "Ms. Lexington, a pleasure to finally meet you. I'm Senator Logan Carmichael."

"Senator." She takes his outstretched hand firmly. "I believe we actually met briefly at a press conference in Sacramento three years ago. You dodged my question about campaign finance reform."

A beat of silence falls over the kitchen before my father laughs. Its genuineness catches me off guard. "I don't recall the incident, but it sounds entirely possible. Please, join us for breakfast."

Jess slides into the chair beside me, and her hand finds mine under the table and squeezes briefly. The simple gesture steadies me in a way I wasn't expecting.

"I look forward to seeing you both at the gala this evening. It's our biggest fundraiser of the year for the foundation," my father continues as he returns to his seat.

"I've been reading up on your education initiatives," Jess says, accepting a plate from my mother with a warm smile. "It's impressive how many people you are able to support each year."

My mother beams. "That's my pet project. Logan handles the political end, but the foundation is my baby."

"It shows," Jess responds. "The retention rates for your scholarship recipients are well above the national average. You must have excellent mentorship components."

The conversation flows surprisingly easily after that, with Jess holding her own as the topic shifts between politics, the foundation's work, and upcoming family events. I find myself watching her—the animated way she talks with her hands when she's passionate about something, how she leans in slightly when listening to my mother describe a recent scholarship recipient's success story.

She fits here, I realize with a start, not in a political-wife, stand-behind-your-man way, but as herself—sharp, engaged, compassionate.

She's the kind of woman I would actually choose to marry.

The thought hits me like a physical blow, and I nearly choke on my coffee.

"You ok there, little brother?" Lucy asks, eyeing me with amusement.

"Fine," I manage. "Just went down the wrong way."

My father checks his watch. "I need to make some calls before the event begins. Lucas, walk with me to the office? There are some gala details we should discuss."

It's not a request. I squeeze Jess's knee under the table and follow my father down the hall to his home office. It's a wood-paneled shrine to his political career, with photos of him alongside presidents and world leaders lining the walls.

He closes the door behind us. "So. Your wife."

I brace myself. "Yes?"

"Not what I expected," he says, settling behind his desk. "Intelligent. Well spoken. Not easily intimidated."

"No, she isn't," I agree, with a hint of pride creeping into my voice.

"And clearly not the type to simply fall in line with the Carmichael agenda." He studies me, his fingers steepled beneath his chin. "This isn't some temporary rebellion against my plans for you, is it, Lucas?"

"Not everything is about you, Dad," I reply as the familiar irritation rises. "I married Jess because I wanted to, not to spite you."

"And the timing? Just when discussions with the Bishops were progressing?"

I clench my jaw. "Purely coincidental."

He watches me for a long moment, his expression

unreadable. "Well, she'll certainly liven up our family gatherings. Your mother is quite taken with her already."

"I noticed," I say carefully.

"We'll need to discuss how to handle the press, of course. A hastily arranged Vegas wedding doesn't exactly align with our family's image, but we can spin it as young love, the romance of spontaneity."

"We're not 'spinning' my marriage," I say firmly. "It's not a campaign strategy."

My father raises an eyebrow. "Everything is strategy, Lucas. You of all people should understand that." He rises, signaling the end of our conversation. "The gala begins at seven. Make sure Jessica understands the importance of tonight. Half the state's political establishment will be there."

"Jess," I correct him. "She prefers Jess."

"Of course," he says dismissively. "Jess."

twenty-five

. . .

Jess

THE GRAND BALLROOM is already filling with guests when I arrive at the top of the staircase, taking a moment to observe the scene below, where Sacramento's political elite mingle beneath crystal chandeliers. There are governors, judges, tech moguls, and old-money families whose combined influence shapes the state. I've covered events like this before, but I've never attended as someone's wife.

I smooth down my emerald gown, feeling unexpectedly nervous. Last night changed something between Lucas and me. We crossed a line we'd been dancing around for weeks. His touch was commanding, deliberate, focused entirely on my pleasure in a way that still makes my skin flush thinking about it—the touch of someone who knew exactly what he wanted and took it. In his bed afterward, with his arms around me and his heartbeat steady against my back, I'd felt safe. Adored. Content.

I spot Lucas at the bottom of the stairs, standing tall in his perfectly fitted tuxedo, and my breath catches. He's scanning the room, checking his watch with that slight furrow between his brows that appears when he's concerned. Then he looks up, and our eyes meet.

His expression transforms instantly to surprise, then to appreciation, and then to something darker that reminds me of how he looked last night on his knees before me. His gaze travels slowly up my body in a way that's entirely inappropriate for a political fundraiser and entirely thrilling. He moves toward the staircase without hesitation, as if drawn by an invisible thread, and I descend to meet him.

"You're staring," I whisper when I reach him, unable to keep the pleased smile from my lips.

"Everyone's staring," he replies, offering his arm. "You're breathtaking."

Heat rises to my cheeks. It's not the practiced, professional response I've perfected for compliments, but something genuine that catches me off guard. "Not so bad yourself. I've always had a weakness for men in well-tailored tuxedos."

"I'll make a note of that." His hand covers mine where it rests on his arm, and the simple contact sends warmth up my skin. "Ready to charm the political elite of California?"

"Of course I am," I say, straightening my spine with determination. If there's one thing I know how to do, it's work a room. "Just point me toward the most intimidating person here, and I'll start there."

"That would be California Supreme Court Justice Elena

Martinez. Conservative bench, liberal personal politics, suffers no fools." He nods toward a formidable woman holding court near the bar. "She terrifies most of the men in this room."

"Perfect," I say with a grin. "My kind of woman."

I spend the next hour in my element, moving through conversations with practiced ease. I discuss constitutional protections with a legal scholar, push back thoughtfully when a tech CEO dismisses traditional media, and find common ground with Justice Martinez over our shared frustration with institutional barriers for women. It's the same skillset I use for interviews: listening more than speaking, asking the right questions, and finding the story beneath the surface.

But throughout it all, I'm acutely aware of Lucas and how he watches me from across the room. The weight of his gaze is a physical sensation. When our eyes meet over the rim of my champagne glass, heat pools low in my belly at the promise I see there. This is a side of him I never expected: possessive.

I excuse myself to visit the ladies' room, needing a moment to collect myself. In the elegant powder room, I'm reapplying lipstick when the door opens and Lucas slips inside. He locks it behind him.

"This is the ladies' room," I point out, though my heartbeat accelerates.

"I'm aware." He moves toward me with intent, backing me against the marble counter. "You've been driving me crazy all night."

"That sounds like a personal problem," I manage, though my voice catches as his hands find my hips.

"It's about to become a mutual problem." His lips hover just above mine. "That dress should be illegal."

"Then perhaps you should arrest me." The words come out breathier than intended.

His mouth captures mine in a kiss that's nothing like the restrained displays we've shown in public. This is hungry, demanding, stealing my breath and my composure in equal measure. My hands clutch at his lapels, pulling him closer despite the voice in my head warning about wrinkled tuxedos and smudged lipstick.

When we break apart, both breathing heavily, I'm gratified to see he looks as affected as I feel.

"We should get back," I say, but I make no move to leave the circle of his arms.

"We should," he agrees, pressing a kiss to the sensitive spot just below my ear. "But later..." His kiss continues down my neck.

The promise in those two words sends anticipation spiraling through me. "Later," I echo, gently pushing him back to straighten my dress and fix my lipstick.

He watches me with dark eyes. "You missed a spot," he says as his thumb brushes the corner of my mouth. The casual intimacy of the gesture feels more significant than the passionate kiss we just shared.

We return to the ballroom separately, the perfect picture of propriety, though I know my cheeks are flushed and my pulse is racing. When we reconnect, his hand finds the small of my back again, which is somehow both comforting and electrifying.

I'm discussing entertainment industry tax incentives with

Governor Williams when Logan Carmichael joins us, his smile practiced and his eyes calculating.

"Lucas," he says, acknowledging his son. "Jessica, I overheard your fascinating perspective on the state's approach to entertainment industry tax incentives."

"Jess," I correct him again with a smile that doesn't quite reach my eyes. He's done this deliberately all weekend, a subtle power play that's almost admirable in its pettiness.

"Of course." He nods and then turns to address the governor. "Jess is quite knowledgeable for someone in celebrity journalism."

The dismissal is so expertly delivered that I almost want to applaud. Instead, I keep my voice level and my smile fixed. "Actually, Senator, my work focuses on the business and ethics of entertainment and the economics of content creation, labor practices, and how media shapes public discourse." I sip my champagne. "The celebrities are just a bonus that helps pay the bills."

The governor laughs appreciatively. "She's got you there, Logan."

I catch the momentary tightening of Logan's smile. It's the same tell Lucas has when he's been outmaneuvered. Like father, like son in some ways, though Lucas would hate the comparison.

"Indeed. You've found yourself quite the match, Lucas," Logan says, his tone making it unclear whether this is praise or accusation.

"I have," Lucas agrees as his arm possessively slides around my waist.

The orchestra begins a waltz, and Lucas seizes the opportunity. "If you'll excuse us, Governor, Dad, I believe they're playing our song."

"We have a song?" I whisper as he guides me to the dance floor.

"We do now," he murmurs back, pulling me into his arms.

I follow his lead easily, and as our bodies sync with the rhythm, I'm struck by how naturally we move together. The memory of his touch from last night flashes through my mind, and I fight back a blush.

"Your father doesn't approve of me," I say, meeting his eyes directly.

"My father doesn't approve of anyone who isn't useful to his ambitions," he replies. "But don't let him fool you. He's impressed. He just hates that he can't control the narrative."

"Sounds familiar," I say with a knowing smile.

"What does that mean?"

"Just that the apple didn't fall as far from the tree as you might think." I soften my expression, tracing small circles on the back of his neck with my fingers. "You're both control freaks who hate it when things don't go according to plan."

"I am nothing like my father," he protests, though without heat.

"Not in the ways that matter," I agree, "but in some of the surface stuff? The need to manage perceptions, the strategic thinking, the inability to admit when you're wrong? Pure Logan Carmichael."

I say it lightly, affectionately. It's odd how quickly I've come to understand Lucas's mannerisms, his tells, the subtle ways he operates. Maybe it's the journalist in me, trained to observe and analyze, or maybe it's because of how close we've become.

"If I'm so like him, why do you put up with me?" he asks, his curiosity evident in his voice.

I pretend to consider this, enjoying the slight uncertainty in his expression. "You're much better looking," I decide. "And you have this annoying habit of actually caring about people, not just using them."

"High praise indeed."

"Don't let it go to your head," I warn, unable to keep from smiling.

We dance in comfortable silence, turning slowly beneath the twinkling lights on the dance floor. I'm hyperaware of his hand at the small of my back, his fingers laced with mine, the subtle scent of his cologne. After last night and feeling his mouth on me, his hands exploring my body with such focused attention, every touch between us carries new weight, new memory, and I want more.

"Everyone's watching us," I murmur, noticing the glances directed our way.

"Let them," he replies with surprising intensity. "They're just jealous."

"Of what?"

He pulls back just enough to look into my eyes. "That I get to dance with the most beautiful, brilliant woman in the room."

I roll my eyes, but pleasure warms my chest. "Smooth, Carmichael. Very smooth."

"I've been told I have my moments."

As we continue to dance, his arms steady around me, and I find myself counting the minutes until this event ends, until we can return to our room and this dress can join last night's clothes on the floor. Below that anticipation runs something deeper, something more frightening: the growing certainty that six months with Lucas Carmichael will never be enough.

twenty-six

. . .

Lucas

THE DOOR to my childhood bedroom barely closes before my hands are on her, unable to maintain the restraint I've been clinging to all evening. Watching Jess command the room in that emerald dress for hours, feeling her occasional knowing glances across crowded conversations, has been exquisite torture.

"Finally," I murmur against her neck, inhaling the intoxicating blend of her perfume. "Do you have any idea what you've been doing to me all night?"

She laughs, and the sound vibrates against my lips as her hands work at my bow tie. "I have some idea. Your poker face isn't quite as good as you think."

"Only with you," I admit, finding the zipper of her dress with practiced ease. As I slide it down, revealing the expanse of her back, I recall how my fingers traced this same path on the dance floor, how she shivered then just as she does now.

"Cold?" I ask, echoing our earlier exchange.

Her smile is knowing as she turns in my arms, letting the

dress fall to the floor in a pool of emerald fabric. "Not even close."

The sight of her nearly undoes me—no bra, just the tantalizing curve of her breasts and a thin scrap of lace between her thighs. She's all smooth skin and quiet confidence, standing there like she was made to destroy my self-control. My body responds instantly, straining against my pants as I take in every perfect inch of her. Unlike last night's hesitation, tonight, there's certainty between us, a decision already made, anticipation replacing uncertainty.

"You're staring again," she observes, her fingers resuming their work on my shirt buttons as I reach up to cup one of her bare breasts in my hand and run my thumb over her hardening nipple.

"Can you blame me?" Her hands push the shirt from my shoulders, and I savor the feeling of her hands exploring my chest.

Her smile turns wicked. "It was a strategic decision." Her fingers trace along my ribs. "Every detail."

I walk her backward toward the bed, my hands never leaving her skin. When her legs hit the mattress, I lower her gently, following her down until we're a tangle of limbs and shared breath. The playfulness between us shifts, deepening into something more intense as I look into her eyes.

"I've been thinking about this all night," I confess, my voice rougher than intended. "About you."

"Me, too," she admits, a rare moment of complete honesty without deflection or wit. Her fingers thread through my hair, pulling me down for a kiss that's both tender and demanding.

I take my time exploring her body, relearning the landscape I discovered last night, but with a new purpose. When my mouth travels lower, she arches with anticipation, already knowing where I'm headed.

I press a kiss to her inner thigh and then pause to admire the view. "I believe we have unfinished business from last night."

"If you're expecting another glowing performance review, you'll have to earn it," she challenges, though her voice trembles slightly.

"I never settle for adequate," I remind her, holding her gaze as my mouth finds her center.

Her response is immediate and gratifying: a gasp, her head falls back, and fingers tighten in my hair. I work with deliberate patience, using the knowledge gained last night to drive her higher. This isn't about proving a point anymore; it's about watching her come undone, about the trust implicit in her surrender.

When she's close, trembling on the edge, I slide one finger inside her, then another, curving them just so. The effect is electric, and her back arches sharply as a stream of breathless profanity mingles with my name.

"Lucas," she gasps, her voice breaking. "Please—"

I intensify my efforts, determined to give her what she's asking for without making her beg. When she shatters, it's with an intensity that sends a wave of satisfaction through me that has nothing to do with ego and everything to do with connection.

Before she's fully recovered, I move up her body, capturing her mouth in a kiss that tastes of her. She responds hungrily, her hands roaming down my back to push impatiently at my remaining clothes.

"Off," she commands, and I comply, shedding the last barriers between us.

When I return to her, she surprises me by flipping our positions, straddling my hips with newfound purpose. In the moonlight filtering through the curtains, she looks otherworldly, all sleek lines and with a determined expression, her hair falling in waves around her shoulders.

"My turn," she declares as her hands splay across my chest.

"By all means." I settle my hands on her hips, content to let her take control. "I'm at your mercy."

"Dangerous admission, Carmichael." Her smile is wicked as she leans down to press a trail of kisses across my chest, moving steadily lower. "I'm not known for my mercy."

My breath catches as her mouth follows the path her hands have blazed, exploring with the same thoroughness that she brings to her reporting. Her tongue traces patterns across my skin, pausing to lavish attention on particularly sensitive spots she discovers, cataloging each sharp intake of breath, every involuntary muscle flex under her touch.

When her lips move lower still, past my navel, my hands fist in her hair. She takes me in her hand first, stroking slowly while her eyes never leave mine, watching my reaction with the same intense focus she uses during interviews. Then her mouth follows, warm, wet, and impossibly skilled, and all coherent thought dissolves.

I've been with women before, but never like this, never with someone who seems to understand my body's responses as intuitively as her own. The way she alternates pressure, the small sounds of satisfaction she makes that vibrate against me, the methodical way she pushes me toward the edge, only to ease back before I can fall over it—it's maddening and perfect, and I'm rapidly losing the ability to form words.

My breathing becomes ragged, my body taut as a wire, and just when I'm certain I can't take anymore, I catch her wrist and pull her up to me with a growl of pure need.

"Jess," I rasp, my hands tangling in her hair as I bring her face to mine. "I have plans for that mouth of yours. So many plans. But right now, I need to be inside you."

Her eyes darken at my words, and she shifts upward, settling over my hips with deliberate slowness. "Before we go further—protection?"

The question cuts through the haze of desire, grounding us both in reality. Even in this moment of passion, Jess remains practical, thoughtful.

"Nightstand drawer," I reply. "Unless..."

"I'm on the pill," she says, "and I was tested about two months ago. All clear."

"Same here. Six weeks ago, all negative." I reach to brush a strand of hair from her face. "But I have condoms if you'd prefer. Whatever makes you comfortable."

She considers this for a moment, her eyes searching mine with an intensity that makes my heart stutter.

"I've never done this before," she admits softly. "Without protection, I mean."

The admission catches me off guard. "Neither have I," I confess, realizing as I say it how true it is. "Not once."

Something shifts between us. It's an acknowledgment

that this is uncharted territory for both of us, not just physically but emotionally. The vulnerability in her eyes mirrors what I'm feeling, and there's a connection beyond the physical that terrifies and exhilarates me in equal measure.

"I trust you," she says finally, and the simple statement carries more weight, perhaps, than she intends. "But only if you're comfortable, too."

"I am," I assure her, touched by her consideration. "Very."

A smile tugs at her lips as she positions herself above me. "Together," she says softly, and the single word carries more meaning than any elaborate declaration.

I nod, unable to speak as she sinks down and takes me inside her with agonizing slowness. She's impossibly tight, wrapping me in a warm heat, and the way she fits around me feels like coming home and losing my mind all at once. The sensation is overwhelming, and every one of my nerve endings is alive and singing as she takes me deeper, inch by torturous inch.

When she's fully seated, I can feel her trembling slightly, her body adjusting to accommodate me. For a moment, we remain still, our foreheads pressed together, breathing each other's air, both of us stunned by the intensity of the connection. She feels like silk and fire wrapped around me, like everything I never knew I needed until this very moment.

She sits up and begins to move, finding a rhythm that starts deliberate and measured, I'm captivated by every detail. The way her muscles tense and relax beneath her skin. How her breath catches when I hit a particularly sensitive spot inside her. The soft sounds she makes, half-sigh, half-moan, when my hands slide up to cup her breasts, my thumbs circling her nipples until they harden further under my touch.

She is breathtaking above me, illuminated by the soft glow of the bedside lamp. The light plays across her skin, highlighting her curves, the elegant line of her neck, the flush that spreads across her cheekbones and down to her chest. Her blonde hair falls in tousled waves around her shoulders, and I reach up to thread my fingers through it, anchoring her to me.

"You're beautiful," I breathe, but the words are inadequate for what I'm feeling.

Her eyes meet mine, startlingly clear despite the haze of desire between us. The connection is almost too intense to bear while I'm buried deep inside her. Without breaking eye contact, she reaches down and takes my hand from her hip. For a moment, I think she's going to guide me between her legs, but instead, she presses my palm firmly against her chest, right over her heart.

I can feel the wild flutter of her pulse beneath my palm, matching the frantic rhythm of my own. She doesn't say anything; she doesn't need to. The gesture speaks volumes, catching me off guard with how raw and unguarded it feels.

The sensation of her heartbeat against my hand, her warmth surrounding me, and the sight of her lost in pleasure is almost overwhelming. Something shifts inside me, a fundamental change I can't quite name but can feel transforming me with each shared breath.

She leans down, and her breasts brush against my chest as she captures my mouth in a surprisingly tender kiss, given the intensity of our bodies' connection. The change in angle makes us both gasp. I wrap my arms around her, with one hand splayed across her back and the other tangled in her hair, holding her close as she rolls her hips in a maddening rhythm.

"God, Jess," I groan against her mouth, unable to form more coherent thoughts as she clenches around me. The friction is exquisite, almost unbearable. I'm fighting for control, desperate to make this last, even as every muscle in my body tenses toward release.

"You feel..." I start, but words fail me.

The intensity builds between us, a feedback loop of pleasure and connection. When I feel her tighten around me, I slip a hand between us, circling precisely where I know she needs it most. Her reaction is immediate as she releases a sharp gasp, and her movements become erratic.

"Lucas," she breathes, her voice breaking on my name. "I can't—"

"Let go," I urge, feeling my own control slipping. "I've got you."

She shatters with a cry that I capture with my mouth, following her over the edge a heartbeat later. The pleasure is blinding, overwhelming in its intensity—not just physical release but something deeper, more significant.

As we collapse together, breathing hard and our hearts racing in tandem, I hold her close, pressing kisses to her temple, her cheek, anywhere I can reach. The tenderness I feel should frighten me, but in this moment, with her warm weight against me, it seems natural, inevitable.

When our breathing steadies, she shifts to lie beside me,

her head pillowed on my shoulder, her leg draped over mine. The comfortable silence stretches between us, but I can sense her mind working, processing, analyzing what just happened.

"I can hear you thinking," I murmur, tracing patterns on her bare shoulder.

She laughs softly. "Occupational hazard."

"Want to share with the class?"

Propping herself up on one elbow, she studies my face in the dim light. "What are we doing, Lucas?"

It's the question that's been hovering between us since last night, since Vegas, maybe since that first meeting eight years ago in a baseball dugout.

"Right now? Enjoying each other," I say carefully, feeling my way through unfamiliar emotional territory. "Beyond that, I don't know."

She nods slowly. "This weekend feels like a bubble. Away from reality, from cameras and contracts and complications."

"Maybe it can be," I suggest, the words forming before I've fully considered them. "A bubble. A pause from everything else."

"What do you mean?"

I choose my words carefully, aware of the dangerous ground we're treading. "Maybe what happens here stays here. No expectations, no complications when we go back to L.A."

Part of me hopes she'll argue, that she'll insist that this is more than a weekend fling, but the rational part knows this is safer for both of us. Our arrangement has clear parameters, a definite end date. Allowing feelings to complicate things can only lead to pain when those six months are up.

"A weekend pass," she says thoughtfully, testing the idea.

"Exactly." I try to ignore the hollow feeling in my chest at her easy acceptance. "We get this out of our systems, then go back to reality, or at least the reality we've created."

She studies me for a long moment, and I wonder if she sees through the lie I'm telling us both. But then she nods, her fingers tracing abstract patterns on my chest.

"Ok," she agrees. "A weekend bubble."

I pull her closer, sealing our agreement with a kiss that feels too meaningful for what we've just decided. As she nestles against me, warm and trusting, I realize with stark clarity that I'm fooling myself. This isn't getting her out of my system. It's letting her sink deeper into my veins.

But for now, the fiction of the bubble protects us both. Tomorrow will come soon enough, with its reality and complications. Tonight, I'll hold her and pretend that this is all we need, all we want, knowing already that when our time is up, I won't be ready to let her go.

twenty-seven

. . .

Jess

THE CALIFORNIA COASTLINE blurs past the window as Lucas drives us back to Los Angeles. It's been a quiet drive so far—not awkward silence, exactly, but heavy with everything unsaid between us.

I steal glances at his profile. His jaw is set, his eyes are focused on the road, and one hand rests casually on the steering wheel. This weekend changed things. There's no going back from this, and now we're returning to our fabricated reality with no roadmap for what comes next.

Los Angeles materializes around us, a familiar sprawl of perpetual sunshine and the rhythm of a city that never fully sleeps. By the time we pull into the parking garage beneath Lucas's building, the tension between us is thick enough to touch.

In the elevator, we stand on opposite sides, our overnight bags between us like some kind of barrier—five floors of charged silence that crackles with possibility and uncertainty.

Inside the apartment, Lucas drops his keys in the bowl I

purchased for him. Setting my overnight bag by the door, I take in the familiar space. It somehow feels different now, less like Lucas's apartment and more like somewhere I belong.

"Hungry?" he asks as he shrugs off his jacket. "I could make us something."

"Sure," I reply, watching him move toward the kitchen, my eyes lingering on the broad lines of his shoulders. "I need a shower first. That drive back was longer than I remembered."

He nods, opening the refrigerator. "Take your time. I'll start dinner."

As I head toward the bathroom, my mind races with possibilities. What I really want to do is turn around, grab his hand, and lead him straight into that shower with me. My body craves his touch like it's become essential, and the thought of his hands on me again sends waves of anticipation through my core.

But I hesitate. We agreed that this was all part of the seclusion of the weekend, but my uncertainty about wanting to go back to our boundaries, our agreement, ties my tongue and leaves me second-guessing everything. Since when has Jess Lexington been afraid to ask for what she wants?

Since Lucas Carmichael made her care about the answer, a treacherous voice in my head replies.

I turn on the shower and, as steam fills the room, undress, mentally kicking myself for my cowardice. I step under the hot spray, letting water cascade over travel-weary muscles, trying to wash away my frustration with myself. The heat relaxes my body even as my mind continues its debate. I'm so lost in thought that I don't hear the door open.

"Room for one more?"

I turn to find Lucas standing there, already shirtless, his eyes traveling over me with undisguised appreciation. Relief and excitement surge through me so powerfully that I almost laugh. Of course he would know exactly what I want without me having to say it.

"I don't know," I say, pretending to consider it while my pulse races with joy. "Water conservation is important, but I was enjoying having the bathroom all to myself."

He laughs, stepping out of his remaining clothes with an efficiency that makes me wonder if he planned this all along. When he joins me under the spray, the shower suddenly feels much smaller, with his broad shoulders taking up space in the best possible way.

"Hi," he says softly, pushing wet hair from my face. The gentle gesture stands in stark contrast to the hunger in his eyes.

"Hi yourself." As water cascades between us, I step closer to him. My nerve endings vibrate with anticipation. "What happened to dinner?"

"It can wait." His hands find my waist, and they feel warm against my wet skin. "This can't."

The kiss is slow at first, exploratory, but it quickly deepens into something urgent. His hands slide lower, lifting me with surprising ease until my back meets the cool tile wall, and my legs wrap around his waist instinctively. I can feel him, already hard and pressing against my center. The contrast of temperatures heightens every sensation: the cool tile against my back and his hot skin against my front.

"Ambitious," I murmur against his mouth as water runs between us.

"Impatient," he corrects, his voice rough with want. "I've been thinking about this since we left Sacramento."

My laugh turns into a gasp as he presses closer, his hard length making his intentions clear. "In the shower? That's risky, Carmichael." But it's obvious that I'm just as eager when my hips flex back into him, chasing the friction I know will feel so good.

"I'm a careful man." His mouth trails down my neck, finding the sensitive spot just below my ear that makes me shudder with pleasure. I never told him about that spot. He discovered it all on his own, cataloging my reactions with the same attention to detail that he brings to everything. "Usually."

"And now?" I challenge, wrapping my arms around his shoulders for balance, loving the feel of muscles shifting beneath my fingertips.

His eyes meet mine, dark with desire. "Now I'm tired of being careful with you."

What follows is nothing like our previous encounters. There's no teasing banter, no battle for control. This is pure need, raw and unfiltered. He pushes inside with an urgency that pulls a gasp of pleasure from me, and his hands grip my hips with bruising intensity that I know I'll feel tomorrow. The thought of carrying his marks on my skin sends an unexpected thrill through me.

Water beats down on us, slicking our skin and heightening every sensation. His mouth covers my breast, and his tongue swirls around my nipple until he brings his lips down in a tight pinch, sucking and licking in a way that sends electric currents straight to my core.

My hands move restlessly in his hair, then around his neck, then gripping his arms, seeking an anchor in the storm of sensation. I tug gently at his hair, remembering how that made him groan the first night we were together. It works again, and the sound vibrates through his chest against mine. The knowledge that I can affect him this way is its own kind of intoxication.

The rhythm he sets is relentless, with each thrust driving me higher. I'm not typically vocal during sex, always too in my head, too concerned with performance, but with Lucas, sounds escape unbidden, moans, gasps, his name like a prayer. It's as though he's stripped away all my careful control, leaving me raw and honest in a way that should terrify me but somehow doesn't.

"Lucas," I breathe against his ear, feeling the tension building inside me. "I'm close."

"I know," he murmurs, and of course he does. He's learning my body with the same thorough attention he brings to everything that matters to him. The realization that I'm in that category sends me spiraling over the edge, and pleasure crashes through me in waves that leave me clinging to him, trembling and breathless.

He follows moments later, his face buried in my neck, his breath hot against my skin as he pulses inside me. The intimacy of it and of him letting go so completely in my arms makes my chest ache with emotions.

For long moments afterward, we stay locked together, and as the shower washes away evidence of our passion, our breathing gradually slows. I feel strangely vulnerable, not physically but emotionally. Sex has always been straightforward for me, enjoyable but uncomplicated. This feels like more.

Finally, he lowers me gently to my feet, and his hands steady me when my legs threaten to give out. His touch is tender now, almost reverent as he brushes wet hair from my face.

Concern replaces desire in his eyes. "You ok?"

"Better than ok," I assure him, reaching for the shampoo, "though I'm not sure that counted as water conservation."

Laughing, he takes the bottle from my hands. "Turn around. Let me."

The intimacy of having him wash my hair is somehow more overwhelming than what we just shared. His fingers work through the strands with gentle thoroughness, massaging my scalp until I'm practically purring with contentment.

"You're good at that," I murmur, my eyes closed in bliss.

"I'm good at lots of things," he replies, and I can hear the smile in his voice. "Some of which I haven't shown you yet."

I turn to face him and wrap my arms around his neck. "Is that a promise?"

"Absolutely." He kisses me again, slower this time, with a tenderness that makes my chest ache. "But first, I should get that dinner started."

Twenty minutes later, we're both clean and satisfied, and I'm wrapped in his robe, which swallows me whole. I pad into the kitchen to find Lucas preparing a sheet pan of salmon and veggies. He's thrown on sweatpants, leaving his chest bare in a distractingly appealing way. Watching him move around his kitchen with casual confidence does something strange to my insides.

This domestic version of Lucas, barefoot, his hair still damp, focused intently on chopping potatoes, is a far cry from the polished PR executive the world sees. It feels like a privilege to witness this unguarded side of him.

We eat at the island, trading plans for the week ahead. It's easy, comfortable, as if we've been doing this for years instead of days. After dinner, he insists on cleaning up alone, and I wander into his living room, examining the bookshelves that reveal more about him than he probably realizes. Disney history, baseball memoirs, classic literature, and a surprising number of mystery novels.

I'm so absorbed in my exploration that I don't hear him approach until his arms slide around my waist from behind.

"Find anything interesting?" he murmurs, his chin resting on my shoulder.

"Just confirming my suspicion that you're secretly a nerd," I reply, leaning back against him. "All these books, organized by genre and author. Very telling."

Before I can say anything else, he turns me to face him and captures my mouth with his. I respond in kind, letting my hands explore the contours of his chest, the strong lines of his shoulders. When he guides me to his bedroom, I go willingly, and the robe falls open as he lays me back against his sheets.

What follows is a thorough, methodical dismantling of my composure. After getting lost in one another once again, we lie tangled together, pleasantly exhausted.

The clock on his bedside table blinks past midnight, officially ending our weekend bubble. Neither of us mentions it.

"I should probably go," I murmur against his chest, making no move to leave.

"Or you could stay."

I wait for my brain to argue, but I don't want to leave.

"Ok."

His arms wrap around me, solid and secure, and I feel myself drifting toward sleep. The last thing I register is the gentle press of his lips against my forehead. As consciousness fades, I can't help but think that reality might not be so bad if it includes moments like this.

twenty-eight

. . .

Lucas

THE FIRST RAYS of morning sunlight filter through the blinds, casting golden streaks across Jess's bare shoulder. She's curled against me, breathing soft and even, her blonde hair spilling across my chest. I check the time: 5:45 a.m. Fifteen minutes before the alarm.

I've memorized her morning rhythm by now. The way she burrows deeper into the pillow when the first alarm goes off. How she stretches, cat-like and languid, before padding to the shower. Her adorable grumpiness until her first sip of coffee.

It's been three weeks since Sacramento, and Jess hasn't spent a single night in the guest room. We never actually discussed it; we've just ignored any conversation of living outside of the Sacramento bubble.

I brush a strand of hair from her face, allowing myself this quiet moment of observation. This woman has invaded every corner of my carefully organized life, and I've never been happier.

The alarm chirps, and Jess groans, tucking her face against my neck.

"Make it stop," she mumbles, her voice thick with sleep.

I reach over to silence it before pressing a kiss to her forehead. "Morning, sunshine."

"Nothing sunny about mornings," she grumbles, but then she tilts her face up for a proper kiss. "You're always disgustingly alert."

"Years of early baseball practice."

She makes a face and sits up, letting the sheet pool at her waist. "Shower?"

"You go ahead. I'll start the coffee."

She raises an eyebrow. "That wasn't an invitation to shower alone, Carmichael."

Fifteen minutes later, we're both breathless and clean, with memories of shower tile against my back and Jess's legs wrapped around my waist. Our morning routine is efficient despite the detour: first coffee, then breakfast, and then a quick discussion of the day ahead.

"Dylan's coming by tonight for more confessional footage," Jess reminds me, stealing a bite of my toast. "Seven o'clock."

"Maybe we should actually have something to confess this time," I suggest, watching her over the rim of my coffee mug.

She gives me that look, half amused, half exasperated. "Like how we've been breaking our own rules for three weeks?"

"Like how you snore when you're really tired."

She throws a grape at me, which I catch. "I do not snore."

"Adorably," I assure her. "Like a tiny kitten with allergies."

She rolls her eyes but doesn't fight the smile tugging at her lips. "I've got to go. Meeting with the podcast team about the end of summer lineup."

At the door, she rises on tiptoes for a goodbye kiss that lingers just a beat too long. It's become our habit, these moments of connection before separating for the day.

"See you tonight," she says against my lips. "I'll pick up Thai from that place you like."

And just like that, we're practically married, not just Vegas married. The routine of it should terrify me, but instead, I find myself looking forward to Thai takeout and falling asleep to the sound of her breathing.

I'm completely screwed.

"The Levi Peterson drama is finally contained," I tell Grant as we wrap up our weekly briefing. "His rehab stint is being framed as 'preventative wellness' before shooting starts on season four."

Grant nods while scrolling through the press coverage on his tablet. "Good work on this. The puff piece in *Vanity Fair* was inspired and made him seem responsible rather than reactive."

"That was actually Jess's suggestion," I admit. "After his publicist blew up our original narrative, she suggested that a redemption narrative might play better if he was proactive about it."

Grant sets down his tablet and studies me with that penetrating gaze that's made studio executives squirm for decades. "Speaking of Jess, how's married life?"

"The arrangement is working well," I say automatically. "Dylan's footage is great, and my father has backed off, surprisingly."

"That's not what I asked."

I shift in my chair, uncomfortable under his scrutiny. "It's fine. We're making it work."

"Really?" He leans back. "Because Sophia says Jess has been suspiciously unavailable for their usual Sunday girl brunches, and you've been smiling at your phone like a teenager with his first crush."

Heat creeps up my neck. "We've adjusted the parameters of the arrangement."

"Adjusted the parameters," he repeats, with amusement dancing in his eyes. "Is that what they're calling it these days?"

"It's nothing serious," I insist, not sure who I'm trying to convince. "Just making the most of a temporary situation."

"Ah, I see." Grant nods sagely. "So, you're living together, sleeping together, and apparently giving each other professional advice, but it's nothing serious."

When he puts it like that, it sounds very serious. But acknowledging what's happening between Jess and me means facing what happens when our six months are up. Three months from now, there's no more documentary, no more inheritance contingency, no more reason to stay married.

"It's complicated," I finally say.

"Isn't it always?" Grant's expression softens with understanding. "It wasn't so long ago that I was in your shoes and you were asking what was going on between me and Sophia."

I wince at the memory. "I was doing my job."

"You were right," he concedes, "and I denied it, even to myself, because admitting those feelings meant risking everything. My reputation, my career, and my carefully constructed life."

"This is different," I protest weakly.

"Is it?" Grant leans forward. "Lucas, in the five years I've known you, I've never seen you look at anyone the way you look at Jess."

I stare at the floor, unable to refute his observation. "We only agreed to six months."

"Maybe you should talk." He stands, signaling the end of our meeting. "Before your time is up and it catches you both by surprise."

"It's not that simple."

"It never is." He claps a hand on my shoulder.

I rise to leave, but he stops me at the door. "Sophia's making my mom's meatloaf this Saturday. You and Jess should come over."

"I'll check with her," I say, though we both know we'll be there.

Driving home, I can't shake Grant's suggestion that I should talk to Jess. What would I say? That I look forward to evenings on the couch, to her feet in my lap while we both work on laptops, to occasionally debating the merits of some news story or studio press release?

But he's right. I've grown accustomed to her and her

habits, the way she knows exactly when to push and when to let things go.

And the sex...the sex is fucking incredible. Not just physically explosive, though it absolutely is, but intimate in a way I've never experienced, like we're constantly discovering new things about each other.

I park outside our building—my building, technically, though it hasn't felt that way since she moved in. The elevator ride up feels endless as I rehearse what to say. How do you ask your fake wife if she wants to be your real girlfriend?

The door opens, and the smell of Thai food greets me. Jess, setting containers on the coffee table, has already changed into leggings and one of my old t-shirts, and her hair is piled messily on top of her head.

She looks up with a smile that hits me directly in the chest. "Hey! I got extra spring rolls for you," she tells me in a sing-song voice. And just like that, I know I'm in love with her.

The realization should be earth-shattering, but instead, it feels like the most natural thing in the world, like I'm finally acknowledging what's been true for weeks, maybe even years.

"You ok?" she asks, noticing my silence. "You look weird."

I cross the room in three strides, pull her into my arms, and kiss her like I'm a drowning man and she's oxygen.

When we break apart, she's breathless, and her eyes are wide. "What was that for?"

"Grant invited us to dinner on Saturday," I say because I'm a coward. "Sophia's making meatloaf."

She studies my face, knowing there's more. "And that

warranted a kiss that nearly set the apartment on fire because…?"

"Just happy to be home," I say, which isn't a lie at all.

Smiling, she rises on tiptoes to give me another quick kiss. "Me, too. Now, come eat before it gets cold. Dylan will be here in an hour."

And so, we fall back into our routine of dinner, conversation, her feet in my lap, and my hand on her ankle, all while I try to figure out how to tell her that I don't want this arrangement to end, that I want all of this for real. Forever.

twenty-nine

. . .

Jess

STEAM RISES from Sophia's kitchen island as she tosses green beans with garlic and olive oil. The scent of her famous meatloaf, actually Grant's mom's recipe, wafts from the oven, making my stomach growl in anticipation. Through the window, I can see Lucas and Grant on the patio, beers in hand, deep in conversation beside the fire pit.

"Are these ready to go out?" I ask, arranging chocolate-dipped strawberries on a serving plate.

"Perfect." Sophia nods appreciatively. "You didn't have to bring dessert, though."

"Lucas made them, actually." The words slip out casually, but Sophia's eyebrows shoot up.

"Lucas Carmichael made chocolate-covered strawberries?"

I can't help smiling. "He's full of surprises."

"Speaking of surprises," Sophia says, lowering her voice conspiratorially, "we've missed you at Sunday brunches.

Stella keeps asking if you've abandoned the girl gang for married life."

I focus intently on arranging the strawberries. "Work's been busy. The podcast is—"

"Jess." Sophia fixes me with that no-nonsense Oscar-winning stare.

My shoulders slump slightly. It's oddly relieving to drop the act, even for a moment. "I don't really know what's going on."

"Well, from what I've seen tonight, you two aren't exactly sticking to the 'business arrangement' playbook."

I glance at Lucas again. He's laughing at something Grant said, and the firelight casts his profile in warm gold. My chest tightens in that now-familiar way.

"We've sort of adjusted the parameters," I admit.

"That's exactly what Lucas said to Grant," Sophia says.

"Wait, Lucas talked to Grant about us?"

"You two are hopeless. Yes, apparently, Lucas was equally evasive while simultaneously being completely transparent about having feelings for you."

"He said he has feelings?" The words come out embarrassingly breathless.

"Not in so many words, but Grant said that it's written all over his face." She studies me. "Like whatever's written all over yours right now."

I turn away, busying myself with the dessert again. "It's just physical. We're both adults. No reason we can't enjoy the situation."

"Mmhmm." Sophia sounds thoroughly unconvinced. "And that's why you're blushing like a teenager?"

"I'm not..." I touch my cheeks, which are indeed warm. "It's hot in here."

"Sure it is," she teases, but then she softens. "Look, I get it. Falling for someone when you're not supposed to? Been there. It's terrifying."

"I'm not falling for him," I say automatically, but it sounds hollow even to my own ears.

Sophia just waits, adding butter to the green beans.

"Fine." I sigh. "It's just, he gets me, you know? Not the podcast host or the team owner's daughter, but me. Even the difficult parts." I fiddle with a strawberry that won't stay in place. "And he has this whole other side that nobody sees. He's thoughtful and surprisingly funny, and he makes the best coffee, and—"

"And you're in love with him," Sophia finishes gently.

"I'm in something," I admit. "But in less than three months, the documentary wraps, I get my inheritance, and the arrangement ends. That was the deal."

"Deals can be renegotiated."

The hope that flares in my chest is almost painful. "It's not that simple."

"It never is." She squeezes my arm. "But you should know this better than anybody. Sometimes, the complicated things are the ones most worth fighting for."

Before I can respond to Sophia, the kitchen door bangs open, and a whirlwind of curls and gangly limbs bursts in.

"Is that chocolate? Did someone say strawberries?" Hazel slides across the tile floor in her socks, coming to a dramatic stop at the island. Her eyes widen at my platter. "Those look AMAZING!"

"Lucas made them for dessert," I tell her. She starts to reach for the platter.

"Hands first," I remind her, surprising myself by how naturally the words come.

Hazel grins and spins toward the sink. "You sound just like Sophia now!" She returns with clean hands and eyes the strawberries with undisguised longing.

"One," I tell her, unable to resist that hopeful face. "The rest are for after dinner."

She selects the largest one with careful deliberation. "Dad wants to know if the table should be set outside because it's nice or inside because it might get cold."

"Outside," Sophia decides. "We'll use the heaters if it gets too cool. Want to help Jess take these plates out?"

"Yes!" Hazel announces, with a smudge of chocolate already on her chin. "I'll take the small plates. I'm not allowed to carry the big ones since 'The Incident.'"

"The Incident?" I ask, gathering silverware.

"I may have done a twirl while carrying Dad's favorite serving dish," she explains with a dramatic sigh. "There were many pieces. Much sadness."

I laugh, following her toward the patio. "I've broken my share of dishes, too."

"Really?" Her eyes light up. "Did you get in trouble?"

"Well, not since I was about your age," I admit.

She nods sagely. "Grown-ups get away with everything."

As we step outside, Lucas looks up from his conversation with Grant, and his expression immediately softens when he sees me. He looks at me like I'm something precious he can't quite believe is real, and it makes my stomach flip.

"Lucas!" Hazel announces. "Jess said you made these amazing strawberries, and I already ate one, and it was perfect!"

"My secret talents are revealed," he says, coming over to help with the plates. Our fingers brush as he takes them from me, and even that small contact sends warmth up my arm.

"You guys look at each other like people in the movies," Hazel observes, setting down forks with surprising precision. "Like when the music gets all swoopy and everything else goes blurry."

Grant chokes on his beer while Sophia unsuccessfully tries to hide her smile.

"Out of the mouths of babes," Grant murmurs.

Lucas and I exchange glances, embarrassed but amused.

"Kids," I say with a dismissive laugh that doesn't quite land.

"Say more things, Hazel," Sophia encourages with a mischievous glint in her eye. "What else have you noticed about Lucas and Jess?"

"Sophia," Hazel says, sighing with the exasperation only a seven-year-old can muster. "You're being obvious again."

This breaks the tension, and we all laugh as we settle around the table. Under the guise of reaching for the salt, Lucas's hand finds mine and squeezes it briefly.

"Swoopy music, huh?" he whispers.

"Ridiculous," I whisper back, but I can't stop smiling.

thirty

. . .

Lucas

AS THE PRIVATE elevator to the owner's box rises smoothly, my stomach does the opposite. Jess glances at me, and her lips quirk into a smile.

"Nervous, Carmichael?" She squeezes my hand, and the gold band on her finger catches the light.

"Meeting your father as your husband is slightly different from meeting him as Austin's teammate," I admit, adjusting my collar. "The last time I saw him was after a USC game. He was officially scouting Austin."

"Relax. Dad already loves you by proxy." She reaches up to straighten my shirt, and her fingers linger at my collar. The documentary cameraman shifts position to capture the moment. "He's just thrilled that I'm married to someone who understands baseball."

When the doors open, we're greeted by the expansive luxury of the California Devils' owner's box. Floor-to-ceiling windows overlook the stadium, where players warm up on the field. Sam Lexington strides toward us, his imposing height belied by the warmth in his eyes.

"Lucas Carmichael!" He envelops me in a bear hug that nearly knocks the wind out of me. "About time my daughter brought you around. Welcome to the family, son."

"Thank you, sir. It's an honor to be here," I say, meaning it more than he knows.

"None of that 'sir' business. It's Sam." He wraps an arm around Jess. "You've been keeping this one all to yourself, sweetheart. Married almost four months, and this is the first time you bring him to a game?"

"We've been busy, Dad," Jess says as a blush creeps up her neck.

The blush isn't entirely for show. Last night's activities would have given the documentary crew enough footage for an entirely different kind of film. The memory of Jess arching beneath me sends heat through my body, and I force my thoughts elsewhere before it gets awkward.

Austin appears, and he claps me on the shoulder. "Lucas! Hope you're ready to see some real baseball."

"As opposed to the college ball we played?" I counter with a grin.

"You know what I mean." Austin laughs. "Professional versus amateur."

Garrett, Jess's older brother, approaches with a more measured pace. His handshake is firm, his assessment shrewd. "So, you're the PR guy who swept my sister off her feet," he says, his eyes narrowing slightly. "Interesting career choice for a Carmichael."

"Garrett," Jess warns.

"It's ok," I say easily. "My father had similar thoughts. But I've always preferred shaping narratives to legislation."

Garrett studies me for a moment and then nods. "Fair enough. Jess seems happy. That's what matters."

"She does, doesn't she?" Sam interjects, looking at his daughter with obvious pride. His voice drops as he adds, "Never seen her like this with anyone else."

The comment hits me harder than expected. It hasn't been a charade for a while now, but hearing others observe what I hope to be true is validating.

Jess slides her arm around my waist. "Food's out, guys. Lucas, come meet everyone else."

For the next half hour, I'm introduced to what feels like most of the Devils' administration and more family and friends. Jess remains at my side, her body a warm constant against mine. We no longer use the cameras as the excuse to touch, lean into each other, or share private smiles. None of this is a performance anymore.

There's something about the easy way the Lexingtons interact that enamors me. Sam's booming laugh, Austin's playful ribbing, even Garrett's protective watchfulness—it all feels so natural, so comfortable, nothing like the calculated conversations and political undertones of gatherings at my parents' home.

I watch Jess roll her eyes at something Austin says and then catch her father's knowing wink in response, and something clicks into place inside me. This is what family can be— warm, genuine, connected. I find myself imagining Thanksgiving dinners and Christmas mornings with these people, wondering what Jess would look like opening presents by a tree or how her laugh would echo through a house that's ours, not just mine and with her temporarily inhabiting it.

"So, Lucas," Sam says as we settle into our seats for the first pitch, "how are you finding married life?"

The cameras aren't close enough to catch our conversation over the roar of the crowd. I could give a generic answer, but something about Sam's genuine interest makes me honest.

"It's been surprising," I admit. "In good ways."

Sam nods, his eyes on the field. "Love's like that. Knocks you sideways when you least expect it."

"Dad's the resident expert on great love stories," Austin adds, leaning over with a beer. "Still wears Mom's ring on a chain."

Sam's hand drifts to his chest, where I can now see the outline of something beneath his shirt. "When you find the real thing, you know it," he says simply. "Seems like you two found it, too."

I'm saved from responding by the crack of a bat. Everyone jumps up as the Devils' leadoff hitter sends one deep into right field. Jess cheers loudly, her professional composure forgotten in her enthusiasm.

"She's been like this since she was little," Garrett tells me during the seventh-inning stretch. We're standing by the bar, watching Jess and Austin argue good-naturedly over a disputed call. "Baseball in her blood, journalism in her heart."

"Like your mother," I observe, remembering what Jess has told me.

Garrett looks impressed. "She told you about Mom?"

"Some. I know how much she influenced Jess."

"She doesn't talk about Mom with just anyone." Garrett studies me over his scotch. "You must be something special, Carmichael."

Austin said the same thing, and the weight of his approval feels significant.

Later, as the game winds down with the Devils ahead by two, Jess leans against me and lays her head on my shoulder. The documentary crew has moved to capture fan reactions, giving us a rare moment of privacy.

"Having fun?" she asks, her voice soft.

"More than I expected," I admit, playing with her fingers. "Your family is great."

"Even Garrett, with his interrogation techniques?"

"Even Garrett." I find myself running my thumb over her knuckles, memorizing the feeling. "I like it here. With them. With you. It feels...right."

The admission surprises me almost as much as it seems to surprise her. I've never been one for sentimentality, always keeping relationships at a safe distance, but sitting here, surrounded by her family, watching her in this element, I'm seeing pieces of Jess that I never knew existed, and I want more. I want all of it.

"Your dad said something earlier," I continue quietly, "about never seeing you this happy with anyone else."

Her body tenses slightly before relaxing. "Dad's got a romantic streak a mile wide."

"Is he wrong, though?" The question slips out before I can stop it.

She looks up at me, her expression unguarded in a way

that makes my heart stutter. "No," she says finally. "He's not wrong."

The moment stretches between us, with neither of us wanting to be the first to break the silence. I'm struck by the realization that four months ago, I was perfectly content with my meticulously ordered life. Now I can't imagine going back to that solitary existence.

For the first time in my life, I'm thinking about a future that has nothing to do with career goals or familial expectations, but just the simple, terrifying possibility of waking up next to the same person every day. A person who challenges me, frustrates me, and somehow makes everything in my world sharper, more vibrant, more real.

"Grant's end-of-summer party in the Hamptons is next weekend," I say, changing the subject before we venture into territory too dangerous for a public setting.

"I know. Blair's already planning our annual trip. We usually stay at Brandon's family's place." She sits up straighter. "The documentary crew won't be there. Grant doesn't allow filming at his private events."

"I know." I take a breath. "I was hoping you'd stay with me at Grant's guesthouse. I can meet you there when your flight gets in."

The question hangs between us. This is more than our arrangement requires. I'm asking her to share a space with no cameras or witnesses for an entire weekend. The crowd erupts as the Devils clinch the win. In the commotion, Jess leans close, and her lips brush my ear.

"Just us sounds perfect," she whispers.

thirty-one

. . .

Jess

"SO, you're telling me that you voluntarily chose to stay with Lucas at Grant's instead of here with us?" Blair raises an eyebrow as she tosses another bottle of sunscreen into our shopping basket.

I roll my eyes but can't quite suppress my smile. "It's more convenient. The party runs late."

"Mm-hmm," Sophia hums knowingly, examining a display of local honey. "Convenient. That's what we're calling it."

Blair, Sophia, Stella, and I have escaped the testosterone-heavy atmosphere of Brandon's beach house for a grocery run. The house is gorgeous, all weathered shingles and panoramic ocean views, but with Brandon, Wyatt, and Jake debating the merits of various grilling techniques, we needed a break.

"I don't know why you're both looking at me like that," I protest, grabbing a box of crackers. "Lucas and I are married. Staying together shouldn't be news." I look back to make sure

Stella isn't in earshot. The guilt creeps up my neck. I feel terrible lying to her.

"Let's not forget that she's wearing his college hoodie," Sophia points out. "Voluntary husband clothes stealing is a critical relationship milestone."

I glance down at the faded USC Baseball sweatshirt I'd thrown on this morning. "It's comfortable," I mutter. "And he doesn't mind."

"I can't believe you won't be staying with us this trip!" Stella pouts as she lingers behind us, oblivious to our conversation. "Next year, maybe you and Lucas can stay with us at Brandon's house."

"You two are actually working out," Blair says as we walk a few more steps ahead of Stella as Sophia slows to hang back with her. "Can't say I'm surprised. Which is actually surprising."

I start to object, but as we turn the corner into the wine section, I freeze so suddenly that Sophia bumps into me from behind.

"Jess, what—" she starts to say and then follows my gaze.

Senator Logan Carmichael stands by the premium cabernets, his hand resting on the lower back of a woman who is decidedly not his wife. She's younger, maybe early forties, with sleek blonde hair in an elegant twist. They're standing close, too close for a professional relationship, and the intimacy in their body language makes my instincts ping loudly.

"Is that...?" Blair whispers.

"Lucas's father," I confirm as a protective anger flares in my chest. I think of Katherine Carmichael, and something hardens in my resolve.

"Jess, maybe we should..." Sophia begins, but I'm already moving forward.

"Senator Carmichael!" I call out, my voice bright with false warmth. "What a surprise!"

The pair jumps apart slightly, and Logan's politician mask slides into place so quickly that it would be impressive if it weren't so practiced.

"Jessica," he says, recovering smoothly, though I don't miss the momentary panic in his eyes. "What a pleasant surprise. I didn't realize you'd be in the Hamptons this weekend."

"I could say the same," I reply, extending my hand to the woman beside him. "I'm Jess Lexington-Carmichael, Logan's daughter-in-law. And you are...?"

The woman takes my hand, and her grip is firm. "Diane Mercer. I work with the senator on his education initiative."

"Diane is my director of legislative affairs," Logan adds, his tone perfectly calibrated between professional and friendly. "We're preparing for a donor meeting tomorrow about Katherine's scholarship foundation."

It sounds legitimate. It probably is legitimate. But something in the way the woman won't quite meet my eyes sets off every warning bell I possess.

"How wonderful," I say, matching his political smoothness. "Katherine's foundation does such important work. Is she here with you this weekend?"

A flicker of discomfort crosses his face. "Unfortunately, no. She's at a conference in Chicago."

"Such a shame that we'll miss her," I reply, letting my

gaze linger on Diane. "Lucas didn't mention you'd be in town, Senator."

"I didn't realize Lucas would be here, either," he says with a slight edge in his voice. "He tends to make decisions without consulting the family calendar these days."

The implication is clear. Logan blames me for the distance with his son. I smile wider.

"Grant Hall's summer party," I explain. "Lucas never misses it. We're staying at Grant's guesthouse."

"Interesting," Logan says, his smile not reaching his eyes. "I thought these industry parties weren't your usual scene, given your...journalistic integrity concerns."

It's a subtle dig, but I don't rise to the bait. "I go where the stories are, Senator. Speaking of which, I'm working on a piece about political families maintaining authentic connections in the public eye. Perhaps you'd be willing to comment? Your family presents such a united front despite different career paths."

Logan's smile tightens. "I'm afraid I'm rather busy this weekend, Jessica. Perhaps another time."

"Of course." I nod understandingly. "Well, I won't keep you and Diane from your...preparations. I'll be sure to tell Lucas that I ran into you. I'm sure he'll want to find time to see his father while you're both here."

The barely concealed alarm in Logan's eyes gives me a petty satisfaction.

"That's not neces—"

"It's no trouble at all," I interrupt sweetly. "Family is so important, don't you think?"

Blair clears her throat beside me. "Jess, we should probably finish up. We've got that thing..."

"Right," I agree, never breaking eye contact with Logan. "Senator, Diane, enjoy your weekend. I'm sure we'll cross paths again soon."

As we walk away, I can feel Logan's eyes burning into my back. The moment we're out of earshot, Stella explodes in a whispered frenzy.

"Oh, my God, was he having an affair? Did we just witness—"

"We don't know that," Sophia cuts in diplomatically, though her expression is troubled.

"We don't," I agree, though everything in me suggests otherwise. "But I know what I saw."

"Are you going to tell Lucas?" Blair asks quietly.

I nod without hesitation. "Of course. He should know his father is here."

"It could just be work," Sophia offers, but her tone lacks conviction.

"Maybe," I concede, though I'm already mentally replaying the body language, the guilty start when I called out, the way Diane's hand had lingered on Logan's arm. My reporter's instinct rarely steers me wrong, and right now, it's screaming that there's more to this story.

"What are you thinking?" Blair asks, studying my face. She knows me too well.

"I'm thinking," I say slowly, "that I'll tell Lucas I saw his father with a colleague and let him decide what to make of it."

"Just the facts?" Stella asks, sounding disappointed by my restraint.

"Just the facts," I confirm. "It's not my place to make accusations or start digging into his family without his permission."

As we're checking out with our groceries, my phone buzzes with a text.

LUCAS

Can't wait to see you tonight.

I stare at the message, with warmth and dread coiling together in my stomach. Four months ago, I wouldn't have hesitated to pursue this story, to expose Logan Carmichael's hypocrisy. Now, with Lucas in my life, the boundaries have shifted.

"You're really not going to investigate?" Sophia asks gently as we load bags into the car, knowing me well enough to read my internal struggle.

"I'm going to tell him what I saw," I say firmly. "Just the facts, that I ran into his father and a legislative staffer. What happens after that is Lucas's call, not mine."

"That's surprisingly restrained for you," Blair observes, her eyebrows raised.

"He's my husband," I say simply; the word still feels strange on my tongue. "His family, his decision."

As we drive back to Brandon's, I can't shake the image of Logan's face when I mentioned telling Lucas about our encounter. For a man who's spent his career controlling narratives, he'd looked genuinely afraid.

I respond to Lucas.

JESS

I'll be there soon 🖤

His response comes quickly.

LUCAS

Whenever you want. Door's always open for you.

I smile at his message, even as I'm wrestling with what to say when I see him. Just the facts, I remind myself. No accusations, no journalist digging. Not unless he asks.

But something deep inside me, the part that's grown increasingly protective of Lucas over these past months, hopes he doesn't ask. Some truths are better left uncovered, at least for now.

thirty-two

. . .

Lucas

"YOUR FATHER IS HERE in the Hamptons."

Jess's words hang in the air between us. She's perched on the edge of the guesthouse sofa, still in her beach clothes, her hair tousled from the ocean breeze. I've been looking forward to seeing her all day, but the moment she walked in, I knew something was wrong.

"What?" I set down my drink. "That's impossible. He's in Sacramento until Tuesday."

"I saw him at Citarella about an hour ago," she says carefully, "with a woman named Diane Mercer. He said she's his director of legislative affairs."

Something cold settles in my stomach. "Blonde? Mid-forties?"

Jess nods, her expression neutral. Too neutral. I recognize her journalist face, the one she uses when she's keeping her thoughts carefully guarded.

"What else?" I ask, my tone sharper than intended.

"Nothing else. I introduced myself, and we chatted

briefly. He mentioned that they were preparing for a donor meeting tomorrow for your mother's foundation." She pauses. "He seemed surprised that you were in town."

I run a hand through my hair as the familiar tension gathers at the base of my skull. Diane Mercer. I've met her at campaign events. She's always hovering at the periphery of my father's circle, always a little too attentive to be just staff.

"Are you ok?" Jess asks softly.

"Fine," I say automatically and then catch myself. "Sorry. I'm just surprised."

Jess watches me, her reporter's instincts visibly battling with something else. Concern, maybe. "Lucas, I'm just telling you what I saw. That's it."

"But you think there's more," I say. It's not a question.

"It doesn't matter what I think."

"It matters to me."

She sighs, tucking a strand of hair behind her ear. "Look, I don't know anything for certain. But yes, something felt off."

The confirmation stings more than it should. I've heard the rumors for years, whispers about my father's indiscretions, carefully buried by his PR team. I've never had proof, never wanted it.

"I'm not investigating him," Jess adds quickly. "I just thought you should know that he's here."

"Are you sure? Seems like a great story for your podcast." The words are unfair, and I regret them immediately.

Hurt flashes across her face. "Is that what you think? That I'd go after your family?"

"No," I say, closing my eyes briefly. "I'm sorry. That was out of line."

"I told you because you're my husband." She stands and moves closer. "Whatever this is between us, I wouldn't cross that line. Your family is off-limits unless you tell me otherwise."

The sincerity in her voice cuts through my defensiveness. She's standing before me not as Jess Lexington, relentless journalist, but as Jess Lexington-Carmichael, my wife and the woman who's somehow become essential to my life.

"Thank you," I say quietly, reaching for her hand. "I know this goes against your every journalistic instinct."

"It does," she admits with a small smile, "but some things are more important than a story." She squeezes my fingers. "I promise, Lucas. I won't dig into this on my own. If something real surfaces, I'll come to you first."

I pull her into my arms and bury my face in her hair, breathing in the scent of salt and sunscreen. "Just when I think I have you figured out, Mrs. Lexington-Carmichael."

"I've got to keep you on your toes, Mr. Carmichael." She leans back, studying my face. "We should get ready. Grant's waiting for us."

Grant's annual summer gathering is, as always, a carefully orchestrated blend of intimacy and exclusivity. The sprawling oceanfront property glows with tasteful lighting. Servers glide between guests with trays of champagne, and the low hum of conversation is punctuated by occasional laughter.

Under normal circumstances, I'd be in my element here,

networking, facilitating introductions, and keeping an eye on potential PR opportunities. Tonight, though, I'm going through the motions, as my thoughts continually drift to the revelation of my father's presence nearby.

Jess appears at my side with a fresh cocktail. "You're a million miles away," she murmurs. She looks stunning in a simple white sundress and with her hair swept up to expose her shoulders.

"Just distracted," I admit, accepting the drink. "Sorry."

"Don't apologize." Her hand finds mine, and our fingers interlace with practiced ease.

Her teasing smile draws me back to the present moment. "Have I mentioned how beautiful you look tonight?"

"Twice," she says, her eyes sparkling. "But I don't mind hearing it again."

Grant passes by, and he raises his glass in acknowledgment. "Thanks for putting words on paper for me again this year, Lucas."

I nod. "Of course."

As he moves on to mingle with other guests, Jess tugs gently at my hand. "Let's step outside for a minute. You need to recenter."

I raise an eyebrow at her. "Recenter?"

Her smile turns mischievous as she raises her fresh cocktail to her lips. "I think I can help with that. I know just the spot." She drains the glass in one long swallow, her eyes never leaving mine. Then she grabs my glass and sets both on a passing server's tray.

She leads me through the party and out onto the terrace, where she finds a secluded corner hidden by potted palms and where ambient lighting doesn't quite reach. The moment we're alone, Jess pushes me against the wall, and her mouth finds mine with urgent heat.

"What are you doing?" I mumble against her lips, though my hands are already spanning her waist.

"Getting you out of your head," she whispers, nipping at my lower lip. "Is it working?"

"Getting there," I manage as her hands slide beneath my jacket.

She laughs softly, and the sound vibrates against my throat, where her lips now explore. "Challenge accepted."

Her fingers make quick work of my belt, and the metallic click of the buckle is unnervingly loud in the quiet corner. My breath catches as her hand slips beneath my waistband and finds me already hard.

"Someone's eager," she teases.

"Can you blame me?" I reply, struggling to keep my voice steady as her fingers wrap around me.

I should stop this. We're at Grant's party, surrounded by industry executives, some of whom I work closely with. But rational thought dissolves as Jess sinks gracefully to her knees and looks up at me with those impossibly blue eyes.

"Jess..." My protest dies as her mouth replaces her hand, warm, wet, and perfect. My head falls back against the wall, and my hands find her ponytail, finally wrapping around the silky length I've been thinking about touching for months. "Christ."

The sight of Jess, brilliant, sharp-tongued Jess, on her knees before me, utterly focused on my pleasure—it's almost too much. "Someone could see," I manage, though I make no move to stop her.

She pulls back just enough to whisper, "Then you'd better be quiet, Carmichael," before returning to her task with renewed determination.

I bite my lip to suppress a groan, gripping the stone wall with my free hand for support. She's relentless, setting a pace that has me fighting for control within minutes. When she takes me deeper, humming softly in a way that sends vibrations through my entire body, I know I'm close.

"Jess," I warn, tugging gently at her hair. "I'm going to—"

She doesn't stop; instead, her eyes hold mine with a challenge I've never been able to resist. The tension coils tighter and tighter until it finally snaps. My release hits with an intensity that steals my breath, and my muscles tense as waves of pleasure wash through me.

Jess stays with me through every pulse, taking every last drop and only pulling away when I'm completely spent. She rises with the same grace that she kneeled with, straightening her dress as if we've just been discussing the weather. My fingers fumble with my belt, still clumsy from the aftershocks.

"Better?" she asks, looking entirely too pleased with herself.

"Much," I admit, reaching for her. I draw her close and press my forehead against hers. "Though, now I owe you."

Her smile is wicked as she presses a brief, hard kiss to my lips. "I'll collect later. With interest."

I catch her wrist before she can turn away. "Jess." The weight of everything I want to say hangs between us.

"I know," she says softly, as if she actually does. She brushes her thumb across my lower lip.

The sound of silverware tapping against glass drifts from inside, signaling that it's time for Grant's speech. We rejoin the party, slightly rumpled but significantly more relaxed, just as Grant takes his position at the front of the room.

I watch with professional pride as he delivers the words we've crafted together, tweaked, and perfected over the years.

"Every year, I tell myself I won't give the same speech about how much this tradition means to me. And yet...here I am again, clearly unable to help myself."

A wave of quiet laughter moves through the room.

"When I started this celebration twelve years ago, I thought it would be a singular event, a simple way to honor the people who'd been part of my journey, but I underestimated just how meaningful these gatherings would become. This room contains not just extraordinary talent, but something far rarer, genuine humanity and a willingness to support each other through both triumphs and challenges. Those qualities are precious, and your continued presence here year after year confirms I've found them in you."

His gaze sweeps the assembled guests, warm and genuine. "Some of you are first-time attendees; others have been here from the beginning. Regardless, you matter. To me and to each other. I've always believed that our finest moments occur when we're truly seen by those around us, and you've repeatedly shown me the power of that connection."

A smile spreads across his face as he raises his glass. "To connections that matter. Cheers, everyone."

As applause fills the room, I feel Jess's eyes on me. "What?" I ask softly.

She shakes her head slightly. "Nothing. It's just, it's good writing."

"Most of it's recycled," I admit. "He says almost the same thing every year."

"Some things don't need changing," she says, her eyes never leaving mine.

I'm about to respond when my phone vibrates in my pocket.

FATHER

> Heard you're in the Hamptons this weekend. I have meetings all day tomorrow but could move some things around for breakfast if you're free. Let me know.

The casual tone almost makes me laugh. Classic Logan Carmichael, acting as if nothing is amiss, as if we're just two family members coordinating schedules.

"Your father?" Jess asks quietly, noticing my expression.

I nod, showing her the message. "Apparently, he has 'meetings' tomorrow."

Her fingers brush mine as she hands the phone back. "Are you going to meet him?"

I consider it for a moment. "I don't know yet."

I pull up a new message, this time to my mother.

LUCAS

> Hey Mom, quick question. Is Dad working on a donor meeting for your foundation this weekend?

Her response comes quickly.

MOM

Not that I'm aware of, but I'm in Chicago at
an education conference until Tuesday. Why
do you ask?

Something cold settles in my chest. I don't reply, just slide the phone back into my pocket.

Jess watches me. The concern is clear in her eyes, but she doesn't push. Instead, she simply takes my hand under the table, tracing small circles on my palm with her thumb.

"Whatever you decide," she says softly, "I've got your back."

The simple declaration steadies me. For all my years in PR and managing other people's crises, I've always handled my family complications alone. Having Jess in my corner is something I never realized I wanted.

thirty-three

. . .

Jess

"WE'VE GOT SOMETHING."

Kira drops a folder on my desk with the quiet intensity that always means a potentially explosive story has landed. I glance at the documentary camerawoman positioned in the corner of my office, capturing every movement for Dylan's "day in the life of a journalist" segment. Great timing.

"Give me a minute," I tell both Kira. "I need to review this first."

Kira nods, understanding the subtext. Some things need to be assessed before they're discussed on camera. She slips out of the office, closing the door behind her.

I open the folder and scan the contents. My stomach drops. It's a legal brief: "Civil Complaint Filed: Vanessa Martin v. Senator Logan Carmichael—Allegations of Sexual Harassment, Hostile Work Environment, and Retaliatory Termination."

It details allegations from Carmichael's former scheduler, Vanessa Martin, who claims he made persistent unwanted advances, sent inappropriate texts, and eventually demoted her when she refused his overtures.

Shit.

I close the folder and press my fingers against my temples. Of all the stories to land on my desk today, it had to be this one. I can almost hear the universe laughing at me.

A week ago, I promised Lucas I wouldn't dig into his father's affairs. Now his father's affairs have dug their way to me.

I buzz Kira back in, aware of our camerawoman adjusting her position to better capture our conversation.

"What do we know about the source?" I ask, keeping my voice neutral.

"Martin's attorney reached out directly. They want to offer an exclusive interview before the story breaks wide."

"Why us?" The question is automatic; the journalist in me is always suspicious of convenient tips.

"Your reputation from the MeToo exposés," Kira explains. "And apparently, Martin's sister follows your podcast."

I nod, organizing my thoughts. "Verify the filing. Check Martin's employment records. See if there are other complaints we can corroborate."

"Already on it." Kira hesitates. "There's something else. The filing mentions a pattern of behavior with multiple women. Names have been redacted, but they reference incidents in the Hamptons."

My mind flashes to Diane Mercer, the woman I saw with Logan. The timing is too perfect to be coincidental.

"Give me an hour," I tell her. "Then we'll map out a plan."

When she leaves, I sit motionless, staring at the folder. The filming continues silently from the corner.

"Can we pause for a minute?" I ask her.

"Dylan requested that we keep rolling during editorial decisions," she replies apologetically. "For authenticity."

Of course he did. I force a professional smile. "I need to speak with Dylan. Now."

Ten minutes later, Dylan strides into my office, all artistic intensity and caffeine energy.

"Privacy issue," I say firmly. "Can we get some space?"

Dylan nods to the camerawoman, who lowers her main camera and steps outside.

"What's up?" he asks, dropping into the chair across from me.

I slide the folder toward him. "This just landed on my desk."

He skims the contents, his eyebrows rising progressively. "Whoa. This is complicated."

"You think?" I run a hand through my hair. "Dylan, I need to know what we're doing with footage like this. This is sensitive material."

"It's incredible content," he counters, the filmmaker in him instantly recognizing the narrative value. "The personal and professional collision is exactly what made me want to film you two in the first place. That night in Vegas, I saw something special between you and Lucas. And now this, well, it's the ultimate test of a power couple."

His genuine belief in our love story would be touching if it weren't so problematic right now.

Dylan studies me. "Have you told Lucas yet?"

"It just came in," I say, avoiding the real question.

"But you're going to tell him," Dylan presses.

I stand and move to the window overlooking the city. The afternoon sun casts long shadows across downtown Los Angeles. Outside, the world continues with its normal rhythm, while mine feels suddenly off-kilter.

"It's complicated." I close my eyes briefly, remembering. "I promised Lucas that I wouldn't dig into his father. That his family was off-limits unless he gave me permission."

"But this came to you," Dylan points out. "You didn't go looking for it."

"Do you think that distinction will matter to him?" The question comes out more with vulnerability than I intended.

Dylan leans forward. "Listen, Jess. Lucas loves you. He understands who you are."

His words hit uncomfortably close to the truth I've been avoiding.

"Which is why this is so hard," I admit. "If this were any other subject, any other story, I wouldn't hesitate. But this is Lucas's father, and no matter how complicated their relationship is, this will hurt him."

"So, what are you going to do?"

I return to my chair and sink back into it. "I need to verify the claims first. Check Martin's background and employment records, see if there's a pattern of behavior."

"And then?"

I stare at the folder, torn. "I don't know. Journalistically, I have an obligation to pursue this story. But personally..."

"You're worried about Lucas's reaction," Dylan finishes for me.

"Wouldn't you be?" I challenge. "This isn't just any story. This is his family."

Dylan taps the folder thoughtfully. "Maybe wait until you have more information. Know exactly what you're dealing with before you bring it to him."

I nod, relieved that someone else is articulating the same instinct I'm feeling. "I need to be absolutely certain before I drop this on him. The allegations could be exaggerated or politically motivated."

"But if they're legitimate?" Dylan presses.

"Then I'll tell him," I say, though my stomach twists at the thought. "But I need facts first, not just allegations. I owe him that much."

Then I ask, "What about the doc footage? If this becomes a story, I don't want our personal reaction breaking on screen before we've dealt with it privately."

"We'll be careful with it," Dylan assures me. "This is sensitive material. I'm not looking to ambush either of you."

I narrow my eyes. "You say that, but I know that filmmaker instinct of yours, Dylan. The drama of it all must be irresistible."

He grins, not even trying to deny it. "It's compelling, I won't lie. But I respect both of you too much to turn this into reality TV." He stands to leave. "Just keep me in the loop. And remember, great marriages survive challenges like this. Makes for better storytelling."

After he leaves, I buzz Kira back in. "Get me everything you can on Vanessa Martin. Employment history, social media, previous complaints, anything that helps establish credibility. And reach out to her attorney to set up a preliminary call."

"On it. And Lucas?" she asks tentatively, aware of the delicate situation.

"Let me worry about Lucas," I say more confidently than I feel.

When she leaves, I turn back to the folder and flip through the allegations again. They're detailed and specific enough to warrant investigation, but I need more before I can determine if this is a legitimate scandal or a political hit job.

As I work, I try to ignore the gnawing feeling that I'm already crossing a line that Lucas asked me not to cross. But I'm not digging into his father, I argue with myself. I'm verifying a legitimate tip that came to me.

The distinction feels increasingly hollow with each page I turn.

I just hope that by the time Lucas finds out about this story, I'll have enough facts to make him understand why I had to pursue it.

And why I didn't tell him right away.

thirty-four

. . .

Lucas

"IF WE ANNOUNCE during the festival, we get the industry buzz, but the general audience coverage gets diluted," I explain, pacing the length of Alex's office. "If we wait until after, we control the narrative but risk losing momentum."

Alex watches me with mild amusement, his feet propped on his desk. "You've given this more thought than I have, and it's my production deal."

I stop pacing, realizing I've been overanalyzing. Again. It's what I do when I'm trying not to think about something else. Or someone else.

"Force of habit," I admit, dropping into the chair across from him. "So, which option?"

"Festival announcement," Alex decides. "The streaming platforms will be there with checkbooks ready. We'll leverage the bidding war for press."

I nod, making notes on my tablet. "We'll need Sophia to

do the rounds. Her involvement gives the project credibility beyond just another comedy."

"Already on it. She's blocked off the weekend." Alex studies me for a moment. "You seem distracted today. Everything ok with the wife?"

Wife. Five months in, and the word still gives me a strange flutter. "She's fine. Just busy with the podcast."

"Mm-hmm," Alex hums skeptically. "And that's why you just spent twenty minutes overthinking a straightforward announcement strategy? Come on, man. I know you better than that."

I set my tablet down. "She's been off lately. Distant. Working late. Distracted when we're together."

"Have you asked her what's wrong?"

"Multiple times. She keeps saying it's just work stress."

Alex shrugs. "Maybe it is."

"Maybe." I don't sound convinced, even to myself.

"Or maybe," Alex suggests carefully, "she's just adjusting to 'married life.'" He brings his hands up to air quote that last part. "It's only been what, five months? You guys went from barely tolerating each other to a Vegas wedding to living together over the course of a weekend. That's a big transition."

The comment lands harder than it should. Everyone else still talks about our relationship like it's some improbable rom-com plot twist. Alex has been quietly rooting for us since the beginning, calling us perfectly matched like he knows something we don't.

I nod slowly, buying time with a sip of coffee. "You're

right. We've both been busy. The documentary wraps next month after my father's announcement, and..."

I stare into the middle distance like the answer might be hiding there. The truth is, that conversation has been circling us for weeks now, unspoken but constant, a deadline hanging in the air. And lately, Jess has seemed quieter, like maybe she's already preparing for the exit ramp, like maybe she's ready to go back to her old life.

"We haven't talked about what happens after that."

The words come out quieter than I intended, and for a second, I can't quite look at him.

"Then you can finally have some privacy," Alex says. "No more cameras following you around. Just you and the wife." He grins. "Maybe you could go on a real honeymoon? You never took one after Vegas."

A text from Grant asking me to stop by his office saves me from having to respond to Alex.

"Gotta run, man. But, uh, I appreciate the talk. Thanks."

I head across the studio lot to Grant's office, and when I arrive, he's reviewing something on his laptop with an intensity that usually means either very good or very bad news.

"Please tell me we're not in the middle of another PR crisis," I say, closing the door behind me.

Grant looks up, and a smile breaks through. "Quite the opposite. I just watched some early cuts from Dylan's documentary. It's excellent."

I relax slightly. "Good to hear. The crew's been filming less lately. I was worried they were losing interest."

"Hardly. Dylan called it his most compelling project to date. Said he's never captured such genuine chemistry between two people." Grant closes his laptop with a satisfied click and leans back in his leather chair. "I think he's particularly fond of you and Jess. I know you were the last couple that signed on, and I might be biased, but your story is outshining the others by miles."

I manage a smile that doesn't quite reach my eyes, and my chest tightens unexpectedly at the praise. "We aim to please. But it's probably better if someone takes the lead on press for this."

"Sounds like once they wrap with you and Jess, they'll head into post-production. Assuming everything goes well, the series should be airing early next year." Grant taps his fingers against his desk, his expression thoughtful. "Must be exciting, seeing it all come together."

"I think we only have two big shoots left: my dad's announcement and then final interviews." The words feel heavy as I say them, and my heart sinks at the thought of all this wrapping up soon. The documentary ending means our arrangement ends, too—a reality I'm increasingly reluctant to face.

"Everything ok between you two?" Grant's perception is sometimes unnerving, and now he's studying me with the same intensity that he reserves for difficult negotiations.

"Fine. Just the usual work stress." The lie comes easily, too easily, sliding off my tongue like something I've practiced. "You mentioned new footage?"

"It's all set up in the screening room. Dylan said you're welcome to preview anything they've shot. Part of your arrangement, I believe?"

I nod, grateful for the excuse to escape further questioning. "I should take a look. Make sure there's nothing problematic."

"Of course." Grant returns to his work, but then he adds casually, "By the way, Lucas, I'm glad things seem to be going well between you and Jess. You seem really happy."

I pause at the door. "Thanks. I am happy."

He doesn't look up. "Funny how it sneaks up on you, isn't it?"

"Hilarious."

I head down the hallway to the screening room and step inside the darkened room filled with a theater-sized screen and a back row full of monitors. No one's around, but a note from Dylan indicates that they've stepped out for lunch and I'm welcome to review any footage on the main system.

I settle into the chair, where I navigate through recently uploaded files. Most are labeled by date and location: "Dinner Party," "Devils' Game," "Office B-roll." I click through a few, smiling despite myself at shots of Jess laughing at the baseball game, her intensity while interviewing Edie Lang, the way she demolished everyone at charades during game night with our friends.

How did I ever think we could fake this for six months without consequences?

I'm about to close the files when I notice one labeled "OTRC: Sensitive." My curiosity piqued, I click play.

The footage shows Jess's office, filmed from a slightly awkward angle, as if the camera had been placed on a bookshelf. She's sitting at her desk with Dylan across from her, an open folder between them.

"*—just landed on my desk,*" Jess is saying, sliding the folder toward Dylan.

I watch as Dylan reviews something, his eyebrows rising. "*Whoa. This is...complicated.*"

"*You think?*" Jess runs a hand through her hair, a gesture I've come to recognize as stress. "*Dylan, I need to know what we're doing with footage like this. This is sensitive material.*"

Dylan's response about "incredible content" and "personal and professional collision" makes me lean closer to the screen, trying to glimpse what's in the folder.

"*Have you told Lucas yet?*" Dylan asks, and my entire body tenses.

Jess shakes her head. "*It just came in.*"

"*But you're going to tell him,*" Dylan presses.

I watch as Jess stands and moves to the window, her back to the camera. When she turns, her expression is pained. "*It's complicated,*" she says. "*I promised Lucas I wouldn't dig into his father's affairs. That his family was off-limits unless he gave me permission.*"

"*But this came to you,*" Dylan points out. "*You didn't go looking for it.*"

"*Do you think that distinction will matter to him?*"

As I pause the video, a cold feeling spreads through my chest. Whatever this is, whatever she knows about my father, she's deliberately keeping it from me.

I force myself to continue watching.

"*I need to verify the claims first,*" Jess is saying. "*Check Martin's background and employment records, see if there's a pattern of behavior.*"

Martin? My mind races, trying to place the name. A donor? A colleague of my father's?

"And then?" Dylan asks.

"I don't know. Journalistically, I have an obligation to pursue this story. But personally..."

"You're worried about Lucas's reaction."

"Wouldn't you be? This isn't just any story. This is his family."

I stop the video, unable to watch more. The betrayal cuts deeper than I expected. After everything we've shared, after her promise in the Hamptons, she's investigating my father behind my back. Worse, she's deliberating whether to even tell me about it.

I close the files, my mind reeling. Every moment of closeness, of supposed trust between us these past months, has now been cast in a different light. Was I just a convenient source of information? A way to get closer to political stories she couldn't otherwise access?

The rational part of my brain argues that I'm overreacting, that I should wait to hear her explanation. But the part of me that's spent a lifetime watching my father's political calculations, my mother's careful compromises, and every relationship in my orbit reduced to strategic value drowns out that rationality.

I've been a fool to think what Jess and I have could be different. To think that someone whose career is built on uncovering secrets would respect mine. To believe, even for a moment, that our unexpected marriage could survive the collision of our professional worlds.

My phone buzzes with a text.

JESS

Home late tonight. Working on a story.

Of course she is.

I stare at the message, my thumb hovering over the keyboard. I should confront her, demand answers.

LUCAS

No problem. I've got work, too.

And if she thinks our marriage, real or fake, can survive her betrayal, she's about to discover just how wrong she is.

thirty-five

. . .

Jess

I CAN'T THINK STRAIGHT in the office, not with
the documentary cameras hovering and certainly not with the
weight of Logan Carmichael's transgressions sitting in a
manila folder on my desk.

"I'm heading out," I announce, gathering my notes and
laptop.

Back at my apartment, I spread the evidence across my
dining table. I have employment records, text messages, and
sworn statements from Vanessa and two other former
staffers. The picture they paint is damning but not entirely
surprising.

Logan Carmichael, it seems, has a pattern of pursuing
women who work for him—not aggressively enough to trigger
immediate outrage, but persistently enough to make them
uncomfortable. Suggestive comments. Lingering touches.
Private meetings that could be explained away as professional, if not for the context.

And when they don't respond to his advances? Gradual

sidelining. Projects are reassigned. Eventually, reasons are found for them to move on.

It's not Hollywood-casting-couch-level harassment. It's more insidious, the kind of behavior powerful men have gotten away with for decades because it exists in gray areas. Because victims fear not being believed or losing careers they've worked hard to build.

I glance at my phone, feeling the guilt from the text I sent earlier.

JESS

Home late tonight. Working on a story.

And his supportive, understanding reply.

LUCAS

No problem. I've got work, too.

I need perspective.

JESS

Emergency girls' night at my place. Wine and moral dilemmas. ASAP.

BLAIR

There in 30. Wrapping up Sophia's new contract.

STELLA

On my way! Need snacks?

An hour later, my living room is transformed into the war room I desperately need. Blair pours wine while Stella arranges an impressive charcuterie board on my coffee table.

"Ok, spill," Blair demands, handing me a generously filled glass. "What's the emergency?"

I take a fortifying sip. "I have a story about Lucas's father."

Their expressions shift from curiosity to concern.

"What kind of story?" Stella asks, settling onto the couch.

"Sexual harassment allegations from former staffers," I explain, gesturing to the documents now neatly stacked on my dining table. "Three women, similar patterns, credible evidence."

"And Lucas doesn't know," Blair guesses.

"Not yet." I run a hand through my hair. "I promised him in the Hamptons that I wouldn't dig into his father's affairs."

"But this came to you," Stella points out.

"Exactly what Dylan said," I mutter.

"Is he filming all this for the documentary?" Blair asks.

"Some of it." I grimace. "He caught my initial reaction when the story landed on my desk."

"Well, if anyone can handle this kind of sensitive content with integrity, it's Dylan," Blair says confidently.

"True," Stella agrees. "But what are you going to do?"

I let out the deep breath I've been holding. "This is a legitimate story I can't ignore. Senator Carmichael is announcing his gubernatorial run next month. Voters deserve to know who they're electing."

"But..." Stella prompts.

"But Lucas will be hurt. And he'll feel betrayed that I didn't tell him immediately." I sink deeper into my chair. "I've been verifying facts before bringing it to him, but the more I confirm, the worse it looks."

"How bad are we talking?" Blair asks, shifting into the protective mode she uses with her clients. "Criminal? Civil? PR nightmare?"

"Mostly the latter," I explain, reaching for the summary I've prepared. "Based on what I've found, Logan Carmichael has a pattern of making advances toward female staffers and then retaliating professionally when rejected. Not physical assault, but definite harassment and abuse of power."

"And you've confirmed this?" Blair's tone is careful, measured.

"Employment records show the pattern. All three women were rising stars who suddenly departed under vague circumstances. I have text messages that, while not explicitly sexual, show inappropriate personal interest. And their stories align perfectly despite them never having communicated with each other."

Blair nods, processing. "Credible but not catastrophic. A good PR team could manage the fallout."

"So, what are you going to do?" Stella asks softly.

I stare into my wine glass like it might contain answers, but all it reflects is my own hesitation. I've built my life around exposing these kinds of stories. I know how this works. I know the patterns, the power imbalances, and the careful silencing. But this one feels different. It's not just a headline. It's Lucas. It's his family. And the thought of him finding out this way, of me being the one to break it, twists something in my chest.

"If I tell him now," I murmur, "he might try to spin it. Bury it. Not because he's like them, but because he's loyal. Because it's his family. And if I publish without warning..."

There's a chance our marriage might not survive. And I don't want that. I'm not ready for it to end. Not even close. I know it was pretend, temporary, but now the idea of it ending feels like losing something real.

"He cares about you," Stella says gently. "I'm sure he'll understand."

I hope so, because the thought of hurting him makes my stomach turn, and that scares me more than the story itself.

"I just need to be sure," I say finally, setting the glass down. "About what I have. About how I bring it to him. About everything."

Blair suddenly pales, and her hand flies to her mouth. "Excuse me," she mumbles, bolting toward the bathroom.

Stella and I exchange concerned glances as retching sounds echo down the hallway.

"Food poisoning?" I wonder, eyeing the charcuterie board suspiciously.

Stella's eyes widen. "Or something else. She's been looking tired lately. And she skipped wine at a premiere party last week."

Blair emerges from the bathroom looking slightly green. "What are you two whispering about?"

"Are you pregnant?" Stella blurts out, subtlety abandoned.

Blair freezes, her expression cycling rapidly through shock, denial, and then dawning realization. "I'm late. But I've been so busy with Sophia's streaming deal that I didn't even notice..." She sits heavily on the couch. "Oh, my God."

"When was your last period?" I ask.

"Six...no, seven weeks ago?" Blair looks dazed. "Wyatt

and I have been talking about starting a family, but not until next year…"

"Well," Stella says brightly, pulling out her phone, "looks like your timeline got accelerated. DoorDash has pregnancy tests, right?"

Twenty minutes and one very generous tip to a bewildered delivery driver later, Blair emerges from the bathroom clutching a plastic stick, her expression unreadable.

"Well?" Stella and I demand in unison.

A smile breaks across Blair's face as tears well in her eyes. "I'm pregnant."

The next few minutes are a blur of excited squeals, hugs, and happy tears. Blair pulls out her phone, her hands shaking. "I need to call Wyatt."

"Go!" I urge her. "Go tell him now, in person. This isn't phone news."

Blair hesitates. "But your crisis—"

"Will still be here tomorrow," I assure her. "Go tell your husband he's going to be a dad."

As Blair gathers her things, practically vibrating with excitement, she pauses to give me a quick hug. "For what it's worth, Jess," she says quietly, "trust Lucas with the truth. All of it."

After Blair leaves, Stella stays to help clean up, both of us still buzzing with the happy news.

"You'll tell him soon?" Stella asks, gathering wine glasses.

"Yes," I promise.

When they're both gone, I take the coward's way out and decide to spend the night at my place. I scroll to see if I missed any texts from Lucas before sending my own.

JESS

> Staying at my apartment tonight. Blair and Stella came by with some good news to celebrate. Will fill you in tomorrow.

His response comes a moment later.

LUCAS

> Sure. See you tomorrow.

Brief. To the point. Not the usual warmth I've grown accustomed to. But it's been a long day for both of us, and I'm probably reading too much into it.

As I get ready for bed in the apartment that no longer quite feels like home, I replay Blair's parting advice: *Trust Lucas with the truth.* The irony doesn't escape me that what started as a convenient arrangement has somehow become the most real relationship I've ever had. And now I'm risking it all for my commitment to the truth.

thirty-six

Lucas

THE ICE in my glass has long since melted, diluting what remains of the expensive bourbon I've been nursing for the past hour. It's my third glass. Or maybe fourth? I lost count as night settled over the apartment, leaving me sitting in an almost-dark room, with only the city lights filtering through the windows.

I didn't bother turning on a lamp. The darkness suits my mood.

Each time I close my eyes, I see the footage from yesterday of Jess and Dylan hunched over that folder. *I promised Lucas I wouldn't dig into his father's affairs...but journalistically, I have an obligation to pursue this story.*

The betrayal burns worse than the alcohol.

The sound of keys in the door snaps me from my thoughts. The door opens, casting a rectangle of light from the hallway that stretches across the floor. Jess steps in, silhouetted for a moment before she flips on the light.

She jumps, and her hand flies to her chest. "Jesus! Lucas,

you scared me." Her expression shifts from surprise to concern as she takes me in, disheveled, drink in hand, sitting in the dark. "What's wrong?"

I raise my glass in a mock toast. "Waiting for my wife to come home."

Something in my tone makes her pause. She sets her bag down slowly, studying me. "Sorry I didn't make it back here last night. Blair and Stella came over with some news and—"

"Spare me." My voice comes out harder than I intended, but I can't seem to modulate it. The alcohol has loosened something bitter inside me.

"What's going on with you?" She approaches cautiously, like I'm a wounded animal that might strike. Perhaps I am.

"Why don't you tell me, Jess? Isn't that what you do best? Dig up stories? Uncover secrets?" I stand, unsteady for a moment before finding my balance. "Or do you only share those discoveries with Dylan?"

Her face scrunches in confusion. "What are you talking about?"

"I saw the footage." I set my glass down with deliberate care. "You and Dylan in your office, discussing the story you're working on. About my father."

Her face pales. "Lucas—"

"The story you deliberately chose not to tell me about." I laugh, and the sound is hollow and unfamiliar to my own ears. "After promising me, to my face, that you wouldn't investigate my family without talking to me first."

She straightens, her defensiveness visibly kicking in. "It's not what you think. The story came to me. I wasn't digging—"

"Don't." I cut her off, my anger flaring hot and bright.

"Don't try to spin this like you're the victim of circumstance. You made a choice, Jess. You chose your story over your promise to me."

"That's not fair. I was gathering facts before bringing it to you. I wanted to be sure—"

"Sure of what? That my father was worth exposing? That the story was juicy enough to pursue? Or were you just calculating the best way to use our relationship for access?"

Her eyes widen, and hurt flashes across her face before hardening into shock. "Is that really what you think? That I've been using you this whole time?"

"What else am I supposed to think?" I gesture between us. "This entire marriage is built on a lie, a business arrangement with mutual benefits. Why should I expect loyalty when there's a better offer on the table?"

"A better offer?" Her voice rises. "You think I see a story about your father as a better offer than what we have?"

"Don't you?" I challenge. "Your career has always come first, Jess. You've made that abundantly clear from day one."

She flinches as if I've struck her. "That's not true."

"Isn't it? You get access to Wonderland's inner circle, exclusive interviews, and a Reynolds Foundation board seat, all while building your personal brand with this documentary. Meanwhile, I get what? A wife who pursues stories behind my back? Who keeps secrets that affect my family?"

Something shifts in her expression, and the hurt gives way to a cold anger I've seen before. Her entire demeanor transforms, with her spine straightening and her eyes turning to ice. When she speaks, her voice is perfectly controlled, stripped of all emotion.

"I see." She steps back, physically removing herself from the conversation. "You've clearly made up your mind about me."

I see the hurt on her face, but I don't respond.

"I won't defend myself to someone who's already decided I'm guilty. I don't grovel, Lucas. Not for anyone."

The shift is jarring. The passionate, argumentative woman I've come to know has been replaced by this cool, detached stranger.

"You either trust me or you don't," she continues, her voice steady and devoid of the emotion that charged her earlier words. "And apparently, you don't. Good to know where we stand."

"Where we stand is that you broke your promise," I press, unsettled by her sudden composure and wanting, perversely, to crack it. "You chose journalism over loyalty."

"And you chose assumptions over giving me the benefit of the doubt." She calmly picks up her bag. "You know, I expected better from someone who claims to understand the nuances of truth and public perception."

Her control only fuels my anger. "Don't turn this around on me. You're the one who—"

"I'll stay at my place tonight," she says as if I hadn't spoken at all. "Wouldn't want me getting any more inside information for my stories."

The sarcasm is delivered with precision.

"Is that all you have to say?" I demand.

She pauses at the front door. For a moment, I think I see her composure waver, but when she turns, her expression is perfectly neutral.

"What else is there to say? You've made it abundantly clear what you think of me and my intentions." She meets my gaze directly. The quiet dignity in her voice lands harder than any shouting could have.

When she walks out, back straight, head high, the soft click of the door closing feels more devastating than if she'd slammed it.

I sink back into my chair. Suddenly, the apartment is too quiet, too empty. The whiskey glass sits abandoned on the coffee table, and I stare at it, wondering when exactly I became my father, using anger as a shield, driving away the people who matter most.

The thought sobers me more effectively than coffee ever could. I rub my hands over my face as the magnitude of what just happened slowly sinks in.

I've spent my entire career managing crises, crafting perfect responses to imperfect situations. But tonight, when it mattered most, I let my hurt pride do the talking.

And I may have destroyed the one relationship I actually care about losing.

thirty-seven

Jess

THE BLUE FOLDER sits open on my desk, its contents spread across the surface like evidence at a crime scene. Three women's stories. Three careers derailed. One powerful man at the center of it all.

I haven't returned to Lucas's apartment since our fight. It's been a week, but the pain of his accusations still cuts deep. Thankfully, I've channeled that hurt into something productive: verifying every detail of the allegations against Senator Logan Carmichael.

Poking her head into my office, my assistant announces, "Ms. Martin is here."

I nod, gathering the papers into a neat stack. "Send her in."

Vanessa Martin enters with the careful composure of someone who's spent months preparing for this moment. She's younger than I expected, maybe early thirties, with a straight-backed posture that speaks of resolve rather than fear.

"Thank you for meeting with me," I say, gesturing to the chair across from my desk.

"Thank you for taking my story seriously." She settles into the seat, her hands folded in her lap. "Not everyone has."

"I've reviewed the documentation you provided." I tap the folder. "Your employment records, the text messages, the timeline of events. Everything checks out."

Relief flickers across her face. "So, you believe me?"

"I do." I lean forward. "But I need to understand what you want from this story. Justice? Vindication? Revenge?"

Her shoulders square. "Truth. That's all. The senator presents himself as a family-values candidate while treating women who work for him as disposable. People deserve to know who they're voting for."

The clarity in her voice makes my chest tighten. It's the same familiar story, the one I've told over and over: the mask of charm, the unchecked entitlement, the way powerful men operate just beneath the surface of plausible deniability. Hell, I've even experienced it personally with men like Marcus.

I study her, looking for any signs of ulterior motives, political rivalries, personal vendettas, or financial incentives. I find none, just the quiet dignity of someone who's been wronged and seeks only acknowledgment.

"I'll publish the story," I tell her, "but not until after he announces his candidacy for governor. And I want to give his team plenty of time to respond."

"They'll deny everything," she says with certainty.

"Most likely. But we have evidence." I hesitate. "Ms. Martin, I should disclose that I have a personal connection to this story. The senator is my father-in-law."

Her eyes widen slightly. "I'd heard you were married to his son, but I wasn't sure if it was true. Does that complicate things for you?"

"It does." Honesty seems the only appropriate response. "But it doesn't change my commitment to the truth. This story will run, regardless of my personal circumstances."

She nods, and a look of respect crosses her features. "That's why I came to you. Your reputation for integrity, even when it's difficult."

After Vanessa leaves, I stand at my office window, watching Los Angeles traffic crawl below. The wedding band on my finger catches the light, a constant reminder of what's at stake. I spin it absently. The now-familiar weight suddenly feels heavier.

My phone vibrates on the desk. Dylan's name flashes on the screen.

"Hey, Dylan."

"Jess! Just checking in about the Carmichael announcement shoot. We'll plan to meet the two of you there and can run through the shot list before everything starts."

My stomach tightens. The gubernatorial announcement is our last major documentary obligation before the final interview. Despite everything, Lucas will be standing dutifully beside his father.

"Yes," I say, my voice steady though everything inside me feels off-kilter. "We'll be there."

We've agreed to these shoots, signed off on them weeks ago. Even with whatever's unraveling between us now, we won't break our commitment.

"Great. This should be fantastic material. The power

couple supporting family despite professional challenges. It's the perfect narrative arc."

"See you in two weeks," I say, fighting my instinct to correct him.

My phone rings again. Unknown number.

"Jess Lexington speaking."

"I'm confused? Is it Lexington or Carmichael?" The voice is instantly recognizable. Logan Carmichael's practiced political tone is a blend of authority and folksy approachability.

"What can I do for you, Senator?"

"I understand you're working on a story that concerns me."

"Yes, I'm investigating allegations of workplace harassment from several former staffers. Would you like to comment?"

A pause, followed by a short laugh. "Always the professional. I was hoping we might speak off the record, as family."

"I'm afraid I can't do that, Senator."

"Logan, please. We are family, after all." His voice drops slightly. "Family that looks out for each other."

The implication hangs in the air between us.

"If you'd like to provide a statement for the record, I'm happy to include it in the story," I say, keeping my voice neutral.

"Jessica," he says, his tone harder now, "you know how this works. These allegations are baseless—disgruntled former employees looking for a payday. Publishing them serves no one but harms many, including my wife. Including Lucas."

My chest tightens, but I don't let it show in my voice. "Then maybe you should've thought about that before you used your position to take advantage of people who trusted you."

A beat. Then he drops the last card he has.

"You really think the political world's going to embrace a tabloid journalist who married into the scandal she exposed? You'll lose access. The calls will stop coming. You'll be the story no one wants to touch."

I smile, sharp and steady. "That's the difference between us, Senator. You're scared of losing access. I'm not scared of telling the truth."

The charm vanishes completely. "I expected better from you after welcoming you into our family."

"If the allegations are baseless, then you have nothing to worry about," I reply evenly. "Your official statement will be included prominently."

"I see. Well, I hope you're prepared for the consequences of your choices, Ms. Lexington. Good day."

The line goes dead.

I set the phone down, my hands steady despite the subtle threat in his words. Logan Carmichael is used to controlling narratives, to making problems disappear through influence and intimidation. He's met his match.

As afternoon fades into evening, I work methodically through the evidence, crafting the story that will likely end my marriage but uphold everything I believe in professionally.

My phone buzzes, and for a minute, hope surges at the thought of Lucas reaching out.

AUSTIN

Surf Sunday morning?

I'm disappointed when I don't see his name on my screen.

JESS

Yes, I need it. 6AM. Zuma.

I glance at the wedding ring on my finger one more time, remembering Lucas's face when he accused me of choosing my career over him. The pain of his words still stings, but underneath it all is a deeper hurt—that he could believe, even for a moment, that I was using him.

I return to my keyboard, and my fingers fly across the keys with renewed determination. If Lucas can't see me clearly through his pride and pain, that's his choice, but I won't compromise who I am—not for him, not for anyone.

The story will run. The truth will come out.

And whatever happens after that, I'll face it standing on the foundation of integrity I've built my entire career upon.

thirty-eight

. . .

Lucas

I'M STILL STARING at the divorce papers when I realize that I can't put this off any longer. My attorney's logo is emblazoned across the top of the documents spread across my coffee table, "Mutual Consent Dissolution of Marriage," dated and ready for signatures once our six-month arrangement officially ends in two weeks.

The sight of them should provide relief. Instead, they feel like a death sentence.

But right now, I have a more pressing obligation, one I've been dreading since Jess and I had our fight a week ago.

I dial my mother's number, and my stomach churns as it rings.

"Lucas, what a lovely surprise," she answers, warmth evident in her voice. "I was just thinking about you and Jess."

"Hi, Mom." I take a deep breath, steeling myself. "I need to talk to you about something. About Dad."

The warmth in her voice shifts to caution. "What about your father?"

This is the conversation I never wanted to have, the reason that I was so angry at Jess in the first place: not just for pursuing the story but for forcing me into this moment, for making me be the one to shatter my mother's carefully maintained world.

"Jess is writing a story. About him." I push forward, needing to get it out. "Sexual harassment allegations from former staffers."

Silence stretches between us. I brace for a denial, for the protective instinct I expect from a woman who's been married to my father for nearly forty years. Instead, she sighs quietly.

"I see. And these allegations, are they substantial?"

Her calm reaction catches me off guard. "Three women, consistent stories, employment records showing patterns of retaliation." I pause. "You don't seem surprised."

"Lucas, I've been married to your father since I was twenty-three years old. There's very little about him that surprises me anymore."

Understanding dawns slowly. "You knew. About the women."

"I've known who I married for a very long time." Her voice is steady, matter-of-fact. "Your father is brilliant, charismatic, and deeply flawed."

"And you've just accepted it?" I can't keep the incredulity from my voice.

"No," she says firmly. "I've managed it. There's a difference."

"I don't understand."

"Marriage is complicated, Lucas. Particularly public

marriages. Your father and I have an understanding. He keeps his transgressions discrete, and I maintain my dignity and focus on the work that matters to me."

"That sounds like a business arrangement, not a marriage," I say before I can stop myself.

The irony hits me immediately. Isn't that exactly what Jess and I have? Or at least, what we started with?

"Tell me about Jess's story. When does it run?"

"The Sunday after Dad's announcement. She's giving you both time to respond."

"Considerate of her." A pause. "And how are you handling this? It sounds like there's more to this conversation than warning me about a news story."

I stare at the divorce papers again, and my throat tightens. "We had a fight. A bad one. I accused her of choosing her career over me, of betraying my trust."

"Did she?"

"She says the story came to her, that she wasn't digging into it. That she was verifying facts before bringing it to me." I run a hand through my hair. "I found out by seeing footage from the documentary they're filming. She was discussing the story with the director."

"I see. And this betrayal, it's about the story or something else?"

The question catches me off guard. "What do you mean?"

"I mean that, sometimes, when we feel most hurt by someone, it's not about their actions but about our fears."

"She promised she wouldn't investigate Dad without talking to me first."

"And if she had told you immediately, what would you have done?"

The question forces me to really think. "I don't think I would've stopped her," I admit. "Not really. I know who he is. I've always known, even if I didn't want to admit it. And those women deserve to be heard."

"Then what are you really angry about?"

I close my eyes as the truth finally becomes clear. "It's you I worry about. You've spent your life carrying his image, standing beside him. This story isn't just going to take him down; it's going to hurt you, too. That's what I didn't want Jess to be part of."

"So, you're not angry at Jess for doing the right thing. You're angry because you couldn't protect me from the fallout."

"Yes," I whisper. "And because she's caught in the middle of it. It's not fair to her, either."

"And yet, she's standing by her principles anyway."

"She's brilliant," I say, the words tumbling out. "Fearless. Unflinchingly principled. She sees through pretense and demands authenticity from everyone around her."

"Including you?"

"Especially me. She challenges me constantly. Makes me think. Makes me better."

"And now she's doing exactly what you admire her for: standing by her principles, seeking truth, refusing to be swayed by personal connections. And you're punishing her for it."

The realization stops me cold. "I never thought of it that way."

"Do you know what I thought when I met Jess at the fundraiser?"

"What?"

"That she wasn't intimidated. Not by your father, not by our world. She remained entirely observant, sharp, authentically herself. You looked at her that night like she was the only real thing in a room full of carefully crafted images."

"I did?"

"Oh, yes. I recognized that look. It's how I used to look at your father before reality set in."

The comparison unsettles me. "You think I'll end up like you and Dad? In some sort of arrangement?"

"No, I think you have the chance to build something genuine, something based on accepting each other completely, flaws and all. Real partnership means loving someone not despite who they are, but because of it."

I hear her moving around, perhaps to a more private part of the house. When she speaks again, her voice is softer, more vulnerable.

"Before I was Katherine Carmichael, political wife, I was Kate Reynolds, education activist. I had fire, purpose. I compromised too much of myself for your father's career, for the family image. I don't regret the family we built, but I do regret losing parts of who I was."

"Why are you telling me this?"

"Because I see Jess heading down a path I didn't have the courage to take. Standing by her convictions, even when it costs her personally. And I see you at a crossroads, deciding whether to be the man who supports her strength or the man who isn't strong enough to embrace it."

I glance at the divorce papers again, and my chest tightens. "What if it's too late?"

"Then you fight for her. Not by asking her to be less, but by being brave enough to love her exactly as she is—brilliant, principled, and occasionally inconvenient to your peace of mind."

"When did you get so wise about relationships, Mom?"

"Forty years of mistakes are a powerful teacher." I can hear the smile in her voice. "Your father will survive this story, Lucas. Our family will adapt. But you may not recover if you let pride drive away the woman who clearly holds your heart."

After we hang up, I sit in the silence of my apartment—our apartment, though Jess hasn't been back since our fight. The divorce papers mock me from the coffee table, ready and waiting for signatures that would legally end what started as a convenience but became something I can't imagine living without.

Part of me wants to drive to her office right now and beg her forgiveness, but I know Jess well enough to realize that grand gestures won't fix what I've broken.

I pick up the divorce papers and tear them in half.

The announcement party is in two weeks. We're both expected to be there, both still maintaining the pretense of our marriage for the cameras and the crowd. I don't know if Jess will forgive me. I don't know if we can rebuild what my accusations have damaged. But now, I know what I want. I just hope that when I tell her, she wants the same things, too.

thirty-nine

. . .

Jess

DAWN BREAKS over Zuma Beach in a spectacular display of pink and gold, the kind of sunrise that would typically fill me with peace. Today, though, the beauty barely registers as I paddle out beyond the break, with my mind churning as restlessly as the ocean beneath me.

"You're going to wear yourself out before we even catch anything good," Austin calls from a few yards away, watching as I paddle aggressively through the swells.

Ignoring him, I scan the horizon for the next set. The familiar burn in my shoulders is a welcome distraction from the hollow ache in my chest. It's been two weeks since my fight with Lucas. Two weeks of sleeping at my apartment, of throwing myself into work, of pretending I'm not falling apart.

I haven't heard from him. No texts, no calls. Just silence. Thankfully, most of the documentary filming is wrapped. All that's left now is the announcement party and the final sit-down interview. And thank God for that because the idea of faking my way through another "happy couple" segment right now might actually break me.

A promising wave approaches, and I turn my board and position myself. The catch is perfect, the ride smooth as I pop up and find my balance, cutting across the face of the wave. For these brief, glorious seconds, nothing exists but water, motion, and the rush of adrenaline.

Then the wave peters out, and reality crashes back. I paddle back toward Austin, who's watching me with that annoying mix of brotherly concern and curiosity.

"That was nice," he says, "but you're surfing angry. Never a good strategy."

"I'm not angry," I lie, wiping salt water from my face. "I'm focused."

"Yeah? You've got this little crease right here"—he touches the space between his eyebrows—"that only shows up when you're pissed about something. Had it since you were like, eight."

I splash water at him, which he dodges effortlessly. "Maybe I'm just getting old. Wrinkles happen."

"Bullshit. What's going on? You and Lucas have a fight?"

The direct hit makes me flinch. Austin knows me too well; he's always been able to read me.

"It's not..." I begin, then stop. What's the point in hiding it? "Yeah."

"Trouble in paradise?" His tone is light, but his eyes are serious. "I thought you guys were solid."

I stare out at the horizon, watching the waves form and break in endless cycles. "It's complicated."

"Marriage usually is," he says with the confidence of

someone who's never been married himself. "Want to talk about it?"

Part of me wants to unburden myself completely, but I'm not sure how I would even begin to explain everything up to this point.

"We had a fight," I finally say. "A bad one."

"About?"

"Work. His father." I hesitate. "I'm running a story that he thinks is a betrayal."

Austin whistles low. "Heavy stuff. What kind of story?"

"The kind that reveals inconvenient truths about powerful men." I run my hand along the edge of my board. "Lucas thinks I chose my career over loyalty to him."

"Did you?"

Somehow, the question hits harder coming from Austin than it did from Lucas. "No. But I didn't compromise my principles, either. Maybe I'm not built for compromise," I admit. "Not the way people want me to be. Maybe that makes me hard to love."

Austin gives me a look. "You know what Mom used to say about you?"

I raise an eyebrow. "This better not end with 'she's a pain in the ass.'"

"She said you were fire," he says, "and people who get close enough to love fire are always at risk of getting burned. But that doesn't mean you stop burning. It means you find someone who knows how to hold the heat."

That undoes something in my chest.

"I thought Lucas was that person," I say, quieter now.

"But maybe he wanted the version of me that only burns on command."

Austin sighs. "Maybe. Or maybe he just needed time to figure out the difference between warmth and control. And maybe he's doing that right now."

His insight, delivered with the straightforward clarity that's always been Austin's gift, brings unexpected tears to my eyes. I blink them away quickly, grateful for the salt water that disguises them.

"Lucas is a good guy," Austin adds. "But he's got his own baggage. That father of his..." He shakes his head. "Talk about complications."

"You have no idea," I mutter.

A larger wave approaches, and we both turn to position ourselves, pausing the conversation as we catch the ride. This time, I surf with less anger and more deliberation, and the tension in my body eases slightly as I carve across the water.

Back on our boards, floating in the lull between sets, Austin picks up where we left off.

"So, what happens now? You and Lucas will work it out, yeah?"

The unfinished question hangs between us. I've been asking myself the same thing.

"I don't know," I admit. "Maybe I'm not cut out for this whole marriage thing."

"Because of one fight?" Austin looks skeptical.

"Because it's hard." I stare at the water. "Being that vulnerable with someone. Letting them see all of you, even the parts that might disappoint them."

"That's what marriage is supposed to be, isn't it?" Austin asks. "The whole 'for better or worse' thing?"

"Yeah, well, they don't warn you how much 'worse' there might be," I say, trying for humor but landing somewhere closer to raw truth.

Before he can respond, my phone chimes from its waterproof pouch. I pull it out, expecting a message from the office. Instead, I see a production note about the announcement event.

Reality crashes back with brutal force. The party. The documentary. Lucas and I standing together, playing the perfect power couple while his father announces a gubernatorial run that my story might derail.

"Bad news?" Austin asks, noticing my expression.

"Just the documentary," I say, tucking the phone away. "A reminder about our next shoot."

"Are you still going?"

"Of course. I wouldn't let him down."

Austin gives a low whistle. "And you'll be working on a story that he thinks betrays his family? That's some serious drama."

"Tell me about it." I stare down at my wedding ring, still on my finger despite everything. "I don't know if I can do this, Austin."

"Do what? The documentary shoot or the marriage?"

"Both." I shake my head. "I don't know how to be someone's wife and still be myself."

"No offense, but from where I'm sitting, it sounds like you might be the one looking for an exit. Are you using this fight as a reason to bail?"

"That's not fair," I protest, though the words hit uncomfortably close to home.

Austin raises an eyebrow. "You've always been a pro at keeping people at arm's length. You focus on work, on uncovering other people's truths while guarding your own."

"I've dated before," I counter.

"Yeah, with guys who were never going to challenge you, who were never going to get close enough to really matter if they left." His voice softens. "Lucas matters. That's why this hurts so much."

I blink rapidly against the sting of tears. "When did you get so insightful about relationships? You avoid them at all costs."

"I watch and learn from other people's mistakes," he says with a grin. "Especially my big sister's."

A perfect wave rises behind us, ending the conversation as we both turn to catch it. This time, I surf with a strange mixture of grief and clarity, with Austin's words echoing in my mind.

You might be the one looking for an exit.

Am I? Have I been sabotaging this relationship by holding back, by keeping one foot out the door, protecting myself from the vulnerability that comes with truly loving someone?

Back on the beach, as Austin and I towel off beside our boards, he bumps my shoulder gently. "For what it's worth, I think you and Lucas make sense together. You challenge each other. Keep each other honest."

"Even when it hurts?" I ask, thinking of the pain in Lucas's eyes during our fight.

"Especially then." Austin unzips his wetsuit.

I want Lucas. The question is whether he wants me, too. This whole thing started as a performance, a strategy, a marriage that wasn't supposed to mean anything. And maybe I convinced myself that as long as I kept it framed that way, temporary, tactical, I could protect myself. That when it was over, I could walk away clean.

But I can't.

And the truth is, I don't want to.

As we gather our gear and head toward the parking lot, my phone buzzes again.

KIRA

Final edits on the Carmichael piece complete. Legal has signed off. Ready to publish the Sunday morning after the announcement.

The timeline is set. I'll be standing beside Lucas at his father's event, knowing what's coming the next day. The thought twists my stomach into knots.

However, now, I feel something beyond anger and hurt: a flicker of determination. Whatever happens next, I need to face it head on.

I don't know if he'll forgive me. I don't know if we can rebuild what's been broken. But I know I have to try, starting with showing up on Saturday and then telling him how I really feel. It won't be easy, but nothing worth fighting for ever is.

forty

. . .

Lucas

I'VE NEVER BEEN SO aware of a tuxedo in my life.

Every stitch feels too tight, every collar point like it's angling toward my jugular. I tug at the cuff links and try to focus on my breathing: slow, deep, even. The same kind of breath you take before walking into a press conference, a courtroom, or, apparently, a political coronation wrapped in designer florals and jazz quartet renditions of Bruce Springsteen.

The Carmichael estate is a masterpiece of optics tonight. Lanterns line the driveway. Champagne flows like water. There's a red, white, and blue step-and-repeat in front of the koi pond because subtlety has never been my father's strong suit.

This is the official launch of Logan Carmichael's gubernatorial run.

And I'm drowning in it.

I shake another hand, smile for another photo, nod at another donor with teeth that are too white and a handshake that's too smooth. The press is kept in a velvet-roped corner, sipping catered cocktails while trying not to look like they're recording everything. The documentary crew is less discreet; their cameras roll freely as Dylan circles the perimeter like a well-dressed hawk.

I see Sophia and Grant arrive. Alex is here somewhere, probably making snide remarks in a corner and texting me memes from ten feet away. The guest list is a carefully balanced mix of power, press, and plausible deniability.

And then there's him. My father. He's working the room like a man running for president instead of governor. Perfect posture. Crisp smile. Every word tailored to his audience. It's disgusting how easy it is for him.

"Lucas!" he says, gripping my shoulder like we're starring in a campaign ad together. "Glad you could make it."

"I was on the invite," I say dryly.

He claps my back with mock affection. "Just remember to look happy for the cameras, son. The voters like seeing a united family."

I don't answer. I don't need to.

And then I see her.

She stands just inside the main entrance, and my heart stops. She's wearing a deep blue dress that makes her eyes look like sapphires, and her hair is swept up elegantly, exposing the graceful curve of her neck. Even after weeks apart, even from across the room, the sight of her still knocks the breath from my lungs.

As she shifts her weight and tucks a strand of hair behind her ear, something silver glints at her wrist. The bracelet. My bracelet. And just below it, her fingers catch the light, and I see that her gold wedding band is still there.

She could've taken them off. But she didn't.

My heart races. I've spent weeks rehearsing what I'd say when I finally saw her again, but now that she's here, all those carefully crafted phrases evaporate.

Our eyes meet from across the crowded room, and everything else fades away. For a heartbeat, we're both perfectly still, suspended in this moment of recognition. Then she begins moving toward me, weaving through the crowd with purpose, and I find myself doing the same.

We meet in the middle of the room, stopping just a foot apart. We're close enough to touch, but neither of us is quite brave enough to bridge that final gap.

"Hey," she says, her voice soft but steady.

"Hey, yourself," I reply, drinking in the sight of her. "You're here."

Her lips curve in a careful smile. "I said I would be."

"You look beautiful," I tell her, because it's true and because I've spent weeks thinking about all the things I should have said.

A blush touches her cheeks. "You clean up pretty well yourself, Carmichael."

"Not working tonight?" I gesture to her outfit and her lack of press credentials.

"No." Something vulnerable flickers in her expression. "Tonight, I'm just here as, well, as your wife."

The word sends a rush of warmth through me. "Does that mean I get to keep you by my side all evening?"

"If you want to." There's a question in her eyes, hesitant and hopeful.

"More than anything," I admit, offering my arm. When she takes it, her hand warm against my sleeve, everything feels right for the first time in weeks.

As we move through the crowd together, I'm acutely aware of her presence beside me. The subtle scent of her perfume. The way her fingers occasionally tighten on my arm when someone approaches. The small, secret smiles we exchange over particularly ridiculous political small talk.

"Senator Reynolds has been telling me about his golf handicap for ten minutes," she whispers, leaning close enough that her breath tickles my ear.

"Amateur mistake," I murmur back. "Never let him start on golf. I once missed an entire Lakers game because he cornered me about his new putter."

She laughs, and the sound ripples through me like sunshine. God, I've missed her laugh.

My mother approaches, elegant in midnight blue that uncannily matches Jess's dress. "Lucas! And Jess, how wonderful to see you both." She embraces each of us quickly before being pulled away by another guest, leaving us in our own bubble once more.

Dylan spots us from across the room and makes a beeline for us, camera crew in tow. His expression is delighted.

"There you are! Our star couple." He gestures to his cameraman. "We're getting some fantastic B-roll tonight. This event is perfect for the documentary's final chapter."

Jess glances at me with a hint of nervousness in her eyes. I place my hand gently on her lower back in silent support.

"Actually," Dylan continues, "while I have you both, we just need a few staged moments by the garden. Some intimate conversations, maybe a dance? And I wanted to confirm our final interview tomorrow afternoon, say around three? We're wrapping principal photography this week."

"The story drops in the morning," Jess says, her voice steady but with an undercurrent of tension.

"Even better," Dylan replies. "We'll capture the authentic aftermath. The real conversations. It's what makes this documentary special."

I look at Jess, searching her face. "That works, right?"

She nods, and her eyes meet mine with unexpected warmth. "Right."

Dylan directs us toward the garden, where he positions us near blooming roses with strategic lighting. "Just act natural," he instructs. "Talk to each other like we're not even here."

As soon as the cameras start rolling, we fall into position easily, muscle memory from months of being filmed. But something's different tonight. The way Jess leans slightly into me when I place my hand at the small of her back. The way her eyes linger on mine a beat longer than necessary.

"You know," I say quietly, our faces close enough that the microphones won't catch it, "tomorrow's going to be intense."

"I know." Her expression is a mix of determination and regret. "The story has to run, Lucas."

"I understand." And surprisingly, I do. "You're doing the right thing."

Surprise flickers in her eyes. "You think so?"

"Truth matters," I tell her simply. "Even when it's inconvenient. Even when it hurts."

Something shifts in her expression, a softening that makes my heart race. Before she can respond, Dylan calls out, "Perfect! That chemistry is exactly what I'm looking for. Could you two move toward the fountain?"

As we follow his direction, I lean close to her ear. "After the interview tomorrow, would you stay for dinner?"

She looks up at me, searching my face. "Dinner?"

"Just to talk. About us. About what happens next."

She hesitates, and for a moment, I fear that I've pushed too far, too fast. But then she nods, and a small smile plays at her lips. "I'd like that."

Hope blooms in my chest, fragile but real. Before I can say more, a campaign aide appears at my elbow.

"Mr. Carmichael, your father is requesting all family members for a portrait by the main staircase."

"We'll be right there."

The aide glances at Jess and then back at me. "Family only, sir."

Something protective and defiant rises in me. "Jess is my wife. She is family."

Jess touches my arm lightly. "Lucas, it's ok. Go ahead."

"No." I cover her hand with mine. "If they want a family photo, you're in it." I turn to the aide. "Tell my father we will be there momentarily."

As the aide walks away, Jess looks at me with a mixture of surprise and something deeper. "Are you sure? Your father won't be pleased."

"I'm not concerned with what pleases him." I hold her gaze steadily. "I care what pleases me. And having my wife by my side pleases me very much."

Her eyes widen slightly at the conviction in my voice. "Lucas..."

"Come on," I say, offering my hand. "Let's go crash a family portrait."

She takes my hand, and as her fingers interlace with mine, the simple contact sends warmth spreading through me. "Lead the way."

Hand in hand, we cross toward the staircase, where my family is gathering. My father's expression tightens when he sees Jess with me, but my mother makes a point of shifting to make space for us right beside her.

As the photographer arranges us, I lean close to Jess. "Thank you for coming tonight. For being here as my wife."

"I had to make a choice," she replies, her voice barely above a whisper. "Tonight, I chose us."

The simple words send hope soaring through me. "I choose us, too," I tell her. "Tonight, tomorrow, for as long as you'll have me."

Her eyes widen slightly, but before she can respond, the photographer calls for our attention. "Everyone, smile please!"

Jess and I turn to face the camera, smiling not because we're told to, but because, for the first time in weeks, there's something real to smile about. As flashbulbs pop, I feel her fingers intertwine with mine, a silent promise for tomorrow.

Tomorrow, everything will change: my father's reputation, the Carmichael name. But with Jess's hand in mine and the promise of dinner tomorrow night, I find myself looking forward to it.

forty-one

. . .

Jess

"ALLEGATIONS OF SEXUAL Harassment Against Gubernatorial Candidate Logan Carmichael."

The headline stares back at me from my laptop screen, stark black letters against a white background. Simple. Factual. Life-altering.

Even though I arrived back in LA last night at a decent hour, I couldn't sleep. I've been awake since four in the morning, making final edits and signing off on the legal review before the story went live at six a.m. sharp. Now, three hours later, I'm watching as it ripples through the political and entertainment ecosystems like a stone dropped in still water.

My phone hasn't stopped buzzing: colleagues congratulating me on the story, competing outlets requesting interviews, and political commentators seeking additional details. I've responded to none of them, letting my assistant field the inquiries with practiced efficiency.

This is what journalists dream of: publishing something that matters, that disrupts, that pulls truth into the light.

But the victory feels different from what I expected. There's professional satisfaction, yes, but also a new sensation that I'm still trying to identify. For the first time in my career, I wish I had someone beside me to share this with, someone who understands both the weight of the truth and the toll it takes to bring it forward.

"You look like you haven't slept," Kira observes as she sets a fresh cup of coffee on my desk.

"Thank you for noticing," I say dryly, reaching for the cup. "Hazard of breaking major political stories."

"Worth it, though. The response has been huge." She hands me a printout of headlines from various news sites, all picking up the story with appropriate attribution. "Even the *Times* is crediting us with the exclusive."

I scan the headlines, feeling a complex blend of emotions. The story is solid. It's meticulously researched, thoroughly vetted, and powerful in its restrained presentation of facts. It's exactly the kind of journalism I've built my career on.

"Senator Carmichael's office released a statement," Kira continues, pulling up the response on her tablet. "The usual denials, calling the allegations politically motivated, questioning the timing of the story."

"Predictable," I murmur, skimming the carefully crafted non-denial denials. Logan Carmichael's communication team is good. They've created just enough ambiguity to give his supporters room to doubt, while avoiding specific refutations that could be disproven later.

My mind drifts to Lucas: last night at the campaign launch, the way he looked at me, the way he held my hand during the family photos, the unexpected warmth in his voice when he asked me to stay for dinner tonight. I wonder what he's thinking now that the story is actually out. Is he still standing by what he said about understanding why I had to publish it?

"His campaign manager is requesting an interview to respond," Kira adds. "Should I schedule it?"

"Absolutely. We always offer equal time for response." I pause, considering. "But make sure it's with someone else on the team, not me. I need distance from the follow-up coverage."

She raises an eyebrow but doesn't question the decision. "Brady's already prepping in case you said that."

My phone vibrates with a text from Dylan reminding me of our final documentary shoot today at Lucas's apartment. In just a few hours, Lucas and I will be face to face again, talking about our relationship on camera. Then, after the crew leaves, we'll have dinner together and finally talk about what's real between us.

Lucas's apartment looks exactly as I remember it: sleek, comfortable, subtly masculine but with touches of me scattered throughout. The scent of coffee lingers in the air as I step inside, greeted by the documentary crew already setting up in the kitchen.

"Perfect timing," Dylan says, clipboard in hand. "Lucas is just getting ready. We thought we'd start with some casual domestic footage before the sit-down interview."

I nod, setting my bag down on the counter. It feels

strange being back here after weeks away, yet also familiar, like my body remembers this space even if my mind is still catching up.

Lucas appears from the bedroom, and my heart does an involuntary flip. He's wearing jeans and a simple button-down, and his hair is slightly damp from the shower. When our eyes meet, his expression softens into something that makes my pulse quicken.

"Hey," he says simply.

"Hey, yourself," I reply, suddenly aware of the cameras capturing our reunion.

Dylan claps his hands together. "Let's get started. Just act natural. Maybe make a snack. Interact like you would on any normal afternoon."

Normal. As if anything about this situation is normal.

But somehow, as we move around the kitchen together, it does feel natural. I reach for a bowl of strawberries while Lucas grabs the can of whipped cream. He hands me the cinnamon without my asking. I nudge the bowl closer to him so he doesn't have to reach. Our bodies remember this dance even if our minds haven't caught up yet.

Lucas glances at me and smiles, something warm and genuine that makes me momentarily forget that the cameras are even there.

After we finish the kitchen scene, we move to the living room for the interview portion. I settle into one side of the couch and pull a pillow into my lap, more for comfort than anything else. Lucas sits at the opposite end with his body angled toward me, relaxed but attentive.

Dylan lowers his clipboard. "Ok, ready for the final interview? First, I want to address the elephant in the room. Jess, you broke a major story this morning about Lucas's father. Can you talk about how that's affected your relationship?"

I shift the pillow in my lap, fidgeting with the corner seam.

"Publishing that story was one of the hardest professional decisions I've ever made," I say carefully. "Not because I had any doubts about its accuracy or importance, but because I knew it would impact someone I care about deeply."

I glance at Lucas and find unexpected steadiness in his gaze.

"In journalism, we're taught to separate ourselves from our subjects and to maintain objectivity at all costs. But real life isn't that clean. Sometimes, the truth affects people you love, and you have to find a way to honor both your professional integrity and your personal relationships."

Lucas nods slightly, encouraging me to continue.

"What made it possible was knowing that Lucas respects what I do. He understands that truth matters, even when it's inconvenient. Even when it hurts." I pause, and my voice softens. "That kind of respect and understanding, well, it means everything."

Dylan turns to Lucas. "And from your perspective?"

Lucas takes a breath. "I won't pretend that it was easy to see my family's name in those headlines this morning. But the story Jess published was fair, factual, and necessary. The women who came forward deserved to be heard, and the public deserved to know."

He shifts slightly, and his gaze intensifies. "I've worked in PR long enough to know how rare truly principled journalism is. Jess doesn't cut corners. She doesn't sensationalize. She seeks truth, not headlines, and I've come to admire that about her more than I can say."

The sincerity in his voice makes my chest tighten. This isn't performance. This is real.

"Let's pivot a bit," Dylan says. "What's one thing you've learned about yourself through this relationship? Jess?"

I let out a soft breath as I gather my thoughts. "I've always been proud of being independent. I built a career on asking the hard questions, trusting my instincts, and never needing anyone to validate what I already knew. I thought that was strength, and in a lot of ways, it was."

I look over at Lucas, and something warm unfurls in my chest.

"But somewhere along the way, I started confusing independence with isolation. I forgot that being strong doesn't mean going it alone. Lucas reminded me what it feels like to have someone in your corner. Not because you need them to fix anything, but because they want to stand beside you. No conditions. No agenda."

I pause, just for a second, before adding, "He sees the parts of me I don't always show the world. And instead of flinching, he leans in."

I don't look at Dylan. I look at Lucas when I say it, wanting him to know that I mean every word.

"Lucas?" Dylan prompts.

Lucas clears his throat. "I think I used to believe that being composed all the time was the same thing as being in control, that if I could anticipate every outcome and manage every message, I'd never really have to feel the fallout of anything real."

He glances at me, and his expression is open in a way that makes my heart race.

"I've spent most of my life curating versions of myself. The dutiful son. The steady professional. The guy who says the right thing, even when he's thinking something else entirely. But Jess, she doesn't let you get away with that. She sees through spin like it's glass. Being with her made me realize how much of my life I'd spent editing myself in real time."

He looks back at Dylan and then at me again, his eyes never wavering.

"So, I guess what I learned is, I don't want to be the version of me that just survives the day. I want to be someone who actually lives in it. And that means showing up. Even when it's messy. Even when I get it wrong. Especially then."

"Last question," Dylan says, his voice gentler now. "What does this relationship mean to you?"

I look down, suddenly overwhelmed by the depth of what I'm feeling. When I look back up, Lucas is watching me with such tenderness that it takes my breath away.

"This relationship has shown me that love doesn't have to mean compromise," I say finally. "It can mean expansion. Growth. Finding someone who challenges you to be more authentically yourself, not less."

I swallow against the emotion rising in my throat. "What we have is not perfect, but it is real. And that's what I've come to value more than anything. That's love, I think: seeing someone clearly and choosing them anyway."

Lucas's eyes shine with emotion. "She showed me what it means to stand for something," he says quietly, "and she reminded me that some things, some people, are worth standing beside. Worth fighting for. Worth loving, even when it's hard."

The word "loving" hangs in the air between us, charged with meaning.

"Cut," Dylan says softly.

The crew starts moving instantly, wrapping cables and powering down gear. Dylan smiles at us, clearly satisfied.

"That was incredible," he says. "The way you two interact, it's layered, grounded. Complicated but still full of respect. That's what people connect to. Not perfection—truth."

I can't tell if he knows just how right he is.

Dylan packs up his notebook and gives us a thoughtful nod. "I'll let you two have some privacy. We've got all we need. I'll be in touch, but thanks again. This has been an incredible experience."

As the door closes behind the crew, silence settles over the apartment. Lucas and I sit facing each other, with the weight of everything we've just said hovering between us.

The real conversation is about to begin.

forty-two

. . .

Lucas

THE APARTMENT FALLS silent as the door closes behind Dylan and his crew. For a moment, neither of us moves. Jess sits at her end of the couch, still holding that pillow like it's an anchor, while I remain at mine, suddenly unsure what to do with my hands now that the cameras aren't telling us what to do.

The afternoon sunlight streams through the windows, illuminating dust particles dancing in the air between us. It feels significant somehow—all these tiny, invisible things suddenly made visible in the right light.

"So," I say finally, breaking the silence. "That was..."

"Intense," she finishes, offering a small smile.

I nod, studying her face. She looks tired—the kind of bone-deep exhaustion that comes from weeks of tension and a sleepless night—but there's something else there, too, a cautious hopefulness in her eyes that mirrors what I'm feeling.

"Did you mean it?" I ask, the question slipping out before

I can consider if it's the right one. "What you said about us being real?"

She looks down at her hands for a moment and then back up at me with a directness that's pure Jess. "Every word. Did you?"

"Yes." No hesitation. No careful calculations about how to phrase it. Just truth.

She exhales, and some of the tension leaves her shoulders. "The story—"

"Was fair," I interrupt gently. "Factual. Necessary. I meant what I said during the interview, Jess. I'm proud of you for writing it."

"Even though it's your father?"

"*Especially* because it's my father." I shift closer to her on the couch, close enough that I could reach for her hand if I dared. "I've spent my entire life managing his image, crafting the perfect Carmichael family narrative. But you chose truth over comfort. You did what was right, even when it was hard."

She studies me, searching for any sign of insincerity. "When you saw that footage of me discussing the story with Dylan, I was terrified that I'd lost you for good."

"I was angry," I admit. "Not because you were pursuing the story, but because I thought you didn't trust me enough to tell me first. I felt blindsided, and I lashed out."

"I should have told you immediately," she says. "I was trying to gather all the facts first, to be absolutely certain before I brought it to you. But that doesn't excuse keeping you in the dark."

"And I should have given you the chance to explain

instead of jumping to conclusions." I run a hand through my hair, a gesture she's teased me about countless times. "We've never been very good at timing, have we?"

That draws a genuine laugh from her, and the sound fills up something hollow in my chest. "Terrible. Absolutely terrible."

I gather my courage and reach for her hand. When she doesn't pull away, I intertwine our fingers, marveling at how natural it feels. "I've missed you," I tell her. "More than I thought possible."

"I've missed you, too." Her voice is soft but steady. "These weeks apart...they've been hell."

"Then why did you stay away so long?"

"Pride," she admits. "Fear. I thought maybe you'd be better off without me complicating your life. Without my stubbornness and my need to chase the truth, even when it hurts."

"Better off?" I shake my head in disbelief. "Jess, those are exactly the things I love about you."

The word hangs between us, finally spoken outright after hovering on the edge of so many conversations. Her eyes widen slightly, and I see her breath catch.

"Do you mean that?" she asks, her voice barely above a whisper.

Instead of answering immediately, I move closer until we're face to face. I reach up to cup her cheek. "I wasn't playing a part when I said it during the interview. I wasn't performing for the documentary. I was telling you. I love you."

Her eyes fill with tears, and as one escapes down her

cheek, I catch it with my thumb, amazed at this rare show of vulnerability from a woman who faces down powerful men without flinching, who's built walls so high that I never thought I'd see over them.

"I love you, too," she says, her voice quiet but steady despite the tremor in her hands. "I think I have for months, but I was too scared to admit it, even to myself. I kept telling myself it was temporary, that we'd go our separate ways when the six months were up."

"And now?" I ask, daring to hope.

She smiles then, the first genuine, unguarded smile I've seen from her in weeks. "Now I don't want our contract to end. I don't want to sign those annulment papers. I want to see what this could be when we're not pretending, when we're just us."

Relief and joy surge through me. I wrap my arms around her, and as I pull her against my chest, her body fits against mine with familiar rightness. "I don't want it to end, either," I murmur against her hair. "I tore up the papers already."

A look of relief crosses her face. "Seriously?"

I nod.

"Are you sure?" she asks, pulling back slightly to look into my eyes. "My career will always involve uncomfortable truths. I'll always ask hard questions. I'll always chase stories that matter."

"I know," I say simply, "and I love that about you. I love your integrity, your courage, your refusal to settle for easy answers."

"And your father..."

"My father will survive. He always does. And our relationship has always been complicated. This doesn't change that."

She studies me for a long moment and then nods, accepting my answer.

"What about you?" I ask. "Are you sure about this? About us? Your carefully crafted independence, your aversion to commitment..."

"Not so careful anymore," she admits with a small laugh. "You kind of dismantled all my defenses when I wasn't looking."

"Professional hazard," I tease. "PR guy, remember?"

She rolls her eyes, but her smile remains. "I'm sure, Lucas. I've never been more sure of anything. I want this. I want us. Not because it's easy or because it makes sense on paper, but because loving you feels more right than anything ever has."

I pull her closer, and our foreheads touch. "Nothing about this has been easy," I murmur, "but it's been worth every complicated, messy, beautiful moment."

"We're not perfect," she whispers, echoing her words from the interview.

"But we are real," I finish before closing the distance between us.

Her lips meet mine with six months of history and weeks of longing behind them. It feels like coming home and setting out on a new adventure all at once.

When we finally break apart, both breathless, I brush a strand of hair from her face. "So, Mrs. Carmichael, what happens now?"

She laughs at the formality. "Now we figure out what our

relationship looks like when it's not for the cameras. When it's just for us."

"I think we've got a pretty good start," I tell her, unable to keep the grin from my face. "Want to stay for dinner? I seem to recall promising you pasta."

"I'm not going anywhere," she says firmly. "Not tonight. Not tomorrow. Not ever."

"Good." I pull her close again, marveling at the fact that I can, that this is real, that the woman who challenged and frustrated and fascinated me from the beginning is choosing to stay. "Because I'm not letting you go again."

We'll still have to figure it out—what this looks like in the real world when the pressure's off, when it's just two people building something without a script or a contract or cameras. There will be hard conversations and compromises, and probably some spectacular arguments.

But as I hold her in my arms, I know we can handle whatever comes our way. We're not here to fix each other or change each other. We're here to choose each other. Not because it's easy.

But because it's worth it.

forty-three

. . .

Jess

THE FIRST TIME I walked into Lucas's apartment, I
had no intention of staying. I brought one box of props. I had
one foot out the door even as I stood in the middle of his pris-
tine kitchen, silently judging his Disney decor.

Now, as I step inside again, everything feels different.
The space hasn't changed, but there's something new underneath it: a warmth that I've grown used to, a pull that feels
like coming home.

Lucas drops his keys in the little dish by the front door,
and I smile. I toe off my boots and wander toward the living
room. The lighting is soft, and the city hums beyond the
windows. He comes up behind me and wraps his arms
around my waist.

It's been a week since the doc wrapped and Lucas and I
were finally honest with each other.

"It feels good to be home," I say as I turn my head to look
up at him.

"You sure?"

"About being here?" I ask, arching an eyebrow.

"About everything."

I turn in his arms and slide my hands up his chest, my fingers brushing against the open collar of his shirt. "I'm not interested in going backward. Or starting over."

His expression becomes serious as his gaze locks on me. "What are you suggesting?"

"I think we just stay married."

His breath catches. "Seriously?"

"Why not?"

Lucas studies me for a second, like he's waiting for the catch.

"There's no media angle," I add. "No documentary. No campaign event. Just you and me."

A slow grin tugs at his mouth. "You proposing, Lexington?"

"You wish, Carmichael."

He laughs and pulls me flush against him. "Are we sealing this with a kiss, or…"

"Hmm." I tilt my head, pretending to consider it. "I was thinking something more binding."

Not wasting another second, he picks me up, throws me over his shoulder, and walks us down the hall to the bedroom. When he lays me on the bed, his mouth finds mine like he'll never get enough. There's nothing hesitant about it, no slow build, no holding back, just heat and hunger and urgency.

"You're obsessed with me," I murmur as he lifts my sweater over my head.

"One hundred percent."

His fingers trail fire across my skin as he undresses me

with deliberate slowness, and his eyes darken as each new inch of skin is revealed. When I'm finally naked beneath him, he takes a moment to just look, his gaze traveling from my face down my body with such blatant appreciation that I feel myself flush despite our familiarity.

"Your turn," I tell him as I reach for his shirt buttons. He helps me, shrugging out of his clothes until he's gloriously bare, all lean muscle and warm skin that I've come to know intimately over these months.

I run my hands over his shoulders and down his chest, feeling the rapid beating of his heart beneath my palm. When he lowers himself to cover my body with his, the contact of skin against skin is electrifying. The weight of him, the heat, the perfect fit of our bodies, it's overwhelming and exactly what I need.

"I'll never get enough of this," he whispers against my neck, his voice rough with desire. "Enough of you."

"Prove it," I say, arching up to press my breasts against his chest.

His mouth finds mine again, hungrier now, as his hand slides between us to touch me where I'm already wet and aching for him. I gasp against his lips as his fingers work their magic, knowing exactly how to touch me, where to apply pressure, when to ease back. The man has made a study of my body, methodical and thorough in a way that would be almost clinical if it weren't so devastatingly effective.

"Lucas," I breathe as my hips rise to meet his hand. "I need you inside me. Now."

"So demanding," he teases, but I feel the tremor in his arms as he positions himself between my thighs. When he finally pushes into me, we both groan at the sensation of being joined again, making up for lost time.

Moonlight spills through the bedroom window, painting Lucas in silver and shadow as he moves above me. Our bodies slide together with practiced familiarity, yet each thrust still sends electricity racing across my skin. This is something deeper, more deliberate, with each movement a promise, each kiss a vow.

"I love you," he whispers against my neck, and the words are still new enough to make my heart stutter.

"Show me," I say, arching up to meet him.

His eyes lock with mine as he adjusts his angle, hitting that perfect spot that makes my breath catch. "Like this?" he asks, with a hint of his usual cockiness returning.

"Getting warmer," I gasp, digging my nails into his shoulders as he increases his pace. The familiar pressure builds low in my belly.

Lucas knows my body now. He knows exactly how to touch me, where to kiss me, when to slow down, and when to push harder. He dips his head to capture my nipple between his lips, using just enough teeth to send a jolt of pleasure-pain through me. My back arches reflexively, and a moan escapes before I can stop it.

"There she is," he murmurs against my breast, sounding supremely satisfied. "No holding back tonight, Jess. I want to hear you."

"Make me," I challenge, though the words come out breathier than intended.

He grins, that devastating half-smile that first caught my

attention in a tunnel leading to a baseball dugout years ago. "Gladly."

With surprising strength, he flips us so I'm straddling him, with my thighs bracketing his hips. The change in position drives him deeper, and we both gasp. His hands settle on my waist, guiding but not controlling as I begin to move.

"God, you're beautiful," he says, his voice rough with emotion. In this position, I feel powerful, cherished, and seen all at once.

Planting my palms on his chest, I set a rhythm that has his eyes rolling back. The solid warmth of him inside me, beneath me, surrounding me, it's overwhelming in the best possible way.

"Look at me," I demand as I feel him getting close and his muscles tense beneath my fingers.

He does, and his gaze burns with such naked adoration that it almost hurts to witness. Six months ago, I would have run from that look.

"I love you," I whisper. Though still unfamiliar on my tongue, the words are utterly true. "God, Lucas, I love you so much."

Something breaks in his expression, and he rises to capture my mouth with his. The change in angle hits exactly right, and suddenly, I'm falling as pleasure radiates outward in waves that leave me trembling. He follows a heartbeat later, and his release triggers aftershocks that prolong my orgasm.

We collapse together, breathing hard, our hearts racing in tandem. His arms come around me, and he holds me close against his chest in that protective way I once resisted but now crave. For several minutes, we lie in silence as his fingers trace idle patterns on my back.

"What are you thinking?" he asks finally, pressing a kiss to my temple.

I consider deflecting with a joke—old habits die hard—but instead, I offer him the truth. "That I never expected this. You. Us."

"Regrets?" There's a hint of vulnerability in his voice that most people would never notice but that I've learned to recognize.

"Not a single one," I assure him, propping myself up to meet his eyes.

"I used to think we hated each other."

"Oh, we did," I reply with a smirk.

He laughs. "And yet, you married me."

I shrug. "You were the only man who ever kept up."

As we lie there in the calm, the comfort of our usual banter softens into something deeper.

"I admired you," he says finally. "Even when we were at each other's throats. You never backed down. Never sold out. I hated how much I respected it."

"I knew you were in love with me the second you saw me in the home team tunnel at USC." I tease him.

"I'm pretty sure the drool on your face was all the proof I needed that you wanted me."

I roll my eyes and then shift closer, suddenly serious. "I love you," I say, not as a declaration but as a truth. An offering.

"I love you," he echoes, pulling my hand to his lips. "And I like you, too. Even when you're insufferable."

"Same," I reply, smiling into his collarbone. "Especially then."

I sit up suddenly. "Oh! I almost forgot."

Lucas raises an eyebrow as I scramble out of bed and pad across the floor to where my bag sits abandoned near the door.

"What are you doing?" he asks with amusement.

"I got you something," I call over my shoulder, digging through the bag until my fingers close around the envelope. "Stay there."

I duck into the closet and rummage through the drawer where I stashed the ridiculous purchase I made on a whim three days ago. When I emerge, Lucas's expression shifts from confusion to disbelief, then to absolute delight.

"Are those—"

"Mickey ears? Yes." I place the sparkly headband on my head, feeling both silly and strangely liberated. I spent years crafting the perfect professional image, and now here I am in Disney merchandise, standing before the man I love. "I've been told they're essential attire."

Lucas sits up, and his eyes are bright with a childlike joy I've come to treasure. I hand him the envelope, suddenly shy.

"What's this?" he asks.

"Open it."

His fingers carefully break the seal, and he pulls out two tickets. His eyes widen.

"Paris?" he whispers, looking up at me. "You got us tickets to Disneyland Paris?"

"For our honeymoon," I say as warmth floods my chest at

his expression. "A real one this time. I figured if I'm going to love a Disney adult, I might as well go all in."

Lucas is out of bed in an instant, lifting me off my feet in a spin that sends the Mickey ears flying. When he sets me down, his eyes are suspiciously bright.

"Jessica Lexington-Carmichael," he says, his voice rough with emotion, "you continue to surprise me."

"That's the plan," I reply, reaching up to touch his face. "For as long as you'll have me."

Outside our window, Los Angeles continues its eternal performance, its lights and glamour concealing complexity beneath. But here, in this space we've made our own, we've found something beyond the carefully constructed narratives we've both built our careers upon.

We've found the truth.

epilogue

. . .

Jess - Six Months Later

Honey Pine Farms
Grant and Sophia's Wedding

THE SKY over Honey Pine Farms is dusted in gold, the sun just starting to dip behind the mountains, as the ceremony shifts into the reception. Rows of white chairs are still scattered across the hillside, and guests mingle with champagne flutes and camera-ready smiles while fairy lights blink awake above the dance floor like they've been waiting for this exact moment.

I slip my hand into Lucas's as we wander toward the main lodge and the soft murmur of conversation rises around us. His fingers squeeze mine, a quiet pulse of affection. He looks effortlessly polished, as always, in a crisp black tux, with his tie slightly loosened now that the vows have been said, and his eyes are warm when they land on mine.

"You doing ok?" he asks, dipping his head slightly to catch my eye.

I nod. "I'm good. Just a little in awe."

He smiles, slow and knowing. "You mean from Grant actually pulling off an emotionally intelligent ceremony without needing to quote *The Breakfast Club*?"

I nudge him with my shoulder. "I meant Sophia's vows, smartass."

"To be fair, they were excellent," he concedes. "And Hazel stole the whole show."

"She always does."

We fall into step again, quiet for a beat as guests trail past us. Blair and Wyatt are among them, strolling with their hands linked, Blair glowing and very, very pregnant.

"She's practically floating," I say. "They both are."

Lucas glances over and grins. "Wyatt's about one false labor call away from wrapping her in bubble wrap."

"Classic first-time dad energy."

Brandon and Stella pass next, deep in conversation. Or rather, Stella's talking, animated and dramatic as always, while Brandon looks hypnotized by her story.

"I'm just saying," she says, tugging at Brandon's sleeve, "that you're a dating ninja. The least you could do is teach me how to flirt like a normal human."

"I'm not a ninja," Brandon replies, looking both smug and unbothered.

"You got that girl from 4B to ask you out by recommending a podcast," she huffs. "I recommended banana bread to my crush, and he asked if I was ok."

Lucas chuckles beside me. "What do we think? Two weeks before she ropes him into giving her dating lessons?"

"Two weeks if he resists. Forty-eight hours if she bribes him with croissants."

Across the lawn, Jake is nursing a whiskey, watching the reception unfold with the tired eyes of a man still trying to figure out what happens after marriage falls apart. Lucas catches him looking toward the catering tent, where Natalie, Stella's yoga friend with the dimples and killer arms, is arranging a tray of lemon bars.

"Should we be concerned?" Lucas asks, nodding in Jake's direction.

"It feels like a stretch," I reply, "but this is LA. Anything could happen, I suppose."

Because, yeah, some things have happened in the last six months.

After I received my inheritance, I accepted the Reynolds board seat. Not because I wanted the prestige, but because I wanted the voice. I wanted the seat at the table. And with it came a chance to shape something, so I did.

My first order of business? A thought piece on workplace harassment in the entertainment industry. Turns out, Marcus Delgado's unwanted advances weren't limited to me. When several other women came forward with similar stories, Wonderland Studios couldn't ignore the pattern. Last month, they quietly showed him the door, though the press release called it "pursuing other opportunities." Lucas helped craft that statement, which makes me laugh every time I think about it.

"I felt like I should thank Marcus," he told me afterward. "If he hadn't been so creepy in Vegas, we might never have fake-married our way into real love."

I pointed out that thanking Marcus felt wrong on every level, but the irony isn't lost on me. Sometimes, the worst people accidentally set the best things in motion.

I donated a portion of my inheritance to Katherine's foundation, and now I volunteer there, too. We're building something better. Smarter. Safer. Jess Lexington-Carmichael, once a rebel with a mic, is now also a rebel with a budget and an agenda.

And Mickey ears, when the occasion calls for them.

Lucas is still at Wonderland and still working with Grant. I expect it'll stay that way as long as they can make it so. He's thriving and bold, still sharp-edged and ruthlessly composed for the press.

Oh, you want to know about the documentary? The buzz got so big the first two episodes premiered in theaters before the entire series went live on Wonderland's streaming platform. It was weird watching us on screen, but Dylan did a wonderful job telling our story. Lucas even cried a bit.

As for the marriage, we didn't renew our vows. We didn't throw a second wedding or plan some splashy PR reversal. That was never the point. What we have now doesn't need an audience—or an ending.

We just kept going.

"Come dance with me," he says now, tugging me gently toward the clearing where strings of warm bulbs crisscross above the wooden dance floor. The music is easy, classic, something old and smooth that makes you sway without thinking.

I follow him out, slipping into the rhythm easily, my body

falling into his like we've been dancing this same step for years.

Around us, couples twirl: Sophia and Grant near the center, Hazel cutting in every so often, claiming her turn with both of them like the star of the show she is.

After a moment, he pulls me a little closer, and his hand settles at the small of my back, steady and warm.

"Can I tell you something?" he asks, more serious now.

"Always."

"I used to think we were strongest when we pushed each other, like rivals who never let the other get too comfortable."

"And now?"

He looks at me, and his eyes are steady and clear. "Now I think we're strongest because we see each other. Because we never had to pretend. Even when we hated each other, we knew exactly who we were dealing with."

I smile. "Guess the line between love and hate really is thin."

"Paper thin," he murmurs. "And wildly combustible."

We stop moving, letting the music swirl around us, and he gently presses his forehead to mine.

"I love you," he says.

"I love you, too," I whisper.

We kiss while the mountains stretch around us, the stars blink overhead, and the people we love dance beside us.

This time, it's not for the story. It *is* the story. Our story.

Not ready to say goodbye to Jess and Lucas?
Scan the QR code to join my newsletter family and unlock
an exclusive bonus scene that wasn't in the book! You'll also
be the first to hear about upcoming releases, behind-the-
scenes peeks, and special offers. No spam, just bookish joy
delivered straight to your inbox!

The Backlot Series

Second Act – *Available Now!*
Center Stage – *Available Now!*
On the Record - *Available Now!*
Behind the Scenes (Stella and Brandon) - Fall 2025
Off Script (Natalie and Jake) - Spring 2026

Thank you!

I hope you fell in love with Jess and Lucas's journey in *On
The Record*! If their story captured your heart, I'd be so

grateful if you'd consider leaving a review. Reviews are like literary fairy dust for indie authors—they help other readers discover our books and help open doors we sometimes can't open ourselves without social proof. Thank you for being part of this adventure! 🤍

acknowledgments

FOR IMMEDIATE RELEASE

Local Author Survives Third Book Launch; Publicly Thanks Everyone Who Helped Keep Her Semi-Sane

Press Release Issued from Author's Writing Cave While Wearing Her Favorite Pajamas

TEXAS, JULY 7, 2025 — Following the completion of her third novel, local romance author Kimberly Page has officially declared herself "somehow still standing," and is pleased to report that love, caffeine, and a few very good people got her through it. The following acknowledgments are heartfelt, sincere, and at times slightly unhinged — just like the author herself.

EXECUTIVE SUMMARY OF GRATITUDE:

To the usual suspects who keep showing up: My mom, who believes in me more than I believe in myself some days. My sisters, Kristy and Jamie—thank you for cheering, texting, and providing nonstop sibling subplot inspo. And my daughter, who lends me her Gen Z wisdom so I can appear semi-relevant online. You're all contractually obligated to stick with me through Book 4. No take-backs.

KEY PERSONNEL ACKNOWLEDGMENTS:

Nicole, Developmental Editor Extraordinaire

This story would've been a beautiful mess without you. You don't just make the book better—you make it worth reading.

Staci, Cover Designer Supreme

The literal first impression queen. People judge books by covers, and thanks to you, this one practically demands to be picked up.

Jefferson, Copy/Line Editor & Grammar Wizard

You've saved me from comma crimes and "lay/lie" humiliation more times than I can count. May your red pen forever be gentle.

STRATEGIC PARTNERSHIPS & RIDE-OR-DIE SHOUTOUTS:

To my beta readers—your notes made this book sharper, funnier, and sexier. Thank you so much for your honesty, enthusiasm, and top-tier trope takes.

To my ARC readers—you are my unpaid marketing department, and I could not love you more for it. Your reviews and posts are the reason new readers find me. Please don't ever stop. Special thanks to my early and continued readers and supporters: isabel.reyes.34, bookishlatinajenn, c_swirl1, life.byt, gemmalouisebooksxx, nala.reads, and joaneeloves (big love y'all!!)!

To indie bookstores, especially *The Plot Twist, Blush Bookstore*, and *Love Stories OKC*—thank you for shelf space, support, and making me feel like a Real Author™ even when I showed up with sweaty palms and an awkward smile.

To Cami and Holly—best friends, first readers, and emotional life rafts. Thank you for reading terrible drafts and having conversations like, "Does this character feel emotionally avoidant or just normal?"

INDUSTRY RELATIONSHIPS & COMMUNITY LOVE:

To my new author friends in Romancelandia: thank you for making this journey less lonely and infinitely more fun. I feel lucky to be in this wild, wonderful community with you.

To every follower who's liked, shared, commented, reviewed, or messaged—your support is *everything*. Truly. You make it all feel possible (and a lot less like screaming into the social media void).

ENVIRONMENTAL FACTORS:

This book was built on a mix of real-life chaos and plot twists: playoff hockey in the background, edits written in the Notes app while idling in the school pickup line, and final edits wrapped in beachside humidity that nearly melted my laptop. (Totally worth it.)

Book events turned out to be way more fun than I ever expected (even if I still get the pre-event jitters). Chatting with readers, meeting booksellers, and connecting with fellow romance lovers has become one of my favorite parts of this whole ride.

So if this story feels a little sun-drenched, slightly sweat-stained, and full of heart... that's because it is. Thanks for being the reason it's all worth doing.

CLOSING STATEMENT:

It takes a village to bring fictional people to life. If you're reading this, you're part of mine. Thank you for helping me write love stories worth believing in.

Want to stay up to date on all the behind-the-scenes fun?

Sign up for my newsletter at **authorkimberlypage.com** or follow along @iamkimberlyjpage on Instagram and TikTok.

Disclaimer: No publicists were harmed in the making of this acknowledgment. All formatting liberties and tense changes were taken with full creative license. Turns out, when you self-publish, no one can stop you from drafting thank-you notes like a fake press release issued from your couch. I regret nothing.

about the author

Kimberly Page is a contemporary romance author who loves writing about strong heroines and the irresistible heroes who fall for them. After a career spent crafting stories for major players in the entertainment industry, she decided to create stories of her own.

When she's not writing, you can find Kimberly planning for beach time, at a theme park with her daughter, or getting lost in a good sports romance book. Follow her on TikTok and Instagram for news and updates.

www.kimberlyjpage.com